HEIR OF RA

BLOOD OF RA BOOK ONE

M. SASINOWSKI

KINGSMILL PRESS

ISBN 978-1-7324467-1-7

ISBN 978-1-7324467-0-0 (ebook)

This is a work of fiction. Names, characters, and incidents are the product of the author's imagination, except in the case of historical figures and events, which are used fictitiously.

To Heather, for decades of friendship

I am Horus. Son of Isis and Osiris. I shall know no fear.

LORD GEORGE RENLEY studied the carving in the stone door, his lips pursed in an expression of perpetual disapproval. *A bird of prey?* Every detail was exquisitely crafted, from the wings, unfurled gracefully in flight, to its curved talons locked around a glimmering, triangular object.

He leaned closer, his skin tingling. Goose bumps skimmed all the way from his toes to the nape of his neck, where the hairs stirred and tried to lift off.

"*Sahib?*"

Renley flinched at the sound behind him, the echo of the long tunnel giving the voice of his Arab guide a ghostly quality. He shot a glance toward Hazim.

"Mind the light," Renley said.

He pulled out a leather-bound notebook and flipped through the pages, eyes darting between the meticulous drawings and the translucent object in the bird's talons. He handed the notebook to Hazim and took the torch. The triangle sparkled, reflecting the dancing light of his torch, shimmering like a firefly flickering in and out of existence.

Renley coughed, his throat parched from the stale air. His face tightened at the drops of sticky wetness the cough left on his fingertips. He raised his hand—and stared at the red blots on his palm.

"*Sahib!*" The cry behind him sounded distant. Renley turned and recoiled. Blood streaked from the other man's nose. He groaned and stretched out a hand to Renley.

"This place…" Hazim backed away with dread in his eyes. "The oracle spoke truth!"

Renley's vision blurred. A slash of pain in his head mingled with the ear-piercing scream of his guide. He watched Hazim reel then rush for the entrance, the sound of his footsteps disappearing into the tunnel.

"Hazim!" Renley's voice grated in his throat, his tongue heavy. Time seemed to slow as darkness enveloped him and the tunnel began to spin. He reached for the wall only to find that his body refused to obey his command and he sank to the ground. His knees hit the limestone floor. Fear came as a surprise, an unknown sensation, when Lord Renley grasped that he would die alone, buried under the great Sphinx with pain and shadow his only companions.

———

HAZIM STAGGERED along the wall of the tunnel. He dared not look back. After an eternity in the blackness, he reached the entrance and collapsed to the ground. Groaning, he forced his body toward the narrow opening chiseled into the bottom of the stone door.

His head appeared beneath the open sky and he hungrily sucked in the cold air of the desert night. He looked up at the other men through the crimson haze.

"*Saa'idni*," he pleaded, blood gurgling in his throat. The workmen gasped at this apparition of horror, blood streaking from its eyes and mouth. The men backed away to the far wall of the large excavation pit then rushed for the ramp as one and scattered into the desert.

Hazim's clawed fingers raked the sand in his futile struggle to pull himself free of the cursed tunnel. Halfway through the opening, he collapsed. With a final, desperate effort, he rolled onto his back and peered into the vastness above him.

Tears mixed with blood dimmed his vision as he prayed to his god, his eyes staring sightlessly at the stars, divine witnesses to his death. He did not see the small boy warily approach him and snatch Lord Renley's notebook from his lifeless grasp before scurrying after the men into the moonlit desert. He did not feel the sand covering his face as the desert reclaimed her land, reshaping it in the image of the wind.

PART 1

AWAKENING

WE ARE BORN NAKED, wet, and hungry—then things get worse.

Alyssa licked the salt from her lips. A-ha's *Hunting High and Low* blared from her earbuds as she wiped her forehead on the sleeve of her vintage Willis & Geiger top—last year's sweet sixteen present from her father. She had tagged along on plenty of his digs since they moved to Egypt seven years ago. None of them were exactly vacations, but this one was definitely in a league of its own.

Stop feeling sorry for yourself.

She dipped her hand into the colorful chalk bag hanging from her hip and lifted her head to study the steep wall above her, scoping out the next handhold. Alyssa shook off the excess chalk and pushed her fingertips into a small crevice above her head. She ignored the pain of the rock digging into her skin and used her legs to push up her weight before clipping her safety line into the next anchor.

A cool breeze lifted her hair and tickled her neck. She smiled and closed her eyes then pushed her feet against the rock and leaned back, letting the rope support her weight and giving her drained muscles a much-needed break.

As if the daily climbs to catalog the *Chinisiri* mountainside graves weren't grueling enough, two days ago her father had been urgently called back to their home in Cairo and put *her* in charge of the entire dig in his absence—much to the bafflement of the rest of the team. He probably had no clue that his students were placing bets on the price tag of her first screw-up. *Thanks a lot, Old Man... No pressure.*

They all conceded that, though just a senior in high school, she'd had far more field experience than most of his college students. She had certainly put in her dues. While her class-mates at Cairo International Academy were busy swapping stories about their exotic summer vacations and fussing over their back-to-school mani-pedis, she kept mostly to herself, callused palms hidden in her pockets, fighting to extract week-old dirt caked under her fingernails—and quietly thankful she hadn't picked up some bizarre flesh-eating bacteria while digging in the armpit of the world. Not to mention the countless hours she spent arranging visas and work permits for digs in countries with names most people couldn't even pronounce. Still, there was plenty of grumbling from everybody in the camp about her father's decision to leave her in charge... herself included.

Well, better not screw this one up.

She reached for the next handhold when the music in her earbuds faded and a buzz announced an incoming call. She glanced at her smartwatch.

Speak of the devil... She rolled her eyes and pushed the button to answer the call.

"You know, you don't have to check up on me every—"

"Alyssa," her father's voice sounded almost effervescent, "the Council of Antiquities accepted my appeal."

Alyssa's heart seemed to freeze, and then it began to pound. She tightened her grip on the rope securing her to the mountain.

"Alyssa, do you copy?"

"What?" she gasped. "How? Why now?"

"It's the council… who knows?" He laughed. "As long as those desk jockeys give us the permits. We're going in!"

"Who else?"

"We're keeping it small and low-key, for now. Ed Wallace and his team sent us the last set of the satellite images. They're wheels up from JFK with the equipment, arriving here tomorrow morning." He sighed. "Of course, the council is sending observers. The minister wants to make sure we do everything by the book."

She checked her watch. "I can make the early morning flight from Cusco. I'll be there tomorrow evening."

"They only gave us a twenty-four-hour window."

"Twenty-four hours? I'm on the face of a mountain, half a world away!"

"I need you to stay and finish cataloging—"

"What? You run off and leave me in charge of this dig to plead with the council, but—"

"Alyssa—"

"This'll be the biggest thing since Tut! You've been dragging me around the world with you ever since Mom—"

"I'm sorry. The schedule is set. We go in first light tomorrow."

Her mind raced. "If I leave now, I can still catch the evening flight and be in Cairo in the morning."

"It's too dangerous. Jacob told me you're a thousand feet up in the air. It'll take you a couple of hours just to get—"

"Dangerous?" Her voice cracked. "Dangerous? What about Masada? Hiding from mercenaries in the world's first toilet drain? That wasn't dangerous?"

"Alyssa, please, just—"

"I'll be there, Kade. Don't you go in without me." She clicked the button and ended the connection. She switched the headset to the walkie talkie.

"Jake, talk to me."

The voice of her father's grad student filled her earbuds. "Forget it, *Wallerina*."

"I don't care what Kade told you," Alyssa shot back.

"Your—*dad*—told me not to let you do anything stupid," Jacob said.

"I'm going."

"No chance. I've been following your ascent through the scope. You just cleared the large headwall on the south face, elevation 358 meters. Even if you rush, you'll never make—"

"Not rappelling." Alyssa's lips curved into a mischievous smile. She reached to her waist and pulled the large Bushcrafter knife from its sheath.

"Oh, no…" She could hear the panic creeping into Jacob's voice as realization dawned on him.

"Better get started on the pre-flight checks, Jake."

"Please don't do this to me, Alyssa."

Alyssa closed her eyes and took a deep breath.

"Your dad is going to kill me!"

She kicked off the mountain as hard as she could and swung out like a pendulum away from the wall.

"Alyssa, don't!" Jake's scream resonated in her ears as she stretched and cut the line securing her to the mountain.

Time froze, then—

The rush of adrenaline surging through her body and the acceleration was instantaneous. The wind howled in her ears as she fell, faster and faster, transforming the side of the mountain into a blur.

Alyssa arched, turning her body in midair, and pulled the ripcord. A split-second later the gut-wrenching jerk of the safety parachute arrested her free fall.

Her body still trembling, she reached up and pulled on the steering lines to guide her away from the wall.

"Woohoo!" Alyssa's voice reflected off the mountain, a huge grin splitting her face.

Alyssa's Bucket List Item #21: Cut a perfectly good life line securing me to the mountain. Check!

"Alyssa, you're friggin' insane!" Jacob shrieked in her earbuds, his voice shaking like a taut rope. "If your dad finds out, he'll never leave you at a dig alone again!" He paused. "And he'll never let me graduate!"

"No worries, Jake, our secret is safe. Now get the Cessna ready." She ended the connection. *Kade will never hear about the BASE jumping lessons you've been giving me in our spare time.*

Her racing heart began to settle. Slowly, her blood found its way into her limbs again. She looked at the ground below, easily spotting their camp and the clearing they had been using as a landing strip for their small Cessna airplane. She steered the parachute toward it and her thoughts turned to her father.

I can't believe he finally got the permits...

His fascination—*no, make it obsession*—with the fabled Hall of Records had cost her any semblance of a normal childhood... and had gotten him into trouble on more occasions than she cared to remember. The Egyptian Council of Antiquities had insisted on solid evidence proving the existence of the chambers before even considering granting a permit for a dig. For years he's been fighting an uphill battle. Then, two days ago and completely out of the blue, he was summoned back to Cairo for a special hearing. A mad rush from Peru to Egypt got him there just in time, so he could present his petition for the excavation.

And a day later they approve the dig? And now he wants to go in by himself? After everything that's happened? After Mom?

Her thoughts were still on her father when she spotted three white Land Rovers speeding for the camp. She squinted, struggling to make out details. Seconds later the SUVs came to a screeching halt in the middle of the camp and several men jumped out.

What the...?

Then she saw the weapons in their hands.

Before her brain fully processed the scene, she pulled the right steering line and her parachute veered sharply away from the camp. A second later she realized her blunder as she stared at the dense rain forest canopy below her. Her eyes darted across the tops of the trees, frantically searching for another clearing. She plummeted closer to the sharp limbs with every heartbeat.

I'm out of time!

The trees were all around her. She grunted, sharp branches scraping her arms and legs. The ground sped at her far too quickly. She screamed an instant before her parachute lines tightened and the harness jolted her upward—then everything stopped.

Still dazed, she looked at the branches around her then down. *Less than fifteen feet. Ground looks soft.* She took a deep breath and released the metal clamp of the parachute harness.

The next second she was lying face-down on the forest floor, spitting furiously to expel foliage in various stages of decomposition from her mouth. Moaning, she rolled onto her back, doing her best not to gag—and to forget her biology lessons about the average number of invertebrates per cubic centimeter of soil in a tropical rain forest.

Okay, so the landings still need some work...

Alyssa slowly sat up. Her body was sluggish, but her brain was in overdrive. *What's happening? Who are those men?*

She wiggled her toes and fingers and flexed the muscles in her arms and legs. She hurt all over, but everything seemed to work. Gingerly, she got to her feet and checked the range of motion in her joints. She examined her body. *A dozen bumps and bruises, but no serious injury.* She shook her head in disbelief.

Better to be lucky than good.

Alyssa glanced at her compass. *The mountains are north, so the camp site should be due east.* She motivated her bruised muscles to budge and set off for the camp.

After a few minutes, the familiar sight of the tents came into view through the dense forest. Alyssa slowed as she approached the clearing. The camp looked deserted, but the three SUVs were still there. She strained her ears.

Nothing.

She waited another minute and surveyed the site.

Where is everybody?

Cautiously, she left the cover of the trees and crept slowly toward the large tent.

"Where is she?"

Alyssa jumped at the sound of the harsh voice, before realizing it came from inside the tent. She swallowed hard and crept closer, holding her breath.

"Who?"

Alyssa froze when she recognized Jake's strained voice.

"Don't test me." The other man's tone was cold as an Arctic lake. "Jacob—is it?"

Alyssa's skin tingled. Without thinking, her hand locked around a fistful of dirt. She saw the shadow of the man behind her an instant before she felt his hand in her hair, and he pulled her up roughly, dragging her toward the tent opening.

"Well, look what I foun—" The rest of his words turned into a groan when she threw the dirt into his eyes. He loosened his grip for a moment, enough time for her to drive her knee into his groin. His face contorted before he doubled over to the ground.

She stumbled backward, struggling to get away from her attacker. She threw a glance into the tent opening—and saw the gun pointed at Jacob's terrified face.

He spotted her.

"Run!" Jacob's scream cut through the air. Alyssa froze for an instant then whirled and took off for the cars.

She gasped when another man surged out of the tent ahead and into her path. She cut sharply to her left, eyes darting from side to side, scrambling to find another escape route.

She spotted the Cessna at the end of the landing strip.

This is a really bad idea…

Before her brain caught up with her, she was already racing flat-out for the plane, the man pursuing her at full speed.

Seconds later she jerked open the door to the plane and dove into the cockpit. She slammed her hand against the mixture-rich and carburetor knobs. She flipped the master switch and turned the ignition key. After an impossibly long second the engine growled and the propeller slowly cranked over before coming alive.

She jammed the throttle forward and ignored the sputters and backfires as the engine grumbled. A second later the plane began inching forward.

She screamed when the door ripped open and the man's hands were on her, pulling hard, trying to wrangle her from the cockpit. Alyssa struggled against him, fighting breathlessly to shove his hands away from her body, not allowing him to get a firm grip.

The man's heavy breaths turned into grunts as he strained to keep up with the accelerating airplane. Alyssa groaned, feeling his grasp on her neck and face. His hand clutched the front of her shirt, just under her chin. She snarled and sank her teeth into his calloused palm. The man's high-pitched howl transformed into a loud grunt as he tripped and dove headfirst into the ground.

Alyssa exhaled sharply and glanced at the speed indicator.

Twenty-five knots… thirty knots… It was creeping up too slowly.

I'm not accelerating fast enough. The engine is cold!

Her eyes darted between the speed indicator and the trees at the end of the clearing.

Forty knots… forty-five knots… Come on! Alyssa's mind cried out as she willed the needle to move toward the sixty-knot takeoff-speed mark.

"Faster!" she didn't realize she was screaming out loud.

She looked up again and gauged the distance to the trees.

I'm not gonna make it!

She killed the engine and slammed both feet on the brakes. The end of the clearing and the trees continued to speed toward her.

Stop! Please stop!

Alyssa drove all her weight onto the brake pedals as she frantically fumbled with the shoulder harness. She heard the buckle click an instant before the small plane crashed into the trees and everything went dark.

GRAYSON BAXTER SCRUTINIZED the microarray robot as the bank of tiny pipettes danced over the thin slide, depositing tiny droplets of DNA onto the glass. He turned his attention from the machine to the student operating it, his eyes traveling from her auburn hair down her body, resting on her long legs. As if feeling his probing gaze, the young woman looked up from her equipment and tugged at her white lab coat.

"Progress, Tasha?" he asked, brusquely.

"Almost half the way done, Professor Baxter," she replied, over-enunciating the syllables in her Russian accent, adding a staccato quality to her speech. "First twenty batches of DNA microarray slides are in quality control stage."

"Halfway? The deadline is tomorrow morning. I need the equipment freed up by noon. New samples are arriving and will need to be processed immediately."

"Tomorrow morning?" She glanced at the clock on the wall. "I estimate another six hours of spotting ahead of us, Professor."

"Then I suggest you plan on staying late."

The young woman opened her mouth in protest but remained silent. She cast her eyes down, nodded, and returned to her task.

Baxter sneered and turned to his computer when the sound of the microarray robot stopped. He looked up from the monitor and scowled when he didn't see Tasha at her workstation.

Where the hell did she go?

"Professor Baxter." Tasha's voice came from behind him.

He turned. "You shouldn't leave the equipment unatten—"

The word froze in his mouth as he stared down the barrel of a black, subcompact automatic pistol.

Tasha's violet eyes locked on him from behind the Ruger, a sly smile on her face.

"I don't think I'll be staying late in the lab, after all, Professor," she said, all trace of the accent gone.

———

KADE MORGAN RUBBED his palms on the khaki cargo pants until they felt dry. Despite the huge air-conditioned tent that enclosed the excavation site, his gray cotton shirt was pasted to his back as if he'd showered in it. His eyes remained fixed on the half-unearthed stone door at the bottom of the thirty foot deep excavation pit in front of him. Yesterday they had located the entrance precisely where the ground-penetrating radar and satellite imaging predicted it to be. After setting up the large dome-shaped tent that made the work in the desert more bearable, they worked through the night, moving sand and constructing the ramp that zigzagged to the bottom of the pit.

Despite their equipment and efforts, the bottom half of the door remained covered by the desert sand.

A line formed between his eyebrows as he studied the door from the top of the ramp while his team continued the excavation. He pored over the close-up images in his hand for the tenth time. *No discernible chiseling patterns, no features.*

"Dr. Morgan!"

Kade lifted his head to his graduate student. Thomas Marshall looked at him, quizzically.

"You okay, boss?"

Kade nodded, ruefully. "I've been waiting for this moment since college, I imagined it a thousand times. I only wish Anja and Alyssa could see this." He shook off the thought. "Whatcha got?"

Thomas handed him a satellite phone. "It's Dr. Wallace."

"About time. He's cutting it close." Kade took the phone. "Where are you, Ed?"

"Our flight from New York was delayed, but we just cleared customs," Ed Wallace was breathing hard. "We'll be there in less than an hour."

"You could never make it to my lectures on time, either," Kade snickered. "Better get a move on. We've got the exterior door almost completely exposed."

"You just can't stop ordering me around, can you?" Wallace shot back with a chuckle. "Just because I was your graduate student doesn't mean—"

"Dr. Morgan!" The booming voice from the entrance of the tent drowned out the rest of the sentence. "What an exciting time!"

Kade whirled. His smile faded when he spotted the middle-aged Egyptian man as he threw the tent flap open and paraded inside, trailed by a film crew. Dressed in his trademark crisp khaki shirt and trousers with a matching wide-brimmed hat that struggled to contain a full head of gray hair, the Minister of the Council of Antiquities gave Kade a flamboyant wave and broad grin.

You gotta be kidding me. He brought the phone close to his mouth. "Get here fast. And start warming up your gear on the way." He ended the call and put on a strained smile as he faced his visitor.

"Minister! Your presence here is quite a surprise."

The other man swaggered up to Kade and grabbed his hand. He shook it fervently, accompanied by the clicking of the cameras.

"Nonsense, Dr. Morgan! This is a monumental occasion in Egyptian archaeology. The ministry is here to support you in any way we can." He leaned in closer and whispered, "And to ensure you do not exceed the twenty-four-hour window the council has granted you." Before Kade could respond, the minister turned around and smiled broadly into the cameras, affectionately putting an arm around Kade.

"Let us have some pictures together. The discoverers of the Hall of Records!"

Kade put on a forced grin as he faced the lenses.

"Let's not get ahead of ourselves, Minister, we've simply located a door that—"

The minister gave him a dismissive wave. He waited for the clicking of the cameras to stop before turning to the exit. "Well, I should let you continue your work as undoubtedly time is of the essence. Please do not mind as we take additional footage outside." He paraded out of the tent, his entourage following closely on his heels.

Thomas waited until they left the tent. He looked up at Kade from the stone door. "Looks like he's already working on his next Discovery Channel special."

Kade shook his head. "For years he's been doing his best to prevent this dig, now he's trying to take credit for it. This was supposed to be kept quiet! Now this blow-dried turd waltzes in here with the press—"

"Whoa!" Thomas exclaimed.

Kade turned to the base of the ramp. His student was motionless, holding on to the trowel he was using to unearth the bottom of the door.

Thomas pointed at the right-hand corner. "Check this out!"

Kade's eyes followed Thomas's finger. He paced down the ramp, his brain struggling to process the two-foot wide horizontal slit that had appeared in the bottom part of the door as the earth was being cleared away from it.

Silently, Kade inspected the slit. He ran his fingers along the edge, tracing the slanted cuts in the stone with his fingertips. He glanced up at Thomas.

"These cuts are relatively new, made by a modern tool." He turned back to the opening. "Look at the front-to-back slant. These marks can't be more than a hundred years old."

He took the trowel from his student's hand and used it to gently clear away the sand from the slit. As he continued unearthing the gap in the stone door, the trowel hit resistance. Automatically, he switched to the round hand brush that Thomas handed him silently, and he gently moved the sand away from the obstruction. After several long minutes, the sand revealed five parallel white bars. Kade held his breath, realizing he was looking at a human ribcage. Dumbfounded, he stared up at Thomas.

"I want a perimeter excavation around the skeleton for a block lift. Make sure to keep the soil from around and underneath it for retrieval of small bones and for sample processing." He swallowed hard. "And let's get some air quality samples from the inside... and gear up, just to be safe. I want PPEs on everybody. Anybody without biosafety gear out of the tent."

————

PROFESSOR GRAYSON BAXTER struggled to control his breathing. He wiggled his wrists as much as the tight rope allowed, trying to get blood flowing through his hands again. How long has he been in this room? The hood on his head itched and the faint smell of kerosene in the air made every breath a struggle. He also had to take a leak so bad his teeth were floating.

After this student, or whoever that broad really was, brought him at gunpoint to the parking garage, he was tied up, hooded, and tossed in the back of a car. Half an hour later, he was led to this room inside of what sounded like a big hangar and locked up. Since then he's been waiting, running through dozens of scenarios in his head about why he'd been kidnapped. He had certainly pissed off enough people in his life. At least he hasn't been hurt. Yet.

His heart rate quickened at the sound of the key in the door. Footsteps. *High heels?*

Baxter blinked as the hood was pulled off his head. He squinted to block out the glare from the lamp shining into his eyes. Tasha took a step back and aimed the Ruger at him with a condescending smirk.

"Somebody would like to meet you," she said, pointing with her head at the man behind the light.

Baxter squinted again, trying to make out the silhouette behind the lamp. The man standing there looked remarkably tall. Baxter lowered his head to avoid the light, glancing at the man's crisply pressed pants and handmade shoes.

"What do you want from me?" Baxter asked, unable to keep the tremor out of his voice.

The tall man regarded him in silence. Finally, he cleared his throat and spoke, his voice ringing with a British accent. "Professor Baxter, I apologize for the unusual circumstance of our meeting, but I wanted to ensure that we had your undivided attention. I am Lord George Renley IV." He pointed at the woman. "I believe you have already met my associate, Miss Mendeva?"

Baxter shot a glance at Tasha. The young woman gave him a shrug.

"We have a saying in the old country, Professor, 'be careful whose toes you tread on today for they might be connected to the foot that kicks your *zadnitsa* tomorrow,'" she said, her voice mocking him as she again exaggerated her Russian accent.

"What the hell is this about? Who are you people?"

Renley appraised him for several moments. "Professor Baxter, your work on the reconstruction of ancestral DNA generated headlines throughout the world. Some argue that your efforts should have earned you the Nobel Prize in biology."

"What does that have to do with anything?"

"To put it simply, Professor, we have urgent need of your expertise."

Baxter glared at the other man. "Ever heard of a phone?"

Renley met his eyes calmly before continuing. "You will resign your academic position and enter our employment. If you are successful in our endeavor, you will be rewarded exceedingly generously."

"And if I'm not?" Baxter said without thinking.

"We have complete faith in you."

"What is this… 'endeavor'?"

Renley inclined his head toward Tasha.

"You're going to reverse engineer genes from samples of DNA and introduce them into the genome of living cells," she said.

"What kind of genes? And what kind of cells?"

"More in due time," Renley said.

"Right…" Baxter's voice dripped with sarcasm.

"You will be given a laboratory, a team of technicians, and every resource you require," Tasha said.

"You want me to create a retrovirus and a delivery vehicle into living cells. So, are we talking gene therapy—or a perfect delivery mechanism for a bioweapon?" Baxter swallowed as he realized the gravity of his situation.

"Our means are yours for the asking, but for now, our ends are our own, Professor," Renley said.

Baxter wished he could rub his temples to ward off the three-aspirin headache building behind his eyeballs. "How long do I have to consider your offer?"

The man's lips curved into a smile that did not reach his

eyes. "Until Miss Mendeva grows tired of holding the gun. Then, of course, you can return to your laboratory."

Tasha moved close to Baxter's ear and whispered.

"As a lab specimen."

———

KADE MORGAN STOOD over the skeleton, now displayed in a long plastic container on a folding table. He tried to ignore the increasingly nagging itch on the tip of his nose, silently cursing the bulky white protective bio-containment suit that enclosed his entire body. He continued to examine the skeleton, scrunching his nose, trying unsuccessfully to ease the itch.

"It appears to be a male, approximately five feet, six inches," he spoke into the suit's built-in microphone. "Based on tooth wear, the age at time of death is estimated to be between thirty and fifty years." He focused his helmet camera on the arms and legs. "There appear to be no signs of physical trauma to the long bones or the cranium."

Who are you? What were you doing here?

Kade turned to the opening carved into the bottom of the entrance. The rest of the team, all decked out in their own biosuits, observed him silently. *Only one way to find out.* He moved closer to the stone door and crouched awkwardly in front of the exposed hole, the bulky suit preventing him from flexing his knees properly.

Thomas squatted beside him. "Just large enough for a man to crawl through," he said.

Or die in, Kade thought dryly as he ran his fingers around the perimeter of the opening. He peered inside, the light on his helmet illuminating the dark space before him. Hesitating, he glanced back at Ed Wallace and the rest of his team.

"This is your moment," Wallace's voice came through his headset. Kade turned to Thomas, who gave him a thumbs up.

His student flashed him a wide grin. "Lead the way, fearless one."

Kade slid into the opening. The hole was barely large enough to maneuver his body through it. After several long seconds of less-than-graceful shimmying, he emerged on the other side. His skin tingled and the sounds of his own breathing echoed strangely in the helmet of the PPE suit.

He spoke into the suit's mic with a trembling voice, "Morgan to base. I'm on the other side of the exterior door, inside of what appears to be a tunnel."

Kade jumped at the sound next to his leg. Ed Wallace peeked up at him through his glass visor. Ed snaked awkwardly through the narrow opening and stood up. He dusted off his suit and moved next to Kade. Moments later Thomas and three other students shuffled through the narrow opening one by one. They all stood inside the tunnel, spellbound.

Kade peered through the dark corridor, into the narrow cone of light carved by his headlamp.

"Initial observation confirms the data from the ground-penetrating radar," he said. "The corridor slopes down due east —the direction of the head." His skin prickled at his own words.

"Ten-four. This is base," the voice of the female student rang in Kade's headset. "Secondary analysis from your sensors just confirmed no pathogens in the air. Sure you want to keep the spacesuits on?"

"Whatever killed that guy may still be here," Kade replied. "This isn't the time to play the canary in the coalmine."

He turned to the wall and ran his fingers along the smooth surface. "No masonry patterns or features," he said. "No hierograms indicating its origin or period. Just like the exterior door."

"Highly unusual for Egyptian architecture," Ed said.

"Maybe because it's not from an Egyptian period," Thomas countered.

Kade shot him a sideways glance.

Thomas shrugged. "Just calling it how I see it, boss. You know it's on everybody's mind."

"Morgan to base," Kade said into the mic. "We're proceeding down the corridor."

"Roger that," the female student replied. "Your video and audio are coming through loud and clear."

They slowly processed along the narrow corridor, their helmet lights illuminating the sloping tunnel ahead. As they approached another stone door, Kade's light caught an object on the floor. He moved closer, focusing his light on it—and stopped in his tracks when his helmet light hit a body.

Thomas recoiled. "Cripes!" he blurted.

"Relax, Indiana," Kade said. "No snakes around." He cautiously approached the body. Tattered clothes hung loosely on the decomposing man, whose empty eye sockets stared sightlessly upward.

Thomas swallowed hard. "This one is still decaying. But if he died later than the guy in the door, how did he get past him?" he asked.

"They died at the same time," Kade replied. "The desert

environment sped up the decomposition process out there. The lower temperature in the tunnel made for a slower decomposition rate. My guess is they were in the same party."

He looked over his shoulder at Wallace. "The clothes are European," he said. "Early twentieth century? That would make it consistent with our estimate of the timeframe of the tools used to carve the opening in the exterior door."

Wallace seemed not to notice the man or hear Kade. He continued wordlessly past them to the end of the tunnel and stopped in front of another stone entrance. Mesmerized, he moved his hands toward the carving in the center of the door, a bird in flight, its talons locked around a triangular object.

Thomas glanced at Wallace then knelt on one knee beside Kade. "Check out the ring on his hand."

Kade bent closer to the man's left hand. A gold signet ring circled the bone that had once been the man's little finger. Kade struggled to keep his hand steady as he gently slid the ring off the decomposing body and lifted it.

He squinted, straining to focus on the coat of arms engraved into the signet. A half-eagle, half-lion reared on its hind legs, eager to tear into its prey. Kade froze and stared at Thomas.

"A griffin," he whispered. "That greedy bastard found it, after all."

Thomas gave him a blank look.

"The griffin was the sigil of Lord George Renley, arguably the most infamous explorer of the early twentieth century," Kade continued. "He used his inheritance to amass the largest private collection of antiquities in Europe, then he spent his final years and most of his money seeking the Hall of—"

Kade was interrupted by a brilliant blue light that filled the tunnel. He snapped his head to the stone entrance. Ed Wallace stood at the door, his helmet cast in a blue hue that emanated from the shimmering triangular object locked inside the bird's talons. His face glowed through the visor and his lips curled into a thin smile as they moved in a breathless whisper, a single word, barely audible in Kade's headset.

"Finally."

ALYSSA PAUSED the episode of *Bill Nye The Science Guy* that was playing on her tablet and craned her neck to glance over the back of the student sitting in front of her. She sighed loudly when she saw the clock in the front of the large lecture hall. *Five more minutes…*

The young woman sitting ahead of her turned around. "Almost over—hang in there, kiddo," she said. "You're a real champ making it through your dad's lectures."

Alyssa flushed and she buried her head in the tablet as her dad's voice carried on from the front of the lecture hall.

"In 1923, psychic Edgar Cayce made the claim that he had discovered the location of the fabled lost Hall of Records," he continued, "a library purported to have dwarfed the great Library of Alexandria, containing the history and technology— a technology more advanced than even our own—of the lost civilization of… Atlantis."

Atlantis? She lifted her head as she heard several students mutter.

Her dad looked up from his notes at the roomful of undergraduate students that filled the hall. He met her eyes and gave her a wink. Alyssa smiled shyly and hid behind the student in front of her.

"This location was under the Great Sphinx of Giza, which Cayce claimed was actually built in the image of the ruler of this ancient civilization."

A young man in the front row raised his hand. Alyssa's dad nodded to him.

"But, Dr. Morgan, wasn't the Sphinx built by the pharaoh who built the Great Pyramids?" he asked. "Khufu or Khafre?"

"Very good, Mr. Wallace," her dad replied. "Mainstream Egyptology tells us that Khafre, son of Khufu, built the Sphinx. Then, in the late nineteen eighties, respected Egyptologist Francis Chaplain claimed to have evidence proving that the true age of the Sphinx didn't fit into any of the established timetables of the Old or New Kingdoms, casting doubt on its actual age. Unfortunately for him, his echoing of Cayce's earlier claims of an advanced civilization left him marginalized in academia."

"But that's not fair," the student shot back. "He was simply proposing another theory!"

"Scientists are complicated at best, Ed... and ruthless at their worst," her dad responded. "Chaplain found that out the hard way and lived out the rest of his life as a—" he paused, a distant flicker of regret crossing his eyes—"a grumpy old hermit."

"Well, I'll leave you all with that until next time we meet, which is... uh..." he fumbled with his notes.

Alyssa perked up. "Thursday at two p.m., Dad," she said before thinking.

The students in the auditorium laughed. Her dad looked up with an embarrassed smirk.

"Right. Thank you, sweetheart. Yes, see you all on Thursday at two p.m.!"

Alyssa packed her tablet in her backpack and followed the students down the stairs of the auditorium as they rushed out of the room to their next lectures.

"Finally!" Alyssa yelled, darting for her dad. "All this talk about mummies is giving me the creepies!"

"Creepies?" he faced her. "Come on, they're not that scary."

Alyssa put her fists on her hips and frowned. "If having your brain pulled out through your nose isn't creepy, I don't know what is."

Her dad stared at her for several moments. He shook his head and laughed. "You've got a valid point there, kiddo." He turned to the computer connected to the projector and brought up an image of a mummy on the screen.

Alyssa wrinkled her nose when she saw the tattered rags hanging on the shriveled body. "Ewww…"

Her dad stepped behind her and put his hands on her shoulders. "Give it a chance. Try to look beyond the icky factor. What do you see?"

Alyssa forced herself to look at the image. "Some ancient dried-out guy who's been dead for ages?"

"Actually, this is a woman," he said. "We can tell from the shape of the pelvis and the type of ornaments with which she was buried." He pointed at the screen. "Also, do you see how she was laid to rest with her arms crossed? That and the high quality of the wrappings suggest that she was a noble woman, perhaps even a member of a royal family." Her dad faced her. "By studying her, we can learn all about her culture, the diseases and injuries she may have suffered, even what kinds of food she ate. We can even take 3D images of the bones that allow us to reconstruct what she looked like." He scrolled through the files before selecting a computer-generated image of an exotic looking woman with elegant features and jet-black, braided hair and striking brown eyes.

"Wow—she's beautiful!" Alyssa said.

"See, you don't have to be afraid of mummies." He looked at her impishly. "So… you know why mummies are so good at keeping secrets?"

Alyssa cocked her head.

"They keep them under wraps." He winked at her.

Alyssa stared at him, her brow crinkled, then rolled her eyes. "Daaaad… just when it was getting good!"

"Oh, come on—it wasn't *that* bad." He laughed. "For a science geek." He held her gaze for a moment longer then his expression seemed to shift. He swallowed and looked down. When he looked up again, he had turned serious. He picked her up and set her on the big table.

"Sweetheart. I got a call this morning."

Alyssa felt a lump in the pit of her stomach. "Uh-oh. You've got that look again."

"You know the position I applied for? In Cairo?"

Alyssa pulled away from him as realization set in. "No, Dad. I don't want to go to Egypt! I want to stay here!"

"Sweetheart…"

Alyssa began to cry. "Dad, no… please don't make us

move." She felt the tears running down her cheeks. "If Mom was still alive we'd never go. I don't want to go to Egypt. I love it here!"

Her dad pulled her close and held her tightly. "You will love it there, too. You'll see. You just have to give it a chance." He took her face gently in his hands. "Will you give it a chance, Alyssa? For us? For Mom?"

She remained quiet as the tears streaked down her cheeks.

"Alyssa?" her dad repeated, pleading.

———

"ALYSSA?"

Alyssa stirred. She regained consciousness slowly, her brain fumbling for a connection to her senses. The soft hum of the fluorescent lights and smell of antiseptic registered first. Then the soft, regular chirping that echoed her heartbeat. Her head was pounding and her body felt as if somebody had scraped out her gut with a trowel. She slowly opened her eyes, straining to focus. *I'm in a bed... a hospital bed.* She saw the young man sitting in the simple metal chair next to the bed.

His head jerked up and he darted to the door. "Doctor, she's waking up!"

He whirled and rushed back to the bed. "Alyssa, how are you feeling? You scared us to death!"

She was still trying to process his words when her mind registered a woman's voice. "Slowly, *joven*, all in time." The woman's voice was calm but firm as she entered the room, her Spanish accent giving it a fiery tone. She approached the bed.

"*Señorita* Morgan, I am Dr. Raquel Huerta. Do you know where you are?"

Alyssa sluggishly focused on the woman. Thinking felt like running under water. Gradually things began to fill in. *I was doing fieldwork... New Zealand... no... South America. I'm in South America.* She spoke hesitantly. "Peru."

"Bravo*, señorita,* very good." The physician smiled. "You are at *Clinica Panamericana* in Cusco. Do you know why you are here?"

Her memories began to take shape. *The Chinisiri site... Inca graves...* "We were cataloguing grave sites." Her tongue felt thick in her mouth as she spoke.

She saw the young man breathe a sigh of relief. *Jacob.* She gave him a tired smile.

He stared back, the concern not yet ready to leave his face.

"What... happened?" she asked.

"What were you thinking, Alyssa? You've never even flown solo..."

"Flown solo?" Her mind leaped. *The men with the guns!*

She bolted up, ignoring the sudden wave of nausea that hit her. "Who were those men?" She paused and looked at Jacob, exhaling quietly.

"Thank God you're okay." She felt dizzy as the memories came flooding back. "The team?"

"Easy, *señorita,*" the physician said. "You must rest your head. What is the last thing you remember?"

Alyssa struggled to recall. "The plane..." She dropped her head, dejected. "I crashed the friggin' plane." Her shoulders slumped. "Kade's gonna be *so* pissed."

The woman gently touched Alyssa's head and shined a pen

light into each pupil. Alyssa winced at the bright glow. "You suffered a concussion, but you were very lucky to escape serious injury. For now, you must rest. You will be out of the hospital and on your feet before you know it." She turned to Jacob. "You may have a few moments with the *señorita*, but please be brief."

Jacob waited for the doctor to leave the room. He pulled his chair closer to the bed then reached out and touched Alyssa's hand. She flinched, Jacob had never been comfortable with physical contact between them. Even a simple hug made him blush like a beetroot.

"The others are fine. They are outside the room."

"What happened, Jake? Who were those men?"

"After you crashed they just... took off."

Alyssa stared at him, confused. "That doesn't make any sense! They come in, wave guns in your face, then just take off? What did they want?"

He shook his head, seemingly bracing himself for what came next. "Alyssa, do you remember the call from your dad?"

Alyssa's mind leaped again. *The Hall of Records! The flight to Egypt!* Her head spun as another wave of nausea threatened to overwhelm her. "The dig in Egypt! How long have I been out? I need to get to—"

Jacob inhaled sharply. "That was two days ago."

"What? I gotta get out of here!"

"I'm sorry Alyssa, you heard the doc. You aren't in any condition to travel."

She glared at him and pulled her hand back. "Damn it, Jacob! You have no idea how important this was to him. This was his big moment and I missed it. And now I'm stuck in a friggin' hospital on the other side of the world!"

Jacob drew back, startled, and she softened her tone. "I'm sorry, Jake. I know it's not your fault. It's just…" She felt tears well up.

Jacob's eyes never left hers. He reached for her hand again and placed it between his palms. She felt his fingers tight and warm against her skin. "Ally." It was the first time he had called her by her nickname. "I'm so sorry." He hesitated. "There is much worse."

Alyssa stared at him, unblinking, unaware she was holding her breath.

"Something went terribly wrong during the dig," Jacob continued. "Your dad and the rest of his team have gotten very ill. Dr. Wallace… is dead."

Kade is sick, Ed Wallace dead? Alyssa's mind raced. Her body began to tremble. *How…?* She didn't notice the tears running freely over her cheeks. *I should have been there.*

When she finally managed to speak, her voice came out as a cracked whisper. "Tell me everything you know."

He took a deep breath. "Everything was going to plan initially. They were wearing their bio-containment suits, but somehow they must have gotten exposed to something. A few minutes after entering the tunnel, they all started getting sick. The Egyptian authorities suspect a spore-forming virus and have quarantined the area. They're not letting anybody anywhere near the site. CDC and the World Health Organization sent their teams and started their own investigations."

Alyssa stared at him. "I have to go back to Egypt," she said. "I have to see him."

"Alyssa, your dad is in Level 4 isolation. Nobody is allowed to see him." He grimaced, a pained expression on his tired face. "I'm so sorry…"

Alyssa's throat was beginning to close up. The throbbing in her head was unbearable. She clenched her hands until she felt her fingernails bite deep into the soft flesh of her palms.

"Will you bring me my laptop?

"Alyssa. You need to rest. You heard—"

"Jacob…" she stared at him, her jaw set.

His eyes told her that he recognized the futility in trying to argue.

"Yes, of course," he said quietly and left the room.

———

DR. KAMAL KHANNA was completely enclosed in his white Biosafety Level 4 suit as he stared at the large monitor connected to the high-powered microscope, his brow furrowed in frustration. He turned a knob to reposition the slide and analyzed another section of Kade Morgan's blood sample as he adjusted the focus.

His eyes narrowed when he caught the silhouette of a dark pentagon in the corner of the screen. He repositioned the object into the center of the display and increased the magnification. He traced the outline of the strange object with his gloved finger, vexed.

"Is that a capsule, Ahmed?" he said to the other man in the laboratory. "It doesn't match any bacteria or virus I've ever seen."

"None of the blood samples match anything in our database," the other man replied, trying to hide his frustration. "The other teams are running more tests, but so far nothing!"

Kamal opened his mouth to reply when the computer beeped, indicating an incoming call. He sighed and pressed a button to accept it. His expression brightened when he recognized the young woman on his monitor.

"Kamal?" Alyssa said. "How is Kade?"

Kamal's smile faded. "I'm so sorry about this, Alyssa."

"How is he?"

"Not good, I'm afraid." Kamal said glumly. "We're still waiting for results to show any positive leads."

"And Dr. Wallace? Was there nothing…?"

"Ed was pronounced dead at the site."

"I'm taking the first flight back. When can I see him?"

"He is in Level 4 isolation with restricted access. Only medical staff is permitted—"

"He's my father!"

"I'm sorry, Alyssa, I won't allow you to endanger yourself. Until we know what we're dealing—"

"You can't be serious!"

The other scientist gently stepped in. "Miss Morgan…"

"Alyssa, this is Dr. Ahmed Farag," Kamal said, "Egypt's leading infectious diseases specialist. Dr. Farag is leading this investigation."

"Miss Morgan, I can only imagine how difficult this must be for you," Farag continued, "but please rest assured, your father is receiving the best possible care. We simply cannot risk—"

"Whatever!" Alyssa snapped. She took a deep breath. "Can I at least talk to him?"

"He's delirious, not making any sense." Kamal shook his head. "He keeps talking about something he found—"

"Something he found?" Alyssa interrupted. "What did the feeds show?"

"The feeds?"

"The video footage from the dig! Somebody must have looked at it!"

"All of the equipment is undergoing full decontamination before the official investigation."

Alyssa's mouth was set in a thin line, her expression unreadable.

"Alyssa?"

Her frown deepened as the silence dragged on. Finally, she said, "Thank you, Kamal." She ended the connection.

"Alyssa!"

Kamal looked at Farag, his mouth open, then sighed deeply and turned back to the microscope.

————

ALYSSA CLOSED her laptop and stared at Jacob. Her shoulders slumped as she sat in the hospital bed struggling against the achiness building in her chest.

"I should have been there with him."

"You would have ended up in the room next to him. Or worse." He handed her a glass of water and flashed her a tired grin. "So, who's this Kamal fellow? He looked pretty dashing in that spaceman get-up. Should I be getting jealous?"

Alyssa took a small sip of the water and gave him a half

smile. "One of my father's friends, a molecular biologist. He got promoted and now runs a big research inst—"

"*Señorita* Morgan!"

Their heads snapped to the door. Alyssa winced when she met Dr. Huerta's scowl.

"*Señorita* Morgan, what is this?" The doctor pointed at her laptop and gave a heavy sigh. "You must brain rest. It is very important." She approached Alyssa, her arm outstretched. "Your computer. *Por favor.*"

Alyssa grabbed her laptop tight.

"No."

"*Por favor, señorita.*" She scowled and shot a stern look in Jake's direction. "*Señor* Jacob. You are the *señorita's novio*, yes? She must rest."

"Yes, ma'am," Jake stuttered, a blank look on his face. *"Novio?"* he asked.

"No, wait, he's not my—" Alyssa started.

The doctor glanced at Jake. "*Novio*… as you say… *boyfriend*, yes?"

Jake froze and lit up like a red nose on a reindeer. He opened his mouth but no sound came out.

"So as *novio* you must take good care of—" the doctor continued.

"He's not my—" Alyssa repeated.

"No, no—" Jake finally stammered.

"What?" Dr. Huerta's eyebrows squished together in confusion. "You must take care—"

"Yes, of course," he said.

"What?" Alyssa shot him a confused look.

Jake's eyes ping-ponged from Dr. Huerta to Alyssa. "No, I

mean, yes, of course I will take care of… not that I'm your…"
He looked like he was about to hyperventilate.

Dr. Huerta snatched the computer from Alyssa. "I will keep safe," and turned around.

"No, wait—" Alyssa started. "My computer!"

"I'm n-not her *n-novio*!" Jake stammered as the woman continued to the door.

Dr. Huerta turned. "Five more minutes, *Señor* Jacob, then the *señorita* will rest," she said before stepping out of the room.

"I'm not her—" Jake repeated, gasping for air.

"He's not my—" Alyssa hollered.

"*Adolescentes*." Dr. Huerta shook her head as she closed the door.

TASHA STEPPED out of the small office and into the open space.
She pressed a button on the remote control in her hand and the
large metal door of the hangar began to slide open, revealing
the tarmac and pulsing lights of the runway in the distance. She
glanced up at George Renley with a satisfied smirk.

"I told you the professor would collaborate."

Renley stayed silent, studying her face. "What happened
in Peru?"

"Peru?"

"Don't play me for a fool, Tasha."

"Those weren't our men. Why would we care about
the girl?"

The man furrowed his brow. "If not you, then who?"

Tasha shrugged. Renley continued gazing at her silently.
After several moments he nodded to the private jet parked
inside the hangar. "You should go. Drake and the others are
waiting."

Tasha flinched at the name.

"The new leader is becoming impatient... and unpre-dictable," Renley said.

Tasha tried to ignore the thickness in her throat. "He scares me," she said softly.

Renley gently took her head in his hands. "Get close to him," he said.

"Why don't you come with me?" she asked. "The others... they will listen to you. They—"

"His father ruled the Society for four decades. Their loyalty to his legacy runs deep. As long as Drake controls the Society, he is useful to us."

She looked up at him and swallowed. "I will do as you ask."

He kissed her forehead then looked at her somberly. "Don't let his youth fool you. He has been groomed for this role ever since he was born. He may not suspect anything yet, but don't underestimate his intellect—William Drake is as perceptive as he is paranoid."

Tasha leaned into him, biting her lower lip to stop it from trembling. "I will miss you," she said.

———

ALYSSA FORCED herself to unclench her jaw as she watched Dr. Huerta's finger trace out a large "N" in front of her face. Her eyes slowly followed the physician's hand.

"You are making good progress, *Señorita* Morgan," Dr. Huerta said. "A few more days and you will be back on your feet." She made some notes on her clipboard and stepped out of the room.

Alyssa waited for the woman to close the door. She hit the bed with her fists and bolted up. "I gotta get out of here!"

"You heard Kamal," Jacob replied. "There is nothing you can do in Egypt. The best thing for you to do is to rest and get better."

Alyssa glared at him. "You just don't understand!"

Jacob raised his eyebrows. "What are you talking about?"

Alyssa took a deep breath. She closed her eyes, searching for a place to start. Finally, she said, "Do you remember the scoop on Francis Chaplain?"

"The loony with the 'ancient aliens' theories?" Jacob snickered.

"Yeah," Alyssa replied. "That one. He was actually a well-respected archaeologist for most of his career, but people really came down on him when he started claiming that the Sphinx was built by an advanced civilization. After his... downfall, he became a recluse and kept in touch with only a handful of people. There were even rumors of a secret society funded with money from Edgar Cayce and other well-to-dos who believed these stories." Alyssa swallowed hard. "Jake... Chaplain was my mom's father... my grandfather."

"What?" Jacob looked at her dumbfounded.

"When my parents met, my grandfather had already secluded himself, but he and Kade eventually grew close. Kade became interested in his work."

"You can't tell me your dad believed any of Chaplain's ramblings!"

Alyssa shrugged. "Maybe it started out as mere intellectual curiosity," she continued, "but it grew into a compulsion. Kade kept pushing. Finally, my grandfather relented and shared everything he knew."

Jacob's face was caught somewhere between a wince and a smile. "Chaplain... *the Chaplain*... and your dad?" He shook his head.

"Kade realized that the key to proving these theories was the Hall of Records. He and my mom followed a lead to Cambay when she..." Alyssa fought the tightness building in her chest. "My grandfather blamed Kade for what happened to my mom... He never forgave him."

Jacob leaned closer. "Have you?" he asked softly.

Alyssa scowled and pulled back. "If he hadn't dragged her with him—"

"Her death wasn't his fault, Alyssa," Jacob cut in gently. "You know that."

"Everything fell apart after we lost her, Jake," Alyssa said, struggling to ignore the burning behind her eyelids. "After we moved to Cairo, he just..." she trailed off.

Jacob watched her silently as she fought off the surge and crash of bitter emotions that awoke inside her.

"I just wanted to go home, Jake. Go back to Virginia with my dad... finally leave Egypt behind forever."

———

GRAYSON BAXTER barely noticed the constant hum of the twin engines of the Gulfstream VII private jet as he replayed the last several hours of his life in his head. To call it surreal would be an understatement. After he accepted the "offer," he and Tasha boarded the private jet waiting for them in the hangar. He looked at the young woman leaning back in the plush leather chair across from him.

"What's in Egypt?" he asked, mindful to keep his eyes on her face instead of her thighs, exposed by the short black skirt as she crossed her long legs.

Tasha Mendeva returned his gaze, unblinking. Finally, she leaned forward in her chair. "How much do you know about ancient Egyptian history, Professor?"

"Do I look like I give a damn?" he shot back.

Tasha smiled a thin smile. "Would you… *give a damn*… if you could be responsible for the greatest leap in human evolution?"

Baxter gave a bark of laughter but leaned forward and pushed up his glasses.

Tasha took a sip of her drink before she spoke, her voice flat and smooth, and decidedly unrushed. "There is evidence that a long time before Upper and Lower Egypt were unified into a single kingdom, before the climatic changes turned the Sahara into the desert it is now, there occurred a significant influx of technology and expertise that dates back thousands of years. According to Egyptian mythology, a king called Menes unified the two regions and built the Sphinx millennia before the Egyptian civilization…"

"Fascinating," Baxter said in a tone that implied the exact opposite.

"…and he lies buried beneath it," Tasha continued.

Baxter snorted. "Let's assume for a moment that your ludicrous theory about the Sphinx and Menes is true. Why do you care?"

"To unite Egypt and be worshiped as a living god required

more than just good strategic sense. There are clues that the ancient ruling society had genetic attributes that have since been lost."

Baxter's cynical smile slowly faded as he puzzled over this, tapping his fingers on his glass.

Tasha regarded him, her violet eyes sharp as scalpels. "Increased intelligence, extended life span, we don't even know what else is possible. Just imagine melding these attributes with modern technology—and reviving the genetic lineage that influenced Egyptian mythology."

"You want to fuse ancient genetic material into modern DNA to harness the power of an ancient civilization." Baxter pinched the bridge of his nose and squeezed his eyelids tightly, finally beginning to piece the puzzle together. "And you need me to isolate this genetic material from the remains, reconstruct the genes and develop a method to insert them into—"

"Us..." Tasha said as she leaned back in the chair and smiled, revealing her perfect white teeth.

Baxter shook his head emphatically, his gray hair waving in the air. "This has got to be the most ridiculous story I have ever heard." He drained the rest of his drink and set the glass loudly on the polished wooden tray. "The chances of reconstructing genes from DNA that old are zero. Even if we could extract the DNA, it would be degraded beyond any recognition."

She gave him a smug look. "What if I told you that the genetic material has been preserved?"

"What do you mean?" he asked, leaning forward.

"Egyptian mythology claims that Menes never truly died. Instead, he is sealed in a chamber beneath the Sphinx, watching over his descendants... a type of hibernation state that preserved him—and the genetic material."

He laughed. "Are you suggesting that somehow the technology existed thousands of years ago to induce the equivalent of cryogenic sleep?"

Tasha rolled her eyes eloquently. "I'm not suggesting that we can bring him back to life, if that's what you're implying. But we may be able to recover his genetic material."

Grayson Baxter took a deep breath and leaned back into the seat. He crossed his arms.

"Your Menes has been down there for millennia. Why the hurry now?"

———

ALYSSA PEERED at Jacob who seemed to struggle absorbing what he had just heard. She picked her fingernails as her teeth tugged at her lower lip.

"That hall, Jake, it cost our family so much. My grandfather's reputation... and sanity, my mom's life. And now Kade..."

Jacob rubbed his temples, his face betraying an internal battle. Finally, he sat up, swallowing hard.

"I probably shouldn't be telling you this, but you'll find out sooner or later," he said. "Kamal called again to check on you. He said this whole thing has turned into a full-out international turf war. The CDC and World Health Organization have declared the site off limits, pending a full investigation. All the equipment has been shipped to the World Health Organization

in London for a full inspection. Laptops, logs, recordings...
everything."

Alyssa stared at him, her mind racing. "Jake, something
really bad happened during that dig," she said. "I need to find
out what. They won't let me see him, but what about the video
feeds? Maybe they can provide some clues? I need to find out
what's making him ill—or go after anything that may point me
in the right direction." She paused. "I have to."

Jacob sighed. "There's no convincing you otherwise,
is there?"

"Will you help me?"

Jacob stared at her silently, his eyes glued to hers. Finally,
he said, "Of course, Alyssa... anything."

"I need my clothes and backpack."

Jacob nodded slowly. He stood and turned to leave.

"Wait, Jake."

"Yes?" He looked at her over his shoulder.

"You think you can get your hands on my laptop?"

He took a deep breath, nodded again, and reached for
the door.

"Oh, and..." she said, grimacing.

He stopped and turned.

"I need you to distract Dr. Huerta for me."

WILLIAM DRAKE SLAMMED his fist on the long mahogany conference table, spilling the Chateau Petrus champagne from his crystal glass. The sound reverberated through the room as it reflected off the ornate marble paneling decorating the walls.

He raised his head. "How the hell does the World Health Organization just stroll into an Egyptian excavation site and confiscate all the equipment?" He surveyed the dozen men and women sitting around the long table, the vintage wall sconces casting ghostly shadows across their faces.

After several heartbeats, a dark-haired woman at the far end of the table broke the silence. "The Egyptians were also taken by complete surprise," she said, an Italian accent complementing her sultry lips and the graceful lines of her cheekbones. "But this was an international project, involving an unknown pathogen, so the WHO claimed jurisdiction and—"

Drake silenced the woman with a look, his deep-set dark eyes burning into her like the lit end of a cigarette.

"Tell me, Dr. Tibaldi," Drake's words were barely a whisper

through his clenched jaw, "when you were invited to join the Society, was it based on your convictions for my father's theories and your expertise as a leading geologist, or was it based on your ability to make excuses for your incompetence?"

"You done yet?" a brusque voice cut through the room. "When you've finished ranting maybe we can figure out how to fix this mess and get us back on track."

Drake glared at the man sitting in the chair to his right. Grayson Baxter was the only person in the room whose clothes did not look like they belonged in a Vogue magazine ad. A faded, blue, button-down shirt was tucked halfheartedly into his khakis. Running a hand through his gray hair, the American geneticist calmly returned the young man's stare.

"What happened at the dig wasn't anybody's fault," Baxter continued. He threw a newspaper down on the table, pointing at the front page headline. "The Minister of Antiquities decided to make this event his personal public relations campaign, so the eyes of the world were already on the dig. The WHO had no choice but to secure the site and contain the mess."

"You're very clever, Professor, but sometimes your brain goes to your head," Drake replied with forced restraint.

Tasha Mendeva cleared her throat. "He has a point, Will. According to our sources at the WHO, the equipment was flown to their headquarters in London. It's scheduled to arrive there tomorrow morning."

Drake regarded her in silence, lips pressed together. Finally, he spoke.

"The object disappeared from the site. I need to know what happened to it," he said quietly. "Contact our man in England."

"And Kade Morgan?" Baxter asked.

Drake looked at him. "What about Kade Morgan?"

"We need to know what we're dealing with. He may be much more dangerous than those fools in the hospital realize."

Drake considered this then turned to Tasha. "This task seems particularly suited to your talents."

Tasha nodded curtly. "And the girl?" she asked.

Drake studied her for several moments. "She's harmless. For her sake, let's hope she stays in Peru."

———

"THIS IS the final boarding call for LatAm flight 2022 with service to London's Heathrow airport. All ticketed passengers should now be on board. The flight will depart…"

Alyssa tuned out the overhead announcement and gathered every last bit of energy, fighting for breath. *Come on!* She ignored the burning in her legs and willed them to move even faster as she raced through the terminal of the Cusco airport. Finally, she spotted her gate—and the gate agent stepping up to the metal door, closing it.

"Wait!" she yelled at the woman, breathless. "I'm coming!"

The agent looked up at Alyssa as she raced across the terminal, waving her boarding pass, backpack bouncing with every stride. The woman gave a small smile and held the door open.

"Slowly, *señorita*," she hollered to Alyssa. "We will wait."

Alyssa raced up to her, chest heaving. She handed the boarding pass to the woman.

"Thank… you…" she said between gasping breaths. The agent scanned her boarding pass and returned it to her.

"Have a nice flight," she said.

Alyssa nodded gratefully, too winded to muster a reply. She walked through the jetway into the airplane and continued along the narrow aisle toward her seat. She did her best to ignore the curious looks from the other passengers as she collapsed, wringing-wet, into her seat.

She reached for the water bottle and took a long sip, savoring the taste, her heartbeat slowly fading from her ears. *That was close…* She took another sip, pulled out her phone, and dialed Jacob's number.

He picked up on the first ring.

"Made it… barely," she said, her breathing finally starting to slow. "How's it going?"

"Uh… still recovering from the reaming I got from Dr. Huerta," he replied. "My Spanish may be rusty, but I don't think she likes me anymore."

Alyssa chuckled. "Thank you, Jake. I definitely owe you one."

"One?" he replied in semi-mock exasperation. "You have a very short memory!"

"I did just get whacked in the head pretty good."

"Nice try," Jacob laughed. "Anyway, the equipment should have arrived at the WHO this morning."

"Thank you, Jake. For everything."

"Good luck," he said. "Call me as soon as you land."

"Yes, sir," she replied, smirking.

Alyssa closed her eyes and let her breathing slow down, barely noting the plane pulling away from the gate and taxiing toward the runway. She leaned her head into the seat and smiled at the rush of the acceleration as the plane sped up and took to the air.

She allowed herself a few more moments of rest then reached into her backpack and pulled out her laptop. *I suppose there's an upside to all the hours spent getting all the permits for our digs.* She opened it up and began browsing through several directories until she spotted the file she was looking for, a letter from the dean of the archaeology department to her father. She opened the file and scanned the formal-looking Cairo University letterhead and the dean's signature at the bottom of the document. Her lips curved into a smirk before she erased the content of the letter and began typing:

I hereby authorize Dr. Alyssa Morgan to inspect the property of Cairo University, shipped to the World Health Organization...

———

THE HAZY GLOW of the afternoon sun found its way through the wooden shutters of the Thatchers Arms Pub, casting banded shadows onto the solitary patron sitting at the bar. Gavriel's dark gray, tailored suit seemed at odds with the cozy interior of the seaside pub and accentuated his broad shoulders and square face as he studied the brim-filled shot glass with a predatory stare.

He reached for the glass with his gloved hand and brought it under his nose, savoring the smell. He emptied it in one throw, letting the taste of the tequila linger on his tongue before setting the glass down next to the open bottle.

The silence in the pub was interrupted by a soft ringtone. Gavriel ignored the intrusion and slowly refilled his glass before reaching inside his jacket. He pulled out his phone and answered it on the third ring.

"Drake has a job for you." Gavriel felt a smile tilting the corner of his mouth as he recognized Tasha's voice.

"My schedule just opened up," he replied, his voice flat.

"World Health Organization, London. Await further instructions," Tasha said and ended the connection.

Gavriel emptied the glass and placed it on the bar, upside down. He reached to the stool next to him and grasped the 9mm Glock semi-automatic pistol. With unhurried movements, he unthreaded the silencer from his weapon and holstered both into the shoulder harness concealed under his jacket. He stood and strode for the door, taking care to step over the blood encircling the two lifeless bodies on the floor.

ALYSSA GLANCED up from the computer monitor and rubbed the back of her neck, working the knots, trying to persuade her stiff muscles to forget about the ten-hour flight she spent crammed into the middle seat. She fidgeted in the new pencil skirt suit she had picked up at one of the airport boutiques and scrunched her toes inside the high heels. *How can women wear these all day long?*

She glanced at her watch. *3:45 p.m.* Going through passport control and customs at Heathrow had taken longer than she'd hoped. A ride on the express train and the famed London underground had gotten her to the small café across from the World Health Organization building.

I'm cutting it close. Hope I'll make it there before they take off for the day.

She swiped her credit card through the reader attached to the computer then plugged her thumb drive into the USB port and waited for her files to appear on the screen. She double-clicked on the letter she wrote on the plane and read through it one last time.

TO WHOM IT MAY CONCERN:

I hereby authorize Dr. Alyssa Morgan to inspect the property of Cairo University, shipped to the World Health Organization. Please grant Dr. Morgan all necessary rights and privileges required to conduct a thorough evaluation and to catalogue the contents of the shipment.

Sincerely,

Prof. Salah El-Haddad

Dean, Department of Archaeology

University of Cairo

Alyssa took a deep breath and hit the print icon. She waited a few seconds then glanced at the printer attached to the computer. She frowned when she didn't hear the familiar whine of the printer powering up.

She hit the print icon a couple of times and looked at the printer again expectantly.

Nothing.

Fantastic, she sighed a measure louder than she had intended and stood. She craned her head behind the monitor, scrutinizing the cables running between the computer and the printer.

"Having a spot of bother?" Alyssa jumped at the voice behind her and whirled. A young man stood next to her desk and smiled. "Need a hand?"

She eyeballed him. His shoulder-length, chestnut hair

matched his playful eyes. His tweed slacks and Tattersall button-down shirt were a perfect match for his British accent. *Why is it that a British accent always makes guys sound smarter... and look cuter?* He looked like he hadn't shaved in a couple of weeks, but the scruff fit him.

"Uh..." she stammered, "it's not coming out... the paper. Not printing." *Brilliant,* she thought. *Me Jane, you Tarzan.*

"Rough day, huh?" he asked.

You have no idea. "I've had better."

He glanced at the computer. "Probably a software flab," he said. "The new system update buggered up all the legacy drivers."

She gave him a blank look. "I'll take your word for it. Do you work here?"

"Nah," he grinned. "Just grabbing a cuppa and a bite on my lunch break." He pointed at the computer. "Mind if I have a little look?"

"She's all yours." Alyssa moved aside and the young man sat in the chair and opened up a new window on the desktop. He scrolled through the settings for several moments then looked up and furrowed his brow. "Well, the drivers all seem to be in order." He rubbed his chin.

"So what now?" Alyssa asked.

"Could be the connection," he replied. "Let's check it out."

Alyssa watched with a raised eyebrow as he got off the chair and his head disappeared under the table. She didn't try to hide her smirk as she watched him wiggle his way to the cables at the back of the computer.

"Sure you know what you're doing there?" she asked.

"Don't you fret, just give me a minute," she heard him mumbling. "It's darker than a goth party down here."

Did he just say 'don't you fret?' Alyssa thought as she reached into her pocket and took out her phone then turned on the flashlight. She resisted the urge to tap his butt and opted for poking him in the side. "Here, try this."

"Ah—cheers," he said and took it.

"What a mess," he sighed. "Hang on… just got to find the USB port where the printer—"

Alyssa drew a deep breath. "Maybe I'd better get somebody who works here."

"No, no. Just hang tight… almost there."

"Take your time," Alyssa muttered under her breath. "Not like I have to be somewhere."

"What?" he asked.

"What?" Alyssa replied.

"Got it! Here we go," he said—a second before the monitor went black. "Wait, uh… I think that was the monitor cable."

Alyssa rolled her eyes. "Oh, come on!" she groaned and smacked the printer. The young man jumped and she cringed at the sound of his head hitting the underside of the table.

"Ow! What the—?" The noise of the printer powering up froze the next word coming out of his mouth.

The young man emerged from under the desk. Alyssa gave him a sheepish smile as he rubbed his head.

"Well, that'll work, too, I suppose…" he said, grimacing.

Alyssa waited for the print-out and took the letter, folded it neatly and slid it into a folder in her backpack. She logged off the computer and turned to the young man.

"Thanks for your help," she said.

"Uh, seems like you're actually quite self-sufficient." He looked down and fidgeted for a moment. He tugged down his shirt and looked at her, blowing out a long breath. "Care to join me for a coffee? I've got another fifteen minutes." He smirked. "Perhaps you could give me a lesson in your ninja approach to computers."

Alyssa gave him a smile, but it was sad and distracted. "I wish I could," she replied, feeling a bit more rueful than she cared to admit. "But I gotta run."

"You sure?"

"Yeah," she said.

"Very well," he replied, a flicker of disappointment crossing his eyes. "Cheers, then."

Alyssa nodded and turned quickly, surprised at the heaviness in her chest. She stepped toward the counter when she spotted a standing display of reading glasses. She considered for a moment.

This may help.

She approached the display and picked up a cat-eye, leopard print set then put on the glasses and looked at herself in the mirror.

Uh, maybe a bit much, she scowled. *I hope he's not watching me.* She shook off the thought as she reached for another pair, a brown tortoise-shell frame with etched metal temples. She took out her ponytail and shook her hair loose before putting on the glasses. She squinted as she adjusted to her vision going blurry then scrutinized herself in the mirror again. The glasses accentuated her olive skin and high cheekbones, and the tortoise shell brought out the deep brown of her irises. Still, the tired look in her eyes and the glasses added at least five years to her age.

Some strategic eyeliner and I may just be able to pull this one off, she thought, still squinting. *Between the glasses and the high heels, I really hope I won't faceplant crossing the street.*

"They suit you nicely," the young man said from across the room.

I knew it!

She turned to him. "Thanks," she replied, blushing.

"Sure about that coffee? Best latte in Bloomsbury here," he said, regarding her. "You look like you could use one."

"Maybe another time," she said. "Besides, I'm more of an espresso type."

He flashed a pensive smile and nodded as Alyssa grabbed her backpack and turned to the checkout.

———

ALYSSA'S STOMACH fluttered with a quickening sense of anticipation as she passed the water fountain in the heart of the elegant square that served as the entryway to the London headquarters of the World Health Organization. *This is either brilliant or really stupid.* She stepped through the revolving glass door and headed for the reception counter with as confident a gait as the three-inch heels sanctioned.

Here we go.

The security guard lifted his head. "May I help you, Miss—?"

"*Doctor* Morgan," Alyssa replied in her most mature voice and handed him the letter and her research associate ID. Her father had to jump through hoops to get her this ID card, but eventually Cairo University relented to his claims that it was a necessary for her safety when she accompanied him on his digs. *Kade probably didn't exactly have this in mind.*

She pushed the new glasses up her nose with a solitary finger. "My equipment arrived this morning. I'm here to inspect it."

The guard looked at the ID and read the letter then eyed her up and down.

"Doctor... Alyssa Morgan?"

"That's correct," Alyssa gave a frosty smile. "Is there a problem?"

"No, Miss, I mean, Dr. Morgan," He looked at the letter again. "The letter appears to be in order, ma'am, but I do need to verify the request with your institution."

Alyssa gave the guard a nervous smile.

"Is that truly necessary?" she asked. "I've been traveling all night from Peru and am quite eager to start the inspection."

"Yes, ma'am. It will only take a minute. Shall I call the number on the letter?" He reached for the phone.

Alyssa's chest tightened. She stared at the guard as he began dialing the number for the Dean of Archaeology.

I'm so screwed. Her gaze ping-ponged around the lobby, her mind racing for options.

I should have known this would never—

She froze when she spotted the young man from the Internet café walk through the door and stride toward her. *You've gotta be kidding me! Can't this guy take no for an answer?* She opened her mouth.

"Ah, Dr. Morgan! There you are." He hollered and waved at

her before she could say a word. He strolled up to her and gave her a smirk.

"It's so good to see you again," he continued. "Professor Garrison has been expecting you for the inspection of the equipment. I trust you had a smooth trip?"

Alyssa's mouth opened and closed, unable to speak. The young man pulled out his ID badge and gave her a look.

"Uh… yes, thank you—" she pulled her glasses down just enough to make out the name on his ID badge—"Paul. Quite nice."

"So glad to hear that, ma'am." Paul smiled and handed his badge to the security guard.

"Everything is in order, Blake," he said. "Please register Dr. Morgan as a visitor to our department."

The security guard considered for a moment then hung up the phone and took Paul's badge. He scanned it, handed Alyssa a visitor badge and pointed to the X-ray scanner.

"Please place your items on the belt, Doctor."

Alyssa nodded, willing herself to breathe, then laid her backpack on the belt and walked through the security scanner, with Paul following closely behind.

A few seconds later, they entered an elevator. Once the doors closed, Alyssa turned to Paul.

"What…? How did you know?" she asked, baffled.

He flashed her an enigmatic grin.

"I'm serious," she kept her stern look.

Paul reached into his pocket and handed her a couple of folded pieces of paper. Her mouth fell open when she realized they were printouts of the letter she wrote.

"That whack you gave the printer did its job, apparently.

There were a couple files in the print queue that came out right after you left." A flush crept across his cheeks. "I couldn't help taking a look at them. Sorry... curiosity sometimes gets the best of me."

She eyed him guardedly for a few seconds, brows pulling in. "Why did you help me?" she asked, finally.

Paul studied her for several moments. "You looked like you could use it." Then he smirked, his eyes crinkling. "And I desperately want another chance at that coffee—and a lesson in martial arts."

Alyssa continued to eye him quietly. Finally, she extended her hand.

"I'm Alyssa—but you already know that."

"Paul." He accepted her hand with a grin. "But you already knew that, too."

Alyssa found it easy to return his smile. "So, this is where all the techies work?"

"Sort of," he replied. "I'm interning this summer. When I'm not facilitating a level three security breach, that is." He hesitated. "So why the charade?"

Alyssa's smile faded. "It's a long story."

"It's a slow elevator."

"My father... he's an archaeologist. Some equipment was shipped here from a dig in Cairo. I was hoping—"

"Wait, your dad was involved with the cock-up in Cairo?"

"It was his expedition."

Paul whistled. "Brilliant," he said and scratched his scruffy beard. "Well, if the equipment just arrived today, it should still be in storage. It's a good thing shipping and receiving is part of my intern duties." He gave her a mischievous smirk and pressed the button for the basement. "Shall we have a little look?"

———

THE MAN DRIVING the silver Jaguar was acutely aware of his surroundings as he skillfully navigated the sedan through the traffic on the M11 toward London. Gavriel glanced at his watch and allowed himself a brief nod of satisfaction. He was making good time.

A beep on his phone indicated an incoming text. He looked down and read the message.

TARGET LOCATION: WHO STORAGE FACILITY, BASEMENT

SHIPMENT ORIGIN: CAIRO

SHIPMENT ID: 214902

SECURITY CREDENTIALS: PENDING

ALYSSA WAS KEENLY aware of the sound of their footsteps
echoing down the long corridor as they exited the elevator and
paced briskly toward the wide double-door at the end of the
hallway.

"The video footage you mentioned," Paul said, breaking the
silence, "nobody has bothered to check it to see what really
happened down there?"

"I guess they were too busy trying to keep the team from
dying," Alyssa replied dryly. Paul furrowed his brow and she
instantly regretted her tone. Before she had a chance to say
another word, they stopped in front of the door and Paul pulled
out his badge.

"Here we go," he said.

He swiped it through the keypad next to the door, waited for
the short beep, then entered a code.

Alyssa braced herself for the sound of an alarm. For an
unimaginably long second nothing happened. Then the light on
the panel changed from red to green, and the magnetic seals

released the glass doors. They parted with a swooshing sound, opening into the dimly lit room ahead of them. She let out a deep breath, unaware she had been holding it.

Paul flashed her a grin before motioning her to enter the room with an exaggerated gesture.

"After you, Dr. Morgan," he said.

Alyssa smiled a thin smile and held his gaze over her shoulder as she entered the room. A moment later the automated lights broke the darkness. She gasped at the size of the space before her. Dozens of shelves stood in neatly organized parallel rows, each holding scores of crates and boxes of all sizes.

"This could take a while..." she said, sagging.

"Don't you fret," Paul gave her a reassuring look and moved to a computer terminal sitting at a desk near the door. "Our cataloguing system would make Mr. Dewey proud." He swiped his badge across the reader and glanced at the monitor.

"Row 14, Section C," he said after a few seconds. "Let me see if I can access the logs for the shipment."

He keyed in several commands. As he studied the display, his face turned glum.

"What is it?" Alyssa asked.

"Well, the good news is that all the items that were in the tunnel have been moved out of quarantine and have been decontaminated. The bad news is that they are being stored in the secured area."

"Secured area?"

Paul pointed to another door at the back of the room.

"Can we get in there?" Alyssa asked.

He hesitated. "Theoretically, yes. But," he pointed at a

camera monitoring the door to the secure storage area, "the surveillance cameras would pick us up the moment we enter. You need a special requisition to go in there."

Alyssa felt a lump rise in her throat. "What about the laptops? Can we at least get our hands on those?"

"Let's see…" Paul slid his finger down the list on the monitor.

"Got it! Field laptop computer—Kaden Morgan," Paul said. "Item twelve, shipping crate three."

Alyssa lit up. She turned and scanned the numbers on the shelves then ducked into one of the aisles. Paul hurried after her as she paced through the aisle, her eyes moving up and down the labels affixed to the crates sitting on the shelves. She pointed at one of them. "Here it is!"

Paul helped her drag the crate from the shelf and they opened the lid. Alyssa reached inside and pulled out a laptop, a triumphant look on her face.

"It's his!"

Paul grinned and gave her a thumbs up. "What are we waiting for? Let's boot'er up!"

———

GAVRIEL DEFTLY MANEUVERED the Jaguar into the tight parking space along the busy four-lane street outside of the World Health Organization and turned off the engine. He took a deep breath and closed his eyes, savoring the brief respite. He removed the thin leather gloves from his hands and rubbed his temples, trying in vain to tune out the pressure building behind his eyeballs. He reached into his pocket. The touch of the small metal box heightened his anticipation, as he flipped it open and removed one of the small pills. He placed it under his tongue, relishing the familiar burning sensation and awareness of the adrenaline thrumming through his veins.

He forced himself to open his eyes and glanced out of the driver's side window across the diligently manicured grounds and large square toward the entrance of the modern-looking facility. He reached for his phone and typed a message.

ON LOCATION

Gavriel watched the display as the replies came in. A message, a photograph, another attachment. He glanced at the photograph, his contact inside the building. He scanned the message.

SECURITY CREDENTIALS: COMPLETE

ID DELIVERY: BRUSH PASS

RENDEZVOUS: MAIN LOBBY, 5 MINUTES

He opened up the attachment and studied the floor plan, his mind and senses sharp as a razor.

————

ALYSSA AND PAUL sat on the floor of the storage facility staring at the laptop monitor. Paul glanced away from the display and turned to Alyssa. She drew her long, espresso-colored hair into a tight ponytail, exposing her high cheekbones and the graceful lines of her face. Her teeth tugged at her chapped lower lip as she scanned the folders on the desktop. He suddenly realized it was the natural, gentle down-curve of her full lips and her understated elegance that made her so appealing, perhaps even more so because she seemed disarmingly unaware of it.

As if sensing his gaze, she looked at him. She lifted her eyebrows in slight surprise. He quickly turned back to the monitor. If she noticed his embarrassment, she didn't show it. She leaned forward and flicked the touchpad.

"Check this out. It looks like three of them were wearing helmet cams—including Kade." She hesitated for a second before she double-tapped on the file named KM_CAM1.

Paul moved closer to the display. He was distinctly aware of Alyssa's shallow and rapid breaths only inches from his neck as the playback began.

———

GAVRIEL LOOKED up from the floor plan and checked his watch.

Time.

Slowly, he stretched the thin leather gloves over his hands then reached into his shoulder holster and pulled out the Glock semi-automatic pistol. He ensured the seventeen-round magazine was at capacity then threaded a silencer onto the barrel, reholstered the weapon, and stepped out of the car.

———

ALYSSA FELT a pebbling of goose bumps creep up her arms as she stared at the display. The view from Kade's helmet camera showed him and the team moving along a long, dark corridor.

"He was right all along," she whispered, unable to keep her voice from shaking. She gasped as the camera panned to the side and focused on a dead body on the ground, tatters of clothing still clinging to the corpse. Her father bent over the body and examined it briefly then took a ring off the skeleton's finger and held it up. They heard her father's muffled voice when the camera view whirled and the screen showed Ed Wallace standing in front of a tall stone door encased in a blue light.

Paul sat up. "What—?" he started but stopped when Alyssa put her hand on his arm, never taking her eyes off the screen.

They watched breathlessly as Kade rushed to Ed Wallace. The camera view moved from Wallace to the door and focused on its center, the origin of the strange glow. Carved into the stone was a magnificent bird, its talons gripping a triangular crystal, the source of the brilliant blue light that bathed the tunnel.

Alyssa brought her hand to her mouth as her mind struggled to comprehend what she saw. Paul continued to stare at the monitor.

Kade's breathing became labored and he began to cough. A moment later, the camera bounced erratically and the audio feed picked up multiple scattered voices, all talking at the same time. Kade groaned and the scene before them disintegrated into chaos. Grunts and screams filled their ears as the camera caught a glimpse of a person in a biosuit sinking to the floor, clutching his head.

"Everybody out! Now!" her father's strained voice shouted through the audio feed. His command broke through the chaos and brought a brief moment of order. Seconds later the camera picked up the team staggering toward the entrance. Kade turned and lumbered painstakingly in the opposite direction.

"What's he doing?" Alyssa yelled, desperation in her voice. "Get out of there!"

The screen showed Kade stumbling toward the stone door, his hands slowly moving for the triangular object, which still emitted the strange blue light. He grasped it and tugged at it for several long seconds, interrupted by fits of coughing. Finally, he pulled it free and the blue light disappeared. Kade turned and staggered toward the entrance.

Paul flicked the touchpad. Alyssa noticed that his hand was trembling, but he managed to back up the video and pause it. He zoomed in on the object in Kade's palm. It was a transparent crystal, the size of a man's fist, cut in the shape of a pyramid.

Alyssa and Paul stared at the image. She turned to him, unable to find words. He met her gaze, a puzzled expression on his face.

Alyssa pressed the button to continue the video. Her father lumbered toward the exit. He collapsed on the floor only feet in front of the opening in the door and the image on the screen went dark.

"Is this it?" Alyssa asked, dread creeping over her like an icy chill. Her hand shot toward the touchpad. "Wait! His camera is still recording."

She moved the time slider forward and they watched as Kade rolled over and brought the crystal to his face. The camera followed his eyes as he slid the object into a zippered pocket in the front of his suit. A few seconds later, he moved his head toward the opening and the camera focused on two pairs of hands reaching through the opening and pulling him to the other side. Concerned faces looked at them from the monitor. Paul stopped the video.

"You okay?" he asked, touching her shoulder.

Alyssa wiped her eyes with her sleeve. She inhaled deeply

and nodded.

"Please tell me they shipped back the suits," she said.

"Even if they're in there, we'd be picked up by the security camera. Besides, we don't even know if that... thing is still in your father's suit."

Alyssa stared at Paul, her earlier anxiety replaced with determination.

"I'm going after that crystal. If you don't want to help me, please stay out of my way."

Paul shook his head, less surprised at the harshness of her words than the ones about to come out of his mouth.

"That cup of coffee is going to cost me my internship," he said, only half-joking.

"Wicked schemes first. Coffee second," Alyssa replied. "So how do we get in there?"

Paul considered for a moment then smirked. "How good are you at climbing?"

———

GAVRIEL ENTERED the lobby and strode up to the security counter. He barely acknowledged the slight, bespectacled man pacing toward him. As the two men passed each other, the other man covertly handed him a security badge.

Gavriel continued to the checkpoint and scanned in the badge. A second later, the light turned green and he stepped through the gate.

He visualized the building layout he had memorized from the map as he turned right and stalked along the corridor toward the elevators.

ALYSSA AND PAUL flattened their bodies against the wall, staying out of the field of view of the security camera pointing at the door to the classified storage area. Alyssa examined the device as they continued to inch their bodies underneath it. It was mounted in the corner, about ten feet off the ground. If they could get under it without being detected... *This might actually work.*

"You're sure there isn't another one inside the room?" she asked Paul, quietly.

"Positive," Paul whispered back. "I've been in there a couple of times. Just the one monitoring the door." He swallowed. "I suppose this isn't a good time to ask if you've changed your mind?"

Alyssa looked at him in silence, her jaw set.

Paul's brow knotted, eyeing the wall. "And you're sure you can do it?"

"If you give me a boost, I can wedge my feet between the walls. Just make sure you get in and out quickly."

"What if something goes wrong?"

"We run."

"Anything more detailed?"

"We run fast."

Before he could muster a reply, she took out her phone and put it between her teeth. Paul backed into the corner and laced his fingers, making a foothold for Alyssa. She approached Paul and placed her hands on his shoulders. A smile tugged on Paul's lips, but he kept his face straight.

"*Don'-get-any-ideash*," she mumbled in his ear, her teeth clenched on her phone, before stepping her foot into his palms.

Paul grinned and lifted her up. She deftly stepped onto his shoulder with her other foot and pushed herself up, using her hands to balance against the walls.

She took the phone out of her mouth and held it next to the camera, aligning the views. She took a picture then looked at it.

"That's as good as it's gonna get," she said to Paul. She used her free hand to balance herself on the camera mount as she moved her feet off Paul's shoulders and wedged them against the walls forming the corner.

"Here we go," she said and lifted the image on the phone in front of the lens.

"Go," she yelled in a whisper to Paul.

"Hold it steady," he said, sprinting for the door.

"I hadn't thought of that!" she called back. "Just hurry up!"

Paul keyed the code into the pad and disappeared through the door.

Alyssa slowed her breathing and focused on the phone, trying to keep it steady and aligned in front of the lens. She ignored the slow burn starting to creep into her legs and arms.

She barely registered the beeping of the keypad at the far end of the large room.

You gotta be kidding me!

Her brain kicked into overdrive as her eyes darted between the main entrance to the storage facility and the door to the secure area. She glanced at the camera and the wires running into the wall.

Time for Plan B!

She grabbed the wires and yanked them out as she jumped to the ground. She spotted a clipboard sitting on the desk and grabbed it. She faced the shelves just before the main door opened.

Alyssa kept her back to the door, trying to ignore the footsteps approaching her. She methodically moved her gaze between the items on the shelf and the clipboard, checking off imaginary boxes on the paper. The footsteps stopped. Alyssa took a deep breath and turned.

The man facing her was short and stocky, with broad shoulders and a bull neck that bulged beneath the dark gray suit. Close-cropped, wiry hair clung to his head as he eyed her silently.

"Oh, good afternoon, sir," Alyssa's hand flew to her chest. "I'm sorry, I didn't hear you come in."

The man studied her coldly, his lips pressed together.

"I was just finishing an inventory for Professor Garrison," she said with more confidence than she felt. "May I help you find anything?"

The man kept her gaze, unblinking. Alyssa looked back at him and smiled, ignoring the beads of sweat forming on her temples.

———

PAUL KNELT next to a large crate. He froze as he heard Alyssa's voice outside the door.

"... for Professor Garrison. May I help you find anything?"

Paul grunted as he rushed to replace the heavy lid. His mind raced. He glanced around the room then grabbed the box closest to him and rushed through the door.

The stranger wearing a gray suit stood next to Alyssa. His eyes were cold as he shifted them from her to Paul.

"Good afternoon," Paul said to the man and moved closer to Alyssa. "Here's the rest of the inventory for Professor Garrison." He held out the box toward her.

"Perfect," Alyssa replied and read the label—and took half a step back. "Body fluid samples from the cholera outbreak in Yemen."

Paul almost dropped the box.

"Very well." Alyssa turned to the other man. "Are you sure we can't help you with anything, sir?"

The man appraised them silently for several moments then shook his head.

"We'll be on our way, then," she said cheerfully and stepped toward the exit.

As they approached the strange man, he seemed to hesitate for a moment, then he moved aside to let them pass. Paul felt the man's eyes on his back as they continued to the main door and strolled through it. The moment they heard the door close behind them, they broke into a sprint for the elevator.

The ding of the approaching elevator stopped them dead in their tracks. Alyssa stared at the box in Paul's hands then pushed him into a side corridor and jumped after him. She motioned Paul to follow her behind a large crate before she ducked behind it.

They huddled motionlessly and listened to the elevator doors open and the footsteps echoing in the corridor. Alyssa slowly peeked out. She caught a glimpse of a man in a security guard uniform an instant before Paul yanked her down and scowled at her.

Seconds seemed like minutes as the security guard paced toward the storage facility and keyed the code into the pad. A second later the door opened and he entered the room.

"Go!" Alyssa whispered and pushed Paul ahead of her into the corridor. "And leave the box!"

Paul happily obliged and they dashed into the elevator. As the door closed behind them, Alyssa took a deep breath.

"Did you get it?" she asked.

Paul gave her a smirk.

"Well, did you?"

He reached into his pocket and pulled out the pyramid-shaped crystal.

"You did it!" She laughed and threw her arms around him. "That was a close one!"

Paul gaped at her, dumbfounded. "You're completely out of your mind, you know that, right?"

"You're just jealous because the voices only talk to me," she said, then leaned forward and gave him a kiss on his cheek.

She snagged the crystal out of his hand and lifted it up to the fluorescent light. The scattered light from the crystal filled the walls of the elevator with hundreds of dancing fireflies that moved in unison as she rotated it in her hand.

"What in the world is this thing?" she asked.

Paul hesitated for a moment, considering. "I have no idea, but I know just the guy who might be able to help us." He pressed the button for the fifth floor.

———

GAVRIEL STEPPED up to the large crate in the center of the room. The hair on his neck stood up as he spotted the open latch. He kneeled beside the crate and pushed the heavy lid to the side. He studied the white biosafety suit for a moment then pulled it out and read the name tag.

KADEN MORGAN.

His hand moved to the open zipper of the breast pocket before it slipped inside. His fist locked around the suit, his suspicion confirmed.

"Sir?"

Gavriel's head snapped up at the voice in the doorway. He stared over the crate into the eyes of a security guard.

"Sir, this is a restricted area," the guard said, eyeing him warily.

"Good afternoon, Officer," Gavriel replied smoothly, his breathing slowing. "I was just checking my shipment here." He casually lifted the suit up to the guard with his left hand, hiding his right hand beneath it. "It just arrived this morning." Gavriel continued talking calmly while he pulled the Glock from his shoulder holster with his right hand, out of view of the guard. "I wanted to ensure everything was in order." Slowly and deliberately, he stood, the suit covering the pistol as he placed it on the lid in front of him. He lowered the biosafety suit over the gun. "I was just finishing up," he said, cocking the hammer.

The guard approached Gavriel cautiously.

"Your badge, sir? I apologize for the inconvenience, but we had a malfunction with the security surveillance."

Gavriel reached for his ID with his left hand and held it out to the guard.

"Of course, Officer. Here you go."

The security guard took the ID. He scanned Gavriel's picture and the name next to it.

"Dr. Marcos Alves?"

"That's me," Gavriel said, the cold smile on his face not quite reaching his eyes.

The guard squeezed the button on the microphone of his radio.

"Base. This is Brawley. I need a credential check on Dr. Marcos Alves, badge number 19690309."

The two men locked gazes, unblinking. Several long seconds passed. Finally, the static of the radio interrupted the silence.

"Brawley—base. Credentials confirmed. Site-wide clearance."

The guard exhaled and held the badge out to Gavriel.

"Thank you, sir," he said. "I apologize for the inconvenience."

"You're just doing your job," Gavriel replied, coolly, taking his badge.

The guard turned to leave. He looked back at the heavy lid and glanced at Gavriel. "Here, let me give you a hand with that." He grabbed the lid and lifted it. The white biosuit slid down, exposing the pistol in Gavriel's right hand.

The guard froze.

He didn't hear the shot as Gavriel lifted the pistol and fired in one smooth motion. He collapsed in front of Gavriel, a pool of blood forming under him from the gunshot wound in his forehead.

Gavriel glanced down at the guard, an almost rueful expression crossing his face. He took out his phone and dialed a number.

"Do you have it?" Drake's voice was tense on the other end of the line.

"Somebody beat us to it," Gavriel replied.

"It must still be close. Find it!" Drake hissed then ended the connection.

————

"CLAY?" Paul knocked on the partially open door. "You in there, mate?"

Alyssa peeked inside the dimly lit office. The overhead lights were off. The only source of light, besides the two large monitors sitting on the L-shaped desk, was a thin floor lamp in the corner of the office.

"Hang on... be with you in a sec," came a disembodied voice. "Come on in."

Alyssa strained to adjust her vision from the brightly lit corridor. A bookshelf filled with books and software boxes, a locked metal cabinet, and a long folding table covered with various computer parts made up the only other furniture in the room.

A couple of seconds later a head poked up from under the desk.

"Sorry about that. Just trying to install a new video card in my machine and she's not—" When he saw Paul, he flashed him a boyish grin.

"*Haiya*, Paul!"

Alyssa considered the young man—kid, actually—as he stood up behind the desk and ran a hand through his curly black hair. Patchy stubble covered the dark skin on his chin. He straightened out his white button-down shirt and wiped his palms on his faded jeans.

"Hey, Clay," Paul said pointing at Alyssa. "Meet Alyssa Morgan, her dad's an archaeologist at Cairo University." He looked at Alyssa and pointed to Clay. "Alyssa, this is Clay Obono, fellow intern and computer geek extraordinaire. He helps out with our computer needs. If it speaks zeros and ones, he can make it do anything you want."

"Good to meet you, Alyssa," Clay said, his smooth African accent instantly growing on her. "But my good friend Paul is exaggerating a bit," he said with a wide, toothy grin.

"Intern?" Alyssa raised her eyebrows. "Aren't you a bit young?"

"My dad is the director," Clay replied, a hint of embarrassment creeping into his voice. "So you're from Cairo? That's lit. You here for a tour of our virtual reality lab?"

Alyssa smiled. "I'm sure it's fascinating. Maybe some other time."

Paul handed the crystal to Clay.

Clay sat down in his chair and examined the crystal. He let out a long whistle. "It's a beaut." He slowly turned it over in his hand. Finally, he put it down and faced them. "So, what is it, Oxford boy?"

Alyssa looked at Paul and rolled her eyes.

He glanced back and shrugged, lifting his eyebrows in the same motion. "It was worth a shot," he said.

Clay feigned hurt. "You do me injustice." He picked up his large cup of soda and swirled it around, bouncing the ice cubes against the sides before taking a sip. "Whose algorithm boosted your dating profile to the top of every girl's list?"

Alyssa eyed Paul, not trying to hide her smirk.

"I... uh," Paul stammered. "It was a class assignment... in psych..." He stared at Clay and said, a bit too quickly, "Can you figure out what it is?"

Clay spun his chair and pulled a magnifying glass from a drawer. He peered into the crystal. "I don't see any inclusions, cut marks or other signs that hint at how it was made." He picked up a small flashlight and aimed it into the crystal.

"That's curious," he muttered.

"What?" Paul and Alyssa asked in unison.

"I think it's getting warm," Clay replied.

"Warm?" Paul asked. "Is it supposed to?"

Clay gave Paul a look. "Last one I checked stayed frosty cool."

"Bollocks," Paul replied.

"I've never seen this type of facet structure," Clay continued. He scratched the stubble covering his chin as another thought struck him. "If we can determine the angle of refraction, we may get an idea of what kind of material we're dealing with." He reached into a pencil cup on his desk and pulled out a laser-pointer.

"A gift from a friend in China," he smirked, "and about ten times more powerful than the ones at our office shop."

He looked up at Alyssa and Paul. "Don't look directly into the crystal," he instructed.

"What's it gonna do?" Paul asked. "Melt my face off?"

Clay put on a pair of goggles and pointed the laser at the crystal. "Nah... but the beam's reflection might burn a hole in your retina."

Paul and Alyssa quickly looked away as Clay pressed the button on the laser pointer.

The crystal exploded with brilliant light as the green laser beam grazed it, lighting up the office with an image of dozens of people dressed in white robes, congregating in a large, magnificently decorated room. A split second later, the scene was replaced by a view of several adults and children playing in a lush green garden, azure blue waters beyond it in the distance. Before any of them had a chance to take in any details, the face of a dark-skinned woman filled the office, her stunning eyes turning to them in a piercing gaze.

"What the... *Ayy*!" Clay screamed and dropped the crystal to the desk. Immediately the pictures disappeared. He put his fingers in his mouth then popped the lid off his cup and dunked them in the icy drink. "Did that get bloody hot!"

Alyssa and Paul stood frozen in place. The views of the three scenes lasted less than a second, yet nobody in the room seemed to be breathing or moving for much longer afterward.

Finally, Clay took his fingers out of the cup and checked them. His flat voice broke the silence.

"Well, that was unexpected."

Alyssa looked at him, dumbfounded. "What... just... happened? What did you do to it?"

Clay shook the drops of soda from his fingers onto the floor and wiped his hand on his jeans. He looked up at her, blinking. "I'm not entirely certain." He rubbed his forehead, staring at the crystal on the desk.

"There's been some research using frequency variations and highly reflective optical media to store information." He stopped and looked from Alyssa to Paul as they stared at him with blank expressions. "Ah... think of it as a DVD or BluRay, except instead of rotating the disk to get more information, you change the frequency of the laser beam shooting into it."

"So this is a hard drive? With movies?" Paul asked.

Clay shrugged before shaking his head slowly.

"What is it, Clay?" Alyssa asked.

"It's just... the technology to manufacture this kind of medium, let alone the processing power to encode that much information... doesn't exist." He scrubbed his face with his hand. "So where did you say this came from?"

Alyssa wet her lips. "You'd never believe it anyway," she replied hesitantly, glancing at Paul.

"Try me," he said, his eyes crinkling with anticipation.

Alyssa's face was a mask as she looked at Clay. "If my father is correct, from about ten thousand years ago."

TASHA MENDEVA STRODE through the elegant sliding-glass doors into the hospital. She scarcely noted the marble floors and statues that adorned the massive lobby and the thirty foot tall, glass water fountain that welcomed visitors into the atrium. Physicians in white coats, professional smiles pasted on their faces, dodged clusters of concerned families as they scurried to attend to their patients.

Dressed in a gray abaya dress and black shawl, Tasha blended seamlessly into the bustling crowd. She glanced at the signs in the lobby before aiming for the restrooms across from the fountain.

Tasha opened the door and moved inside, catching a whiff of detergent and scented antiseptic. She surveyed the room. Four stalls lined the right wall, a mirror fixed over the sinks covered the entire left wall. *This will suffice.*

She stalked to the first stall and pushed on the door then checked the other three stalls. Satisfied they were empty, she entered the handicapped stall at the far wall and pulled the door closed, leaving a small crack to give her a view of the mirror and the restroom.

Tasha leaned against the wall and began to breathe, focusing on her training. *Inhale... one... two... three... Hold... one... two... three... four... Exhale... one... two... three... four... five... six...* She slowed down her breathing, finding comfort in the familiar pattern, as she allowed her mind to drift.

———

St. Petersburg, Russia—Ten Years Earlier

The young girl's feet were cold and wet as she shuffled through the snow-covered cobbles of the dark alley. The white dampness filled her lungs, clinging to her like the shreds of a ghastly cloak. Her disheveled auburn locks hung upon her tattered dress, her sunken eyes darting anxiously across the shadows.

She stopped and squeezed her eyelids tighter than tight. She imagined stuffing her terrors into a bag and carrying it down a long hallway, past the other locked doors.

Her mother's shuddering screams behind the wall.

Her father, drunk and leering, standing in her bedroom doorway.

Her mother's stare, filled with terror, the bloodied knife in her hand.

The men in uniforms, her mother's face contorted with guilt and fear as they dragged her away.

A great sob knotted up in her chest. She swallowed and took a deep breath, closing another door in her mind. *You've made it this far.*

She tried to ignore the smell of sewage and wet trash as the aching pain deep in her belly pulled her toward a garbage can leaning against the wall.

She began sifting through it for anything that could fill her stomach without making her ill when she spotted an old plastic doll. Hesitantly she reached for it.

The hand around her mouth was as sudden as it was vicious. The girl's blood drained from her face when the attacker lifted her and spun her around to another man, his cruel glare and callous sneer tearing into her.

She tried to scream. Hot tears blinded. Her heart and lungs threatened to burst. She fought the vicious man with all her strength, but her arms were pinned at her sides in his vice-like grip.

Suddenly, the other man dropped to the ground, revealing the tall silhouette of another man behind him, his hard eyes burning into her captor.

The vicious man dropped her. He stared down the tall man, eyeing the crisply pressed suit and polished shoes. His mouth twisted into an ugly sneer before he pulled out a knife.

"*Aristocraty...*" he spat, then lunged at the tall man without warning.

The tall man's move was a blur to the girl as he deftly stepped aside and grabbed the other man's arm. An instant later she heard a sickening sound that grew into a tortured howl. She gasped when she saw her attacker on the ground, his arm at a grotesque angle. The tall man loomed above him as her attacker crabbed away clumsily, holding his broken arm, before awkwardly getting on his feet and scampering into the dark alley.

The tall man turned to her and his face softened. She scooted backward until she hit the alley wall and stared at him, frozen, too scared to look away. Her heart squeezed tightly in her chest and she could no longer take a breath.

"Easy. It's all right. I will not harm you," he said in a comforting voice.

The young girl trembled, not understanding.

He kept his gaze on her and repeated.

"*Ne boysia. Vse horosho.*"

She blinked. The tall man held out his arms to his side, palms facing her, as he slowly approached her. He spotted the doll on the ground and picked it up. He wiped it off, gently smoothing the doll's hair and held it out to her.

The girl hesitantly reached out, her striking violet eyes locked on his, as he continued speaking to her in Russian.

"There, there," he said softly. "You shall never have to be scared again. Would you like that?"

The girl continued to stare at him silently, the terror slowly ebbing from her belly. She nodded, uncertainly.

"What is your name?" he asked.

The girl held his gaze for several moments. Then she spoke, timidly, "*Tasha...*"

————

TASHA'S EYES snapped open at the sound of the door. She bit down on a smile when she glimpsed the white color of a physician's coat before the woman entered a stall. With unhurried movements, Tasha slid her hand inside her *abaya*, pulling out a small syringe. She carefully removed the plastic cap from the needle and waited until she heard the woman flush the toilet and leave the stall. Tasha flushed the toilet a moment later and, palming the syringe, opened the door and strode to the sink next to the physician.

The woman pulled a lipstick out of her pocket and leaned closer to the mirror to apply it. Tasha slowed down for an instant as she passed behind her. Without a warning, she jammed the needle into the side of the woman's neck and emptied the contents of the syringe in one motion. The physician gasped a split second before the paralytic drug took effect and her body went limp.

Tasha deftly caught the other woman before she hit the floor and dragged her into the stall, locking the door behind them. She sat the woman on the toilet and calmly pulled the syringe from the physician's neck. Tasha ignored the terror in the paralyzed woman's eyes as she removed the physician's white coat, ID badge and key card. She leaned the woman against the back wall then climbed nimbly over the stall door.

Taking slow and easy breaths, she strode toward the sink and washed her hands before putting on the white coat. She glanced in the mirror and adjusted her shawl and coat, flipping the ID badge backwards. Her lips curved up into the barest of smiles as she turned to the door and reached into the coat pocket, pulling out a stethoscope. Stepping briskly, she put the stethoscope around her neck and left the restroom.

Tasha crossed the lobby to the information desk in the center of the atrium.

"Kade Morgan?" she said to the clerk then she spelled the name.

"Just a moment, Doctor," the woman replied as she typed

the name into the computer. "Tenth floor, Intensive Care Unit Quarantine, Room 1021."

———

THE ELEVATOR STOPPED on the tenth floor and Tasha stepped out into the brightly lit corridor. The smell of antiseptic and the metallic tang from stainless steel hung in the air, trying in vain to mask the odor of sickness. She read the overhead sign: Rooms 1001-1030 left, 1031-1060 straight, 1061-1090 right. She turned left and paced along the hallway.

Room 1021. She glanced through the window into the small anteroom and into the hospital room beyond. Tasha's breathing quickened when she recognized the man lying in the bed.

She used the physician's key card, entered the small chamber, and pulled out a mask and a pair of blue gloves from the overhead cabinet and slipped them on. She glanced out into the hallway before taking a deep breath and stepping through the second door into the hospital room.

Tasha's senses sharpened as she slowly moved to the bed enclosed in a transparent, plastic canopy. The man lying in the bed appeared to be sleeping. Close-up, he looked much thinner than in the pictures she had memorized. His skin was ashen and his breathing was labored.

Tasha pulled out an empty tube and disconnected Kade's IV line outside the plastic canopy. She hooked up the tube to the port and watched Kade's blood fill the small cylinder. After a few seconds, she unscrewed the tube, carefully placed it in a Ziploc bag, and slipped it into a pocket inside her abaya.

"With respect, Doctor. You can't be in here without a safety gown!"

Tasha whirled sharply and glared at the physician standing in the doorway.

"Are you part of Dr. Morgan's care team?" he asked, closing the door behind him. He approached the bed guardedly. "My name is Dr. Ahmed Farag." He eyed the badge on Tasha's white coat. "What service are you with?"

Tasha remained silent as Dr. Farag continued moving toward the bed. He froze when he spotted the disconnected IV line.

Before he had a chance to react, Tasha lunged at him, ripping the mask from his face. He reeled back, staggering against the wall at the head of the bed.

The thin knife in Tasha's hand appeared as if from nowhere. Terrified, Farag stared into her violet eyes as she stalked toward him. Panicked, his gaze darted around the room. He spotted the code blue button and hit it. An instant later, the sound of the cardiac code alarm filled the corridor.

Tasha glared at the blue light flashing above the bed. The physician held his breath as her glare bored through him before she spun for the door—and stared into the face of the security guard standing in the doorway.

"Hold it!" the guard barked, drawing his pistol.

Tasha darted forward and, in one motion, snatched the gun then spun and flipped the guard on his back. She pointed the pistol at the man, who gaped at her open-mouthed.

"Don't!" The word seemed to burst out of Farag's mouth before he realized it. Tasha's head snapped toward him, a feral look in her eyes.

"Please…" Farag mouthed.

She moved her gaze back to the man lying on the floor, his face a mask of dread as he stared into the barrel of his pistol.

The memories came uninvited.

The attackers in the alley.

The tall man.

You shall never have to be scared again.

Tasha ejected the magazine and cleared the bullet from the chamber then dropped the pistol to the ground before bolting through the door.

ALYSSA SAT on Clay's desk, holding the crystal pyramid. It had cooled off and felt smooth against her skin. It was heavier than it looked, much heavier than a piece of glass or ordinary crystal of that size. She held it up against the light from the floor lamp. *Nothing, no reflection, no internal facet structure,* she pondered. *Just an interesting looking paperweight—until you shine a laser into it.*

She put down the crystal and looked at Clay, pursing her lips in thought. "How did you know to shine the laser pointer into it?"

"Lucky guess... or stroke of genius." He gave a toothy grin. "I had no idea it would actually work. If it really is an optical storage device, I suppose it makes sense that any frequency triggered it since the data is stored across the entire spectrum. I wasn't able to hold the beam steady, I suppose that's why it jumped from one image to another."

"Can you access more of it?"

"I'm not sure. Even if I could put something together, I have no idea how much we'd be able to get, or how long at a time." He saw her darken with disappointment and quickly added. "But we should be able to do better than a laser pointer."

He stood. "There's some equipment in the VR lab that I can appropriate for this." He smiled impishly. "I've got everything else I need at home. Give me a few minutes." He walked through a side door into the adjoining lab.

————

PAUL OPENED the door to Clay's office. Alyssa sat on the desk, cross-legged, peering into the crystal. She had changed her clothes, trading her suit and high heels for a pair of jeans, a gray college sweatshirt, and sneakers. She glanced up. Paul pulled a chocolate bar and a soda can from a paper bag and held it out. "Dinner?"

Alyssa lit up. She hopped off the desk and grabbed the bar, tore open the wrapper, and sank her teeth into it. Paul smiled at her expression as she savored the snack.

The next bite was interrupted by the sound of her phone. A look of disappointment crossed her face. She glanced at the caller ID—and threw the snack on the table and snatched the phone.

"Kamal, any news about Kade?"

Paul watched as she listened for a few seconds before her hand rushed to her mouth and the color drained from her face.

"What? When?"

"What's going on?" Paul asked, a dozen questions racing through his mind. She shushed him and stared through him, fingers touching her parted lips.

"Oh my God... yes... I understand... thank you, Kamal." She put the phone down and slumped into the chair.

"That was Kamal... my father's friend from Cairo," she said to Paul, her hands trembling. "Somebody broke into his hospital room." She brought her knees to her chest, hugging them. "Paul, I think somebody tried to kill—"

"There you are." They jumped at the voice of the man standing in the doorway. Paul's stomach knotted when he recognized him as the man from the storage area. His eyes were two black orbs, locked onto Alyssa with a predator's unwavering attention. He nodded at the crystal and stretched out his hand.

"I'll have that now," Gavriel said.

Alyssa pulled the crystal closer to her chest.

"I've had a long day and am not in the mood for games," Gavriel said.

He pulled out a sinister looking pistol and pointed it at Alyssa.

———

CLAY FLIPPED on the light switch and strolled into the center of the virtual reality lab. The circular area was enclosed by a padded, chest-high railing. An articulated arm above the center of the circle held a helmet attached to a large pair of goggles. Whistling softly, Clay ducked under the railing and stepped into the center. He pulled down the helmet, unhooked the connections, and carefully slid it into his backpack.

He slung the pack over one shoulder and crossed the room to a large metal cabinet on the right-hand side of the room. He opened both doors of the cabinet and pulled out four drawers. He began digging through them, setting aside numerous cables and silver antistatic bags containing electronic cards, before placing them into his backpack.

Clay turned to the metal shelves that lined the entire back wall of the room. "And here is the Grand Poobah," he muttered.

He picked up a heavy box from a shelf and gently deposited it into the duffle bag then started going through the list in his mind, mentally checking off the items: *VR set, LIDAR, spare CCDs, cables, power cells—*

"There you are."

Startled by the strange voice in the adjoining room, Clay ducked and crawled to the door.

He stifled a yelp when he spotted a menacing man pointing a pistol at Alyssa. Clay's gaze swept the room, his mind racing. He paused then locked his fingers around the laser pointer in his pocket.

———

PAUL STARED at the weapon that was pointed at Alyssa.

"Alyssa," he whispered, fighting off the panic rising in his chest.

"I won't ask again," Gavriel said.

A green dot appeared out of nowhere on the wall behind the man an instant before Paul spotted Clay's head poking out of the door of the research lab. Clay pointed with his finger to the laser pointer then the crystal. Paul's skin tingled with under-standing.

"Give him what he wants," he said to Alyssa.

"That's a smart boy," Gavriel said condescendingly.

Alyssa scowled at Paul. He kept her gaze, his lips tight. He could read the conflict in her face, her distrust of him battling within her. Finally, she sighed dejectedly then handed the crystal to Gavriel.

"All that for a shiny paperweight," Gavriel said, eyeing the crystal.

"If you look close, you can even see the images," Paul said. Alyssa shot him a quizzical look.

"What images?" Gavriel brought the crystal to his face. He stared into it.

"Alyssa," Paul's voice was tense, "remember, *the images*."

Alyssa's face was a mirror of her confusion.

"The images!" Paul called out and closed his eyes tightly.

Alyssa gasped and squeezed her eyes shut. A second later Clay fired the laser into the crystal.

The room flared into an incandescent, green glow. Gavriel howled in agony and fell to his knees as the laser bounced off the internal facets of the crystal and reflected into his eyes, burning his retinas. He raised his arms, desperately trying to shield himself from the searing beams.

Paul roared as he covered the ten feet to the door in a single leap and plowed headfirst into the other man. The force of the impact drove them through the door into the corridor, and slammed them both to the floor, knocking the crystal and pistol out of Gavriel's hands.

"Go!" Paul bellowed to Alyssa, scrambling to untangle himself from Gavriel.

Alyssa dashed for the crystal and scooped it up. She turned and held out her other arm to Paul. He grasped it and she hauled him to his feet a second before Clay charged into the corridor, sporting a backpack and a duffel bag in each hand. He froze and stared at Gavriel writhing on the floor.

"Elevator—now!" Paul yelled and pushed Alyssa ahead of him toward the open doors at the end of the corridor. He grabbed Clay by his backpack and pulled him along.

They flew into the elevator at full speed, drenched in cold sweat. Paul jabbed the button for the parking garage. They stared back into the hallway.

Gavriel dragged himself to his feet. He lumbered toward the pistol. He stumbled, reaching for it, then tried again and managed to clutch it with his right hand, his left still covering his eyes. He turned to them just as the elevator doors began to close. He dropped to one knee and lifted the weapon.

"Look out!" Alyssa screamed. She jumped to one side. Paul and Clay flattened their bodies against the other wall.

The bullets flew wide and smashed into the wall next to the elevator. The closing doors absorbed the next round. An eternity later, the cabin started its downward drift.

Clay stood perfectly still. His lips moved, but no sound came out.

"He was shooting at us," he finally uttered. The next sentence crescendoed into a frantic scream. "That guy had a gun and was shooting at us. Those bullets were aimed at my arse!"

"Get a hold of yourself." Paul grabbed his shoulder. "There could be more of them." He glanced at the display flashing the floor numbers as the elevator descended.

Fourth floor.

Clay's face turned into a mask. He stared at the wall behind

Paul. His chest rose and fell in rapid breaths, but he remained silent.

Third floor.

Alyssa tried to keep her voice flat. "Do you have a car?" she asked Paul.

"I'm an intern… at the WHO… I ride the tube." He nodded at Clay. "His old man does. Bomb one, too."

Second floor.

He turned to Clay. "You want to show Alyssa your smartphone trick?"

Clay continued staring at the wall, frozen. "Sixteen years old, never even been to New York City…" he muttered.

First floor.

Paul squeezed Clay's arm. "The car!"

Clay yanked his arm away. "Are you bloody crackers? My father would disown me!"

Basement.

"I bet Alyssa would *love* to see the trick." Paul said, ignoring him. "She'd be quite impressed." He glanced at Alyssa. "Isn't that right?"

Alyssa gawked at Paul for a moment, perplexed, then nodded with exaggerated enthusiasm. "Yes. Yes, totally. I would *love* to see your phone trick, Clay."

Parking garage.

Paul grabbed the front of Clay's shirt. "Now, mate!"

Clay flinched. His eyes focused and he fumbled in his pockets. He fished out a smartphone.

Paul glanced at Alyssa. "He figured out how to use his phone to hack into his old man's car."

The elevator stopped and they flattened against the wall.

The trio stood glued to the sides of the cabin, holding their breaths as the doors slid open. After two heartbeats, Paul peeked out.

"Looks clear," he whispered. "Go!"

They bolted through the garage past a row of parked cars.

"Where is it?" Paul asked, between heavy breaths, as they tore through the garage.

Clay hit a button on his phone. A moment later they heard a chirp and saw the lights flash on a black Porsche 911 parked between a blue Ford hatchback and a silver Volvo.

Alyssa's eyes lit up. She sprinted for the car, ripped open the driver's side door and dove in before Clay could object. Paul jumped into the back seat from the passenger side. Clay stood outside of the car, frozen.

Alyssa turned to him and shouted, "Get in! I'll drive—you tell me where to go!"

"Wh-what?" he stammered.

"You heard her," Paul said. "Get in—now!"

Clay opened his mouth to reply but was cut short by the thud of the stairwell door smashing into the wall. He jumped into the passenger seat and they all ducked down.

Paul gingerly lifted his head and glanced out of the back window. He winced when he saw Gavriel stagger out of the stairwell. The man still looked dazed and steadied himself on the wall, but he surveyed the garage with a predatory stare.

"Shit! Shit! Shit!" Clay whimpered.

"We need to get out of here," Paul whispered. "Get it started, Clay!"

Paul held his breath as Clay typed on his phone. He

watched Gavriel through the rear window, continuing to scan the parking garage. He was approaching their aisle.

"Come on… start her up…"

"I'm trying! I'm trying!" Clay's voice shook like a badly-tuned diesel engine.

"Now, Clay," Paul whispered, his voice strained, as Gavriel glanced into the silver Volvo parked next to the Porsche.

The Porsche's engine roared to life.

"Who's your daddy?" Clay shrieked.

"Go!" Paul yelled a split second before Alyssa slammed the gear lever into reverse. The Porsche's wheels squealed as Alyssa popped the clutch and slung the car out of the parking spot. Gavriel leaped out of the way, narrowly escaping the wide fender.

Alyssa floored the accelerator and the car continued in reverse. Gavriel's confusion lasted only an instant before he began chasing after the car. The staccato sound of the Porsche's rev limiter echoed through the parking deck as they slowly outdistanced their pursuer.

Alyssa steered with one hand, her neck craned over her shoulder, looking out the rear window. "Which way? Quickly!"

Paul turned and stared at the wall at the end of the aisle, growing larger every second.

"Left! Go left!" Clay's frantic voice matched the panic in his eyes.

Paul was thrown against the side of the cabin as Alyssa turned the car sharply. Suddenly, his head slammed against the back seat as Alyssa locked the brakes, barely avoiding crashing into another wall. She gave Clay a look.

"No, no! Other left! Other left!"

As Paul struggled to regain focus, Alyssa's hand grazed the gear lever and the engine revved just before she disengaged the clutch again. The car lurched forward, leaving behind two parallel lines of rubber on the concrete floor.

Paul stared through the windshield at Gavriel standing in the middle of the aisle, blocking their path. Slowly, the man raised his pistol and took aim at the Porsche when a security car, sirens blaring, appeared from a side aisle and screeched to a stop behind him. A guard leaped out, pistol drawn.

Gavriel spun and slowly put his hands up in the air. Paul locked eyes with the security guard, who took his attention off Gavriel for an instant as the Porsche sped past both men. Paul gasped at the sound of the gunshot and the security guard's fatal mistake before the man collapsed to the ground. Gavriel pointed the weapon at the Porsche again.

"Turn!" Paul yelled, before he ducked behind the rear seat. "Get down!"

Alyssa hit the brakes hard, just barely keeping them from locking up. Paul heard the soft chirping of the rubber on the concrete. She released the brakes and turned the car smoothly into an aisle on the right at the same time the shots rang out behind them.

"Can I get out this way?" Her voice sounded strangely calm.

"Right at the end of this aisle then straight," Clay replied. "Follow the exit sign up to the street level."

The Porsche slowed hard and Paul was pushed against the left side as the car turned right. Alyssa accelerated confidently through the apex of the turn, her driving smooth and controlled. Paul shot her a glance. Her moves were a picture of efficiency as they raced past rows of parked cars on either side of them. *I'm sure glad she knows what she's doing.*

He heard and saw the police car simultaneously as it drifted into the aisle thirty yards behind them. The tires of the heavy sedan screamed, struggling to keep the rear from smashing into the parked cars. The car accelerated hard toward them. Gavriel leaned out of the driver's seat and fired his weapon. The bullets exploded into the concrete supports less than ten feet from the Porsche.

Paul looked ahead, staring at the arrows pointing left toward the exit several aisles ahead of them. The Porsche continued to accelerate. The aisles were flying by them on their left, to the right a concrete wall and cars. He glanced back again. The other car had almost closed the gap. Gavriel took aim, determined not to miss this time.

"Turn left!" Clay yelled.

"Are you sure?" Alyssa asked.

"Turn!"

Paul felt himself fly forward as Alyssa squeezed the brakes hard at the last instant and slowed the car just enough to make the turn into the exit aisle. He heard the on-off-on squeal of the antilock system of the police car behind them as the wide tires of the heavy sedan strained to obey the driver's instructions to follow the Porsche. But he carried too much speed and flew past the exit aisle.

Paul glanced back and saw Gavriel struggling to maintain control before he stabilized the car and turned hard into the next aisle left. He was now racing parallel to the Porsche, a row of parked cars separating them. Gavriel leaned out and fired several shots. A bullet shattered the rear side window.

Clay gasped. Paul hoped it was from surprise, not a wound.

"Faster! Faster!" Clay yelled.

The Porsche's engine growled under full acceleration when alarms filled the parking garage. Paul gasped, realizing the heavy gate at the end of the aisle was starting to close, threatening to block their escape. Two armed security guards with guns drawn rushed out of the guardhouse.

Paul's stomach dropped as the Porsche shot up the exit ramp only feet ahead of the closing gate, the security guards scattering out of the way. The police car swerved hard into the exit aisle and shot up the ramp a few car lengths behind them.

"Nonononono!" Clay shrieked just before the Porsche catapulted out of the parking garage, catching air.

Paul's teeth rattled when the Porsche slammed into the street.

The screeching noise and bright lights barreling at him registered all at once. His eyes bulged when he spotted a huge dump truck sliding toward them, brakes fully locked.

He was thrown against the side as Alyssa turned the Porsche sharply, bringing it parallel to the street and accelerated hard, an instant before the police car shot out of the ramp behind them—and crashed violently into the dump truck.

"Hell yeah!" Paul screamed.

Clay stared at the carnage behind them dumbfounded, dazed.

"Holy… shit…" he muttered.

Alyssa glanced into the rearview mirror, taking in the scene behind them.

"Alyssa," Paul said.

She remained silent, her jaw set as the Porsche sped along the street.

"Alyssa, you can slow down." Paul tried to keep his voice calm. "Clay, tell her where to go. Grab whatever you need from your place to get the crystal working. We'll check into a motel tonight when we get out of the city."

Clay faced Paul and opened his mouth. Paul's look silenced any words of protest before Clay could utter them. He turned back and stared at the road ahead.

"Take the next right and then A-2 East toward Bexley. We will be there in about thirty minutes," he said, his voice flat.

———

ALYSSA RESTED against the front fender of the parked Porsche, peering down the narrow cobblestone street in Bexley as she and Paul waited for Clay. She took a deep breath, savoring the crisp evening air when she heard Paul climb out of the back seat. He stood next to her in silence.

"That was some incredible driving," he finally said.

"It was nothing compared to what you did in the building," she replied, softly. "You threw yourself at a guy with a gun and saved my life. All of our lives." She smiled, for the first time in a while. "That was some pretty heroic stuff."

Paul didn't reply. He stood surprisingly still. Alyssa saw tiny beads of sweat break out on his forehead. All of the blood seemed to drain from his face. He staggered as the adrenalin rush came to an end as suddenly as it had set in. A wave of nausea overpowered him and he heaved. Abruptly, he turned away, doubled over, and threw up violently.

"God, I'm sorry. I—" His next words were interrupted by another heave.

Alyssa spent the next two minutes rubbing his back as he emptied the contents of his stomach into the bush. After he recovered and wiped his mouth with his arm, he turned to her, embarrassed.

"Some hero, huh?" he said, a tired smile across his face.

ALYSSA SAT next to Paul on the blue and red plaid sofa and stared at the once artsy wallpaper that lined the walls of the sparsely decorated hotel room. *How many nights have I spent in rooms like this?* She pushed away the thought just as Clay plodded out of the bathroom and placed his backpack and two duffel bags on the small desk in the corner. He stood, facing the faded sunflower painting hanging over the desk. Finally, he turned around, scowling.

"I don't know where you came from, Alyssa, or what you're hiding that makes some goon want to end you *and* everybody else around you." He glowered at her. Alyssa met his gaze wordlessly, chewing her lip.

"Clay, there's nothing we can do to make you help us," Paul said. "I can only imagine how cheesed off you are, but if this thing is as big as we think—"

"Sod off," Clay sneered and turned. After several long seconds, he sighed dejectedly and faced them again, his eyes damp.

"My father's Porsche is totally buggered... probably going to lose my internship... Oh, and some nutter is LARPing Agent 47 on my arse!"

Alyssa and Paul remained silent, regarding him without blinking.

"You really think this thing is from ten thousand years in the past?" Clay asked.

Alyssa nodded. "My father is dying. It's the only hope I've got for trying to help him."

Clay seemed to ponder her words, the conflict plain in his face when his eyes crinkled with some inner gaiety, and he shook his head in disbelief. He put up his hands in a gesture of resignation.

"Only hope for a foxy girl... You do know that's every geek's dream, right?" He almost smirked. "All right, Leia, just promise me, no secrets. You will level with me and tell me everything you know."

Alyssa exhaled loudly. "No secrets," she said.

———

THIRTY MINUTES LATER, they sat on the floor around the coffee table. Clay was digesting Alyssa's words.

"So, let me get this straight," he rubbed his brow. "Fifty years ago, this guy, Chaplain—oh, who also happens to be your grandfather—claims to have found proof of some room under the Sphinx that could prove once and for all when the statue was built, right?"

Alyssa nodded.

"His colleagues discredit him, the Egyptians hate him

because his ideas are insulting to them, and the whole world pretty much thinks he went kook, so he gets cranky and hides for the rest of his life."

"That's essentially it, in a nutshell."

"And in all that time, nobody bothered to check whether your grandfather was right and this supposed room under the Sphinx was actually there?" Clay asked.

"It's not that simple," Alyssa replied. "The Egyptians consider the Sphinx, the pyramids, and the grounds around them their greatest national treasures. Not to mention that for thousands of years grave robbers have plundered archaeological sites without the slightest regard for their historical value."

Clay nodded. "Makes sense, I suppose. Why would they even think about allowing a dig around the symbols of their greatest pride based on shaky evidence gathered by yet another western Egyptologist trying to make a name for himself?"

"Exactly," Alyssa said. "What did they have to gain? The best-case scenario for them was that he was wrong, in which case they would have desecrated the site for no reason. And God forbid if he was actually right, disproving a belief they've revered for thousands of years."

Paul cut in. "So how did your dad get permission to move forward with the dig?"

Alyssa shrugged. "I think it was as big a surprise to him as it was to everybody else."

"So your dad and his team go in," Clay went on. "He finds something that he thinks holds the key to the age of the Sphinx and the origin of its creation. You and Oxford boy nick it from the storage room. And now all you need me to do is figure out how to interface with this doofer... built with ten thousand-year-old technology that we don't have today."

"Can you do it?" Alyssa asked.

"Well, that's why I'm here, I guess." He looked over his gear. "You'd have to be as loony as your grandpa to even think that we have a shot at making this work. But we've made it this far, right? I think I brought everything I need from the lab and my place."

He pulled out a large box from his backpack. "This is a titanium sapphire laser. It's a micropulse LIDAR." He noticed their quizzical looks. "*Light Detection And Ranging*," he explained. "It's basically a laser with a bunch of mirrors and cameras. It's used to produce 3D scans of objects and insides of buildings. I should be able to rig up the lasers to shoot into the crystal and collect the reflected light into the CCDs—"

"What's a CCD?" Alyssa asked.

He reached into the duffel bag and handed her a silver anti-static bag with a rectangular wafer inside. "Don't touch the shiny part," he said. "*Charge-Coupled Device*. Basically, just a fancy name for light collector. Same thing the camera in your phone uses to convert the images into data."

"Okay, cool... so... um..." Alyssa looked at him with a puzzled expression.

"I should be able to collect the images and stream them into the VR headgear as we scan the crystal with the laser. I have no idea whether it'll work, but it's worth a shot."

Paul nodded slowly. "That's bloody ace, Clay," he said.

"It will be if it works," Clay replied. "It'll take a while to hook it all up and calibrate it. We'll still have a problem with the crystal heating up, so we won't be able to hit it for too long at a time, but we'll start with the lowest beam intensity."

"Paul wasn't exaggerating when he said you could do anything," Alyssa said.

"I have my moments, no?" Clay gave her a crooked, boyish grin. "Now if you two will excuse me, I have some work to do." He put his earbuds in and turned to his equipment. He looked over his shoulder. "Please don't interrupt unless that nutter is banging on the door," he said and hunched over his gear.

Alyssa shook her head. "Things sure came a long way since Bill Nye."

"Who?" Paul asked.

"Bill Nye," Alyssa repeated. "The Science Guy?"

Paul gave her a blank stare.

"Come on, seriously?" Alyssa exhaled theatrically. "He was my first crush."

"Ah," Paul replied. "Mine was Princess Zelda."

It was Alyssa's turn to look perplexed.

"Princess Zelda. You know... Zelda, Warcraft, Skyrim. Computer games?"

Alyssa stood up. "A computer did beat me at chess once," she said, "but it was no match for me at kickboxing."

Paul stared at her for a moment then laughed. "I believe I'm detecting a pattern here. Should I be worried?"

"You should be safe—as long as you don't jam on me," she said. "But I may go ninja on your phone if it rings in the middle of the night."

Before Paul had a chance to reply, she strolled to the bed and put the pillow against the headboard then sat down. She rested her back against the pillow and stretched her neck. Paul went to the nightstand and grabbed a bottle of water. He opened it and handed it to Alyssa then sat next to her, his back against the headboard.

"Where'd you learn to drive like that?" he asked.

"The parking garage?" She smiled self-consciously. "That was nothing."

"Come on, that was a lot more than just pushing pedal to the metal."

"A dig in Masada," she said after a while. "A *misunderstanding* with the local authorities required a quick getaway." She chuckled. "I crashed our truck. Kade—my dad—and I spent two weeks in a detention facility before the U.S. consulate finally bailed us out. When we got home, he insisted on tactical driving lessons for me. He wasn't satisfied until I could do a four-wheel drift and J-turn on a dime... blindfolded."

Paul laughed. "Why do you call him Kade?"

Alyssa took a long sip and regarded Paul in silence. Finally, she spoke.

"After my mom... after she died and we moved to Cairo, he kind of freaked. He was a wreck, completely obsessed."

"The Hall of Records?" Paul asked.

Alyssa nodded. "He drowned himself in work and I was left to take care of him. Before long, I was organizing the trips, helping to coordinate the digs." She sighed. "We became associates. I don't even remember when I started calling him by his first name. It felt natural, I guess."

"You never tried convincing him to stop?"

"There was only one way he would. It may have been naïve,

but I had hoped that when he found it, it would provide some kind of closure... for both of us. I had hoped that somehow I'd get my father back and we could salvage whatever was left of our family."

Paul swallowed. "How did your mom die?"

Alyssa's face darkened as locked up memories awoke, gnawing their way to the surface. "It's my turn," she said.

"What?"

"You asked your questions, now it's my turn." She gave him a playful smile, tucking a strand of hair behind her ear, and moved closer to him.

"So what's your story, Mr. Paul Matthews? How did you end up an intern at the World Health Organization?"

Paul grimaced and rubbed the back of his neck. "Single child. Semi-proud offspring of a career diplomat." He chuckled wistfully. "I haven't celebrated my birthday in the same country twice. Science has been the only constant in my life... my escape. I should've realized I had problems when my imaginary playmates wouldn't play with me."

Alyssa laughed. "You turned out fine, just a little twitchy, that's all."

"My dad wants me to follow in his footsteps. Naturally, I'm doing the opposite... I suppose we both want to make a difference in the world. His weapons are statecraft and negotiation. I prefer lab coats and pipettes." He snickered. "I think he's still hoping I'll switch my major from biochem to global governance and diplomacy."

Alyssa looked at him with heavy eyelids. He smiled. "Nothing like my riveting life story to remind you how sleepy you are, huh?" He put his arm around her shoulders. "Why don't you try to get some rest?" he said softly. "You look completely exhausted."

Alyssa sunk into the warmth of his side, appreciative of the simple gesture and too tired to argue. She nestled against his shoulder and looked up at him, her deep brown eyes revealing a hint of optimism for the first time since they met.

"You know, I don't care that you're twitchy, or that you honked all over the bushes when it was all over. You were incredible when it mattered." She kissed him lightly on the cheek. "Thank you. I will never forget what you did for me today."

Within a few moments her breathing slowed and she fell asleep. Paul remained awake for a long time, staring at Clay's back, hunched over the table. Paul closed his eyes and listened to Alyssa's slow and steady breathing, while he relived the most terrifying and exhilarating day of his life. The sun was beginning to rise when his head gently fell against Alyssa's hair and he finally drifted off into an uneasy sleep.

―――――

WILLIAM DRAKE SAT at the intricately carved writing desk, his fists clenched, and stared at the young woman in front of him. Her slim body seemed even more delicate as she stood between the pair of ornate wing chairs that sat on the hand-woven rug in the middle of the dimly lit room. He tightened his jaw, trying in vain to stop the spasms of the muscle in his cheek.

"Let me get this straight," he said, his voice strained. "We had our best London asset pitted against three kids."

Tasha Mendeva regarded him in silence and swallowed. She forced her head up, meeting his glare.

"Yet somehow, those pathetic nerds not only got away with the item from the site—" he took a deep breath—"but they sent our well-paid man to the hospital."

She slowly nodded.

"And we don't know where they are." His voice was as tense as a violin string ready to snap.

She shook her head.

Drake screamed and swept his hand across the desk, strewing its contents across the room.

Tasha cringed imperceptibly, but stood motionless, her head held high, focused on Drake's heaving chest.

Drake breathed loudly through his nose, his nostrils flaring. Gradually his breathing slowed. He ran his hand through his slicked-back black curls.

Silently, Tasha crossed the wood-paneled room to the small bar and filled a glass halfway with single malt whiskey. She returned to the desk and set it in front of Drake.

She leaned toward him. "I would have poured it for you before I gave you the news, but I knew it would go to waste," she said, a sultry smirk on her lips.

Drake silently picked up the glass, took a slow sip and allowed the liquid to settle onto his tongue as he moved it around his mouth. After a moment, he swallowed it and looked up at her. She put her hands around his head.

"We have Kade Morgan's blood," she said softly. "We will succeed."

He pulled her closer and brought his palm to her cheek, his

fingertips skimming the outline of her face. "I cannot fail," he said. "I have sacrificed too much for this."

"We will find them," she said. "We're monitoring their phones and credit cards, even their email accounts." She moved her lips close to his, the pupils in her violet eyes growing. "They can't stay hidden forever."

———

"WAKE UP, sleepyheads! Time for the exciting part!"

Alyssa jerked up. She blinked as her eyes adjusted.

Clay stood in front of her, still wearing the same white button-down shirt and faded jeans, a can of Mountain Dew in one hand. The dark circles under his eyes were new, but he sported a big grin. He held up a can to her face.

"Red Bull?"

Alyssa grimaced. "No thanks… I'm good."

Paul sat up groggily next to her and grabbed the can. "Cheers, mate."

Alyssa shot Paul a glance. His hair was disheveled and he looked scruffier than she remembered. He gave her a sleepy smile.

"How was your nap?" he asked.

"Too short to remember."

"Good to know you were working hard, too," Clay snickered. He held up the crystal. "Ready to see what we're up against?"

They jumped out of bed and followed him to the table. On it, the LIDAR was hooked up to one of Clay's laptops. The VR headset was connected to the other computer. Several neatly crimped cables ran between the LIDAR, the headset and the two computers.

Clay pushed a button on the LIDAR and a small panel slid open. "I replaced the rotating mirror assembly from the LIDAR with a mount for the crystal," he said and placed the crystal inside. He tapped the laptop next to it. "This one drives the LIDAR. I can control the orientation of the crystal and the frequency and amplitude of the laser pulse with it." He pointed to the other computer. "The signals from the CCDs are fed into the second laptop and then streamed to the VR gear."

Alyssa pointed at the earpieces. "What's with the headphones?"

"Ah. Turns out that a subset of the frequencies from the crystal contains encoded audio. I was able to write some code to isolate it and pipe it to the headphones in the VR set."

"So I'll be able to hear stuff, too?" Alyssa moved closer to the gear, taking it all in. She shook her head. "You did this all in, what, five hours?"

"Quite brill, no?" Clay flashed his teeth. "We'll still have a problem with the crystal heating up, so we won't be able to hit it for too long at a time. I'll start with low power, just to be safe."

"Mutt's nuts, mate," Paul sounded equally impressed. "You've really outdone yourself." He paused, considering. "Could this be dangerous?"

Clay scratched his chin. "Uh... well, given that this is the first time this has been attempted, that's... ah... impossible to say." He cleared his throat. "I suppose there's always the risk of sensory overload."

"I'll be the guinea pig," Paul said and took the helmet.

"No way, Paul." Alyssa grabbed the helmet from him. "I started this. This is my thing."

Paul regarded her for several seconds then nodded. "Fair enough… but at the first sign of trouble, we're stopping."

Alyssa nodded. "Let's do this."

A few minutes later Alyssa sat in the chair, VR helmet on her head. Clay flipped a series of switches and turned to the laptop to finalize the calibration. He leaned into a microphone connected to the headphones inside the helmet. "Comfortable?"

"Ever tried walking in high heels?" Alyssa replied.

"Sure you're ready for this?" Paul asked.

She gave a thumbs up.

"All right. Three… two… one… here we go." Clay fired the laser.

Alyssa ripped the VR gear from her head and jumped up out of the chair.

"How? How is this possible?" She staggered.

Clay flipped the master switch to OFF and dashed over to her, but Paul grabbed her first, before she could fall.

"You okay?" Paul's voice echoed the concern in his face. "What happened?"

"Is something wrong?" Clay jumped in.

"What? No…" Alyssa looked at him puzzled, "It was incredible! Like I was right there, looking through someone else's eyes!"

Clay stared at her silently then glanced toward Paul who looked equally astonished. After a couple of moments Paul said warily, "You ripped off the helmet only a second after Clay flipped the switch."

"What? It seemed much longer—at least thirty seconds."

"What did you see?" Clay asked.

"I didn't just see, or hear," she could barely contain the excitement in her voice. "I actually *felt* things, too."

Paul and Clay stared at her wordlessly.

"You think I'm making this up?" she asked.

"No, no, that's not it." Paul shook his head. "It's just—how is that possible? The different time perception, the emotions?"

"Subliminal messages, perhaps?" Clay said. "If someone actually managed to develop technology to record memories, displaying and using subliminal messages to evoke emotions and thoughts would be simple—relatively speaking." He scratched his head.

"What?" asked Paul.

"Well, it's just... that's probably why she felt like she was *there* for half a minute, even though only a couple of seconds went by in real-time. The information must be fed at a staggering rate."

Paul turned to Alyssa. "What exactly did you see?"

"A laboratory—I think." She hesitated. "Well, at least it *felt* like I was in a laboratory. But it didn't look like any lab I've ever seen." She shook her head. "I... I can't explain it."

She stopped and considered. "God, if this crystal is truly as old as we think it is," she said, "do you realize what this means?"

Without waiting for an answer, she continued, "People. I saw people. They were working on something. Something important."

"Anything else?" Paul asked.

"I'm not sure. It seemed like the longer I was there, the

clearer the thoughts and emotions became. As if I was learning to read them better."

She was quiet for a few moments. "Damn! It's like trying to hold on to a dream. The more time goes by, the more I forget. I know there was more." She picked up the helmet. "I have to try again."

"Maybe I should be the one this time," Paul said.

She shook her head. "I'm fine. And I'm going. I know I can get tuned into it easier the second time around."

Paul pointed to the gear. "You're the one who built it," he said to Clay, "what do you think?"

Clay rubbed his chin. "It's impossible to predict what repeated exposure might do." He looked at Alyssa. "I doubt there'll be permanent damage, but you may feel all kinds of wonkers in the short term."

Alyssa nodded. "I understand."

Paul's mouth was tight, but he gave a quiet nod.

"Give me a couple of minutes to recalibrate it," Clay said and turned to the equipment.

"Thank you," Alyssa said.

Several minutes later, Paul and Clay stood at the table, watching Alyssa sitting in the chair once again, the VR helmet in her lap.

"I think I figured out how to access the beginning of the data," Clay said.

Paul scowled. "I have a really bad feeling about this."

Alyssa put her hand on his arm. "I'll be okay," she grinned. "With the *Wunderkind* here and you looking after me, what can possibly go wrong?"

She turned to Clay. "Hook me up."

Clay put the helmet on her head and adjusted it. He hesitated as his hand approached the ON switch for the laser.

"I'm going to start out with the intensity set at fifty percent," he said into the microphone. "You ready?"

"Beam me up, Scotty," came her reply.

Clay toggled the switch.

PART 2

REFLECTION

THERE IS a hint of moist warmth in the air. I lift my head.

"I am ready, *Amah*." My words sound distant.

My mother meets my gaze, her eyes two green orbs, glinting, feline, ever aware. She is wearing her white dress with the high collar. The one she wears but once a year. The fear is present in her face, yet her smile is real.

I reach out and touch her hand.

"Do not worry about me. I am not afraid." It is a lie.

She takes my hand and squeezes it. Strong. Much stronger than ever before.

"You are worthy of your sentinel." The tremor in her voice betrays her concern. "Your body will accept the gift."

I turn and face the triangular stone structure. I look past hundreds of steps to the summit. Two reptilian eyes stare down at me, unblinking. They belong to So'bek, the high priest, he whose sentinel is the crocodile. Few have ever chosen the crocodile as their sentinel. Fewer yet have survived.

I turn back to my mother and try to blink away the tears.

"What if I am not ready?"

She regards me quietly for several heartbeats, her serenity and confidence giving me strength.

"You are destined for greatness, Horus, my son."

I am startled at the sound of my chosen name. The one I shall carry into adulthood from this day forth. She smiles.

"You are worthy of that name, and of the animal companion you have chosen."

Horus. The falcon.

The high priest lifts his scaled arms above the stone altar and beckons. "It is time," he says.

I give my mother a final look. I know I shall never look at her the same way again. I want to cling to her and beg her not to let me go. My legs begin to tremble, and I squeeze her hand hard enough to make her wince.

She pulls me tightly to her and holds me for a long time. The familiar scent of jasmine in her hair and the metopion oil on her skin is soothing. Time seems to freeze. Too soon, she loosens her embrace and holds me at arm's length, her hands resting on my shoulders. She peers down at me, her feline eyes calm and full of confidence.

She places her hands on my head, her thumbs and forefingers shaping a triangle in the blessing of our people, representing the rays of the sun that give life to us.

"You are Horus, son of Isis and Osiris. You shall know no fear."

I take a deep breath and face the summit once again. Slowly, I take the first of the three hundred and forty-three stairs. I count silently as I climb.

One... two... three...

Seven levels of forty-nine stairs separate me from my new beginning. Each of the seven levels symbolizes a year of my life. A year lived without the animal gift. A life incomplete.

44... 45... 46...

With each step, my childhood fades away. Each step brings me closer to my new life. Soon, if my body accepts the gift, I shall join my father and my elder brothers as Horus, a young man bearing the gift of the falcon.

121... 122... 123...

My mind fills with memories. My time inside my mother's womb. The sound of her voice singing to me when she felt how frightened I was of the darkness.

187... 188... 189...

My first glance at my mother, her eyes exhausted, filled with tears and unconditional love. Me, a shivering bundle in her arms, unable to express my true love for her and my gratitude for the gift of life she gave me.

212... 213... 214...

My naming day, seven days after my birth. My father and my brothers looking down at me, their faces bright and gleaming with pride.

256... 257... 258...

My first word. *Haru,* falcon.

299... 300... 301...

The first time I understood our gift, the animal sentinel that our people choose on the seventh anniversary of their naming day.

341... 342... 343—

The stairs end. The robed figure regards me silently, his

pupils two black vertical slits set deeply inside his yellow eyes. Among the stillness is the pounding of my heart in my ears.

Two scaled hands emerge from the robed figure and I bow. The high priest's rough palms are a stark contrast to my mother's soft hands as he repeats the greeting of our people.

I lift my head.

"Are you prepared?" he asks.

"I am." My voice sounds thin.

"Who comes before me?"

I swallow. "Horus, son of Isis and Osiris."

"Horus, son of Isis and Osiris," he says as he lifts his arms, "this day marks the last day of your life as a child. From this day forth, you shall live your life as a man, blessed with the gift of your sentinel."

He pauses, his eyes piercing through me.

"Have you chosen?"

"I have." I try to keep my voice from trembling. I fail.

"What sentinel shall be yours?"

"The falcon," I whisper.

The figure regards me silently.

"I choose the falcon," I say, louder, with more confidence. "My namesake."

He nods. From behind the altar, the acolyte steps forth, on his arm a falcon. My falcon. I sink to my knees as the acolyte moves into his place beside So'bek.

The high priest peers down at me, his face as expressionless as a mask.

"On this day, you shall know if your sentinel accepts you. If you are worthy of his gift and his sacrifice. On this day, you and he shall die and be reborn as one."

Time slows as So'bek lifts a dagger from the stone altar and brings it toward the falcon.

"From this day forth, the two of you shall live as one. The falcon inside you and you inside him," he says.

My body screams for him to stop. I remain silent and stare as he moves the blade toward the magnificent bird.

The falcon's head is hooded, yet he stirs anxiously. I know he feels the threat. He spreads his wings and begins to beat them forcefully, pulling anxiously at the leather jesses tied to his talons.

No, don't! Please don't! I scream in my mind. My lips remain sealed.

I am Horus.

So'bek brings the blade to the falcon.

Son of Isis and Osiris.

I close my eyes.

I shall know no fear!

The pain is unbearable. I will not scream. My memories… I soar into the sky then I am falling. My body is consumed by fire. I scream.

————

WHAT IS ON MY HEAD? Get it off me! I try to rip it off the hood. Strong hands hold me, lift the hood from my head. Two strangers stare down at me, concern welling in their faces.

"Alyssa? Alyssa, are you okay?" I hear a strange voice.

————

ALYSSA GASPED as the waves of pain ebbed from her body. The pain gave way to confusion as the familiar surroundings of the magnificent pyramid disappeared. Slowly, she focused on the drab interior of the motel room. She felt hands on her shoulders as Clay lifted the VR set from her head.

"Alyssa! Can you hear me?" Paul's voice was strained. "You screamed—"

"H-how long?" she stammered.

"Maybe ten seconds. Fifteen max," Clay said.

"That's… impossible—it felt like minutes." She reached out and squeezed Paul's arm. "There were memories within memories!"

"Slow down." Paul's glow betrayed his own excitement. "What did you see?"

Alyssa took a deep breath. "A ritual, some kind of rite of passage. Seen through the eyes of a child… a boy." She struggled to replay the events in her mind. "It was to somehow create a hybrid between the boy and his—falcon." She froze.

Clay and Paul watched her silently with blank expressions.

"His name was Horus," she said.

Paul slowly shook his head, frowning. "Please tell me you're not thinking what I think you're thinking," he said.

Clay blinked a couple of times. "Uh… will someone fill in the techie?"

Paul turned to Clay. "Egyptian mythology," he said.

"Horus was the mythical falcon-headed god," Alyssa continued. "Son of Isis and Osiris. The protector of pharaohs."

Clay gaped at them. "You guys are both off your trolleys! I can *almost* accept a ten-thousand-year-old thumb drive filled with the memories of some ancient chap. But now he turns out to be an Egyptian god? Whatever you've been smoking—do share, please."

"I know it sounds crazy," Alyssa said, "but one of my grandfather's theories was that the gods in Egyptian mythology were merely a portrayal of an advanced civilization that was perceived to be godlike."

"So where did they come from?" Clay asked. "And don't tell me that they're some sort of space aliens."

"I don't know," Alyssa said softly. She stood. A wave of dizziness swept through her and she staggered. Paul rushed to her, but she waved him off. "I'm okay."

He stared at her.

"I'm fine, really." She took a deep breath. "There's only one way to find out what we're dealing with. I need to go back."

"You almost passed out!" Paul said.

"Yeah, you did look bloody wonky," Clay added. "And the frequency keeps bouncing, so I'd need to crank up the power."

"Can you get it going again?" she asked him.

Clay looked to Paul.

"Damn it, Clay, don't look to him for permission!" she said, her voice a measure sharper than she intended.

Clay's face tightened.

"I'm sorry," Alyssa said softly. She put her hand on his arm. "Please, Clay. I really need to do this."

His expression thawed. He nodded. "All right, give me a sec to recalibrate the LIDAR."

"Thank you," she said.

Paul sat motionless, staring at her, eyebrows drawing together.

"Don't worry. I'll be fine," she said to him as she lifted the VR set to her head.

Paul continued gazing at her silently, his expression dark, as the helmet covered her eyes.

"Do not slow down, Horus, we must not lose the others!"

I race at full speed, struggling to keep pace with my mother. As we pass under a lantern, I catch a glimpse of her face, her beautiful features marred by fear, her dress stained a dark crimson.

Father's blood...

I glance behind into the darkness, toward the rough voices of our pursuers. We are the last ones. There is nobody left between us and them. Without a warning, my mother turns into a dark alley and tugs me with her. The sudden jerk almost pulls me off my feet. I blink away my tears and struggle to focus on the narrow path ahead. My lungs are burning. The tears in my throat make the air taste sour.

"We are almost there, my son. You must be strong."

"*Amah*, I cannot go on!" I plead.

I trip again and this time she almost loses her grip, but somehow keeps me from falling. The voices behind us grow louder, their shouts more frequent.

I'm startled when she stops and pushes me into one of the narrow doorways. She looks at me, her chest rising in shallow, rapid breaths. Gradually, calmness replaces the fear in her eyes.

She cups my face with her hands. "Horus, my son, listen well," her whisper is soft, but unwavering. The pounding of my heart and my heavy breathing make it difficult to hear her voice. "You will follow the others to the harbor. I will meet you on the ship, later."

"No, *Amah*..." I want to plead with her not to leave me, but fear and exhaustion rob me of my voice.

She pulls me tightly into her arms and holds me. When she lets go, I see her peer into the darkness behind us, the shimmer in her beautiful feline eyes tainted with pain and fear. She looks at me and her expression shifts.

"I will always love you, my son," she says and places her hands on my head. Once more she turns toward the voices. I can see the pupils grow to cover each iris. She tenses as she sees them, even though they will not spot us in the darkness for a long time. My vision has begun to be worthy of the falcon, but at night, none could match the sight of those living with the gift of the sacred cat.

"Why do they hate us so much? Why do they want to hurt us?" My voice is trembling, my fear and confusion unbearable.

"They fear what they do not understand, my son. And they hate those whom they fear."

"We have never wronged them. What do they want from us?"

"They want to misuse the gifts of the animals. To make themselves strong. To win wars." She looks at me piercingly then holds me tight again.

Every breath I take brings them closer to us. "It is time, my son." She releases me and gently pushes me into the dark corner of the doorway. "Stay hidden here until you do not hear them anymore, then run as fast as you can to the boats. Find Grandfather."

"*Amah...*"

She holds me at arm's length. "You are Horus, son of Isis and Osiris," she says softly, then moves into the alley. She stands and waits for the pursuit to drive close enough to see her.

I press into the corner of the doorway. Breath by breath the voices grow louder. I close my eyes.

A rough voice pierces the darkness. "There's one!"

I fight my terror and open my eyes. I see my mother staring into the darkness toward the pursuers. Somehow, I grasp that the image of her standing there, tall and defiant, will forever be engraved in my memory. She glances at me one last time, I see her lips move. *You shall know no fear.*

She whirls and leaps into the darkness, away from the pursuers. Away from me.

I turn and press my cheeks against the cold rock. My tears wet the rough surface as it digs into my skin. My heart pounds against my chest.

I am Horus.

I hear their feet, only a few arms' lengths away from me. I know they can hear the thumping of my heart.

Son of Isis and Osiris.

I wait for a rough hand to yank me out of my hiding place. I hold my breath and squeeze my eyes shut as tightly as I can.

I shall know—

As soon as it came, the noise is gone. They continue their

pursuit into the darkness. I stay huddled against the rock for a long time before I dare to turn my head and look into the alley. It is empty. I leave the dark doorway and run the opposite way, the wind drying my tears as they streak down my face. I have to get to the harbor. My mother will meet me there.

She said she would.

I continue racing into the darkness. I reach the sloped gardens. The harbor is just ahead. Without warning, strong hands pull me into an alley. I try to scream but my mouth is covered.

"Be still, Horus." I hear a familiar voice. My grandfather, Thoth, the Scribe. I am shaking, too numb to feel. He points at the men by the boats and puts his finger to his lips. I nod in understanding and look to the boats. I gasp at the sight of the bodies of our kin lying at the docks motionless. I recognize the pursuers, standing around them with their weapons drawn.

"Where is your mother?" my grandfather whispers.

"She… she ran inland… to draw them away," I reply, tears streaking freely down my cheeks. "She said she would meet me. She said…"

Anguish fills his ancient eyes as he regards me, his face a shadow of agony. Slowly and deliberately, he pulls me to him and holds me close. When he releases me and I look at him again, his face is a mask, but I shiver at his eyes, two glaring mirrors of terrible pain and unrestrained hatred.

"They slaughtered everyone," he says as he slides his hand into his robe and draws out three glass orbs, the ghostly, purple mist inside them shifting subtly with his movements.

"But *Amah…*"

"We could have all lived together, in peace," his voice

quivers as he gently pushes me back and sets off toward the men.

"We could have been united, one people!" His voice grows louder, startling the men near the boats. They turn and face him for an instant then rush at us, raising their weapons.

"We have never done you harm, yet you slaughtered my brothers... my sisters!" His voice is a shaking crescendo. "You have murdered my sons and daughters! Now you shall answer for your savagery!" He screams and hurls the glass orbs at the running men.

The orbs fly through the air and break on the ground in front of the men as they rush into the barely perceptible mist.

The men continue to rush at Thoth for several strides then their eyes grow large as their legs refuse to obey them.

"Do not look, boy. Turn away!"

I cannot tear my eyes from the nightmare before me. The men's skin turns the color of fire and they fall to their knees, clawing at their throats and faces, blood streaking from their eyes. Then the screams begin. They grow louder and turn to the shrieks of animals. I cover my ears to drown out the sounds, but I can still hear them. I feel Thoth pull me to him and hold my head tight against his chest until the screams fade into a ghastly memory.

The strong beats of my grandfather's heart ring against my ear, their steady rhythm a brief solace in this horror. Finally, he releases me and moves toward the men. I hesitate, drawing him back.

He stops and looks down at me.

"Do not be afraid," he says. "This weapon can never cause you harm. It was made to protect us and bring death to our enemies. Our blood shall keep us safe." He cups my face in his hand. "Do you understand?"

I slowly nod and allow him to take my hand and lead me to the docks. I close my eyes as we walk past the lifeless bodies of our enemies and our kin covering the ground. When we stop and I open my eyes again, we stand before a single-masted sloop, moored at the far end of the harbor.

My grandfather sinks to one knee before me and puts his hands on my shoulders. "Nothing shall ever be again as it was," he says, his voice heavy. "We must leave our home and we shall never return."

I stare at him, unwilling to comprehend.

"They murdered your family." His voice cracks under the weight of his words. "They slaughtered them—all of them. You and I are all that remain of our people, our culture… our blood." He takes my head into his hands. "Our knowledge, what persists inside us, is all we have. I shall teach you all that I know, but I am old and you must carry this burden once I am gone. You must safeguard the memory of our people."

He stands and lifts me up, his arms surprisingly strong, and gently sets me inside the sailboat. He slips the lines off the wooden pylons, climbs in behind me and pushes off. He rows for a long time. The sky is deeper and the stars are brighter when he unfurls the sail and the wind pushes us east. I turn back one last time to the island I leave behind. I am grateful for the darkness as it conceals my tears and I silently curse the only home I have ever known.

———

ALYSSA LIFTED the VR helmet off her head and squinted. The room lights swam like darting fish in a midnight sea. Gradually, the blurriness receded and she slowly focused on the two pairs of eyes looking down at her.

"Alyssa?" Paul's voice broke the silence.

Alyssa stared at him, waiting for the dizziness to subside.

"They killed them," she finally said, her voice trembling. "They killed all of his people." She grimaced, the sound of her own voice strange to her ears. "I saw it. I *felt* what he felt." Her lips quivered. "Paul…" she looked at him, words failing her.

Paul gently placed his hand on her shoulder. She shivered. He reached over and put a blanket around her. Alyssa sat quietly, trying to ward off the ringing in her ears, and lifted her hands to rub her temples. She flinched when she felt wetness on her cheeks. Absentmindedly, she dried the tears with her sleeve.

"I think there was some kind of war, a civil war, on their island. There was an ambush on Horus's people by others who lived there." She winced, recalling the images. "He and his grandfather were the only ones who survived and escaped. His grandfather, Thoth, killed their enemies with a…" She shuddered at the memory of the screams.

She bolted upright. "The mist! It's a weapon!"

"What?" Paul gasped.

"I… I'm not sure," she said, struggling to remember the details. "I can't put it together yet. Maybe if we try again."

Paul shook his head. "You need to rest."

"We don't have time to rest!" She whirled. "Clay, tell him I'm—" The room spun and she staggered. She tumbled to the floor before either of them could reach her.

"Alyssa!" Paul cried as he and Clay rushed to her side. Paul dropped to the floor beside her and gently lifted her head. "What happened?"

"I… I don't know. Just got a bit dizzy," she said. "It's okay. I'm better now."

"It's because of what we're doing, isn't it?" Paul asked, shooting a glance at Clay.

Clay cleared his throat. "Probably a good idea to give it a rest."

"What?" Alyssa bolted up. "We're getting so close to finding out what's going on!"

"You know he's right," Paul said. "We have no idea what this is doing to you. It's too risky."

"We're finally getting somewhere. Please, you have to trust me on this. I think I know what is making Kade ill."

Paul and Clay looked at her wordlessly.

"Go on," Paul said.

"I think it's some kind of a weapon. I'm not sure what it is exactly, maybe it's chemical or biological, not just a virus or bacteria…" She struggled for the right words. "It's man-made, manufactured, somehow." She described the glass balls Thoth used to defeat the men. "He told Horus that it was safe for him, that his blood will protect him."

"That's impossible!" Clay said. "We don't even have the technology to do this now!"

"We also don't have technology to record memories onto a crystal." Alyssa snapped back.

"Biological nanotechnology ten thousand years ago?" Paul said. "You have to admit, that's a pretty long stretch."

"Isn't *all* of this a pretty long stretch?" Alyssa laughed dryly, sounding more sarcastic than she had intended. "If you had told me three days ago that my father was dying and the key to his cure was locked inside a ten thousand year old DVD that contains the memories of Horus, God of Egypt, I would have called you a frigging lunatic!"

She inhaled deeply. "Wherever the crystal came from, their technology is far beyond ours. I think they developed the weapon—whatever it was—to protect themselves. Somehow, it was released and is causing Kade's illness. What if it can spread to others?"

Alyssa shuddered, unsure if it was at the chill or sudden realization. "The people trying to kill us want this technology. The key to it lies in the chamber. I have to get in there... somehow."

"Are you completely looney?" Clay pulled a face. "After what happened to your dad?"

She turned to him. "I can't tell you how sorry I am to have dragged you—both of you—into this. But I cannot continue risking your lives. You should hide for a while, until this is over."

Paul looked at her, resigned. "There's no convincing you otherwise, is there?"

When she shook her head, he sighed. "I'm coming with you to Egypt."

"Paul—"

"No arguments. That's the deal. You'll need somebody to watch your back. We have no idea what we're up against."

She considered for several moments then nodded. "Will you bring me my cell phone?" she asked.

An hour later, Alyssa hung up the phone and gave Paul a tired smile. "Congratulations, Mr. Matthews, you are the proud recipient of an all-expenses-paid, 'Beyond First Class' flight package to Cairo."

Paul gave her a puzzled look.

"All of today's flights to Cairo were booked solid. The only available seats were the obscenely expensive private suites," she said. "It's a good thing Kade and I have been saving up all of our frequent flyer miles for the past five years." She smirked. "I knew they'd come in handy one day." She glanced at the VR goggles. "Besides, it will give us a chance to find out more about Horus while we're in the air."

Paul turned to Clay. "Are you sure we'll be able to take the equipment through airport security?"

"Nothing dodgy there, just electronic bits 'n bobs," Clay replied. "On the other hand, I'm quite certain that it doesn't qualify as an approved electronic device, so you should probably wait to close the door on your fancy suite before turning it on."

Alyssa nodded. "Are you going to be okay?"

He flashed a grin. "Don't you worry about me. I'll be tickety-boo."

"Do be careful," she said. "I can't tell you how grateful I am."

"Of course, you can," Clay gave her an impish look. "But first go and sort out this bloody mess and save the world."

"Deal." Alyssa gave him a long hug and kissed him on the cheek.

Clay cleared his throat, trying to hide the flush that crept across his cheeks. "Just promise me to take good care of yourself. And of Oxford boy." He winked at Paul then turned serious again. "You can do this, you know. I will wait to hear from both of you."

————

TASHA MENDEVA PUSHED the heavy wooden doors and sauntered into the room as they swung open ahead of her. She moved confidently toward the man sitting at the desk, the strapless black dress emphasizing her perfect posture and the graceful lines of her neck.

"If it's not good news, turn around and close the door behind you." Drake's cold voice met her from behind the desk, his gaze remaining fixed on the document in front of him.

Tasha slowly glided next to him and put her arms around his neck, clasping her hands behind his head. She leaned close to his ear.

"The girl just used her cell phone to book two tickets to Cairo," she whispered. "For herself and one of the boys from the WHO."

Drake looked up at her, raising his eyebrows.

"Where is she flying from?"

"Gatwick, London."

Drake sat up and freed himself from her embrace. Reluctantly, she moved back with a sultry expression.

"I want Gavriel on that plane," he said.

"Renley said we needed them alive." She pressed her lips into a fine line.

His hand shot out and his fingers locked around her arm. He pulled her roughly to him until her face was only inches from his eyes.

"I'm tired of Renley's games," he said, his voice low and his gaze filled with a dangerous gleam. "Sometimes I wonder whether your loyalty to your mentor means more to you than your dedication to the Society."

Tasha cast her eyes down. "George Renley gave me a life," she said, her words slow and measured. She looked up. "But you and the Society gave it a purpose." She moved even closer to his face, eyes locked on his. "The Society has my complete devotion." She gently took his hand off her arm and brought his palm to her mouth and kissed it. "As do you."

"Make the calls," he said.

She nodded. Slowly, she stood and straightened her dress then left the room.

Tasha paced briskly along the corridor for several steps before she slowed and staggered. She gasped and reached for the wall, barely catching herself from dropping to the floor.

The hallway spun, but somehow her hands found a door. She fumbled with the handle and stumbled into the empty room, locking the door behind her. Her heartbeat pounded against her temples as she fell against the door, shuddering and breathing hard. Dread crept over her like an icy chill, numbing her brain. Gradually, she sank to the floor, hands pressed against her temples. Slow, desolate tears ran from her unblinking eyes, making wet tracks on her face before dripping off her chin and melting into the black dress.

She leaned her head back and inhaled deeply through the nose and exhaled through her mouth, willing her breathing to slow. She wiped off her tears then pulled out her phone and dialed a number.

"Yes?" George Renley's voice felt like an embrace.

She drew in a deep breath. "They are flying out of Gatwick to Cairo today," she said quietly, struggling to keep her voice composed.

"Well done," Renley replied.

"He wants me to send Gavriel on that plane."

Renley seemed to hesitate for a moment. "That is not wise —and a great risk."

"And what would you have me do, George?"

"The girl may be more valuable than he realizes."

Tasha swallowed to clear the lump in her throat. "I'm falling apart."

"You cannot falter now, Tasha. Remember what's at stake— and remember your training."

She stayed silent, her unfocused gaze staring into the dark room.

"Tasha?"

She blinked, her violet eyes swollen and sore. "I have to go. I need to make the calls," she said, her voice flat, before she hung up the phone.

ALYSSA EYED the two-deck fuselage of the massive Airbus 380 and the two other jetways leading to the coach sections on the lower level. She shook her head. *The Wright Flyer's first flight could have taken off and landed inside this behemoth*, she thought.

She moved away from the window and followed Paul as he continued along the upper level jetway toward the plane. The flight attendant standing in the doorway was dressed in a chic cream-colored blouse and beige skirt. A white scarf and matching red hat and shoes completed her uniform. She greeted them with an elegant smile.

"Your boarding passes, please?" After a quick glance, she looked up at them again.

"Welcome to Meridian Airlines, Miss Morgan and Mr. Matthews. If you would please follow me to your suite."

Alyssa glanced at Paul as the woman led the way. He shrugged and grinned then extended his hand and bowed. "After you, Miss Morgan."

They followed the flight attendant to the front of the plane. The smell of fresh leather enveloped Alyssa as she entered the first class section. A horseshoe-shaped bar at the front of the cabin was flanked by plush leather benches set along the sides of the plane. Alyssa followed the flight attendant past the bar and the waiter with his well-practiced smile.

When she entered the next cabin, she felt like she had been transported into the lobby of a five-star hotel. The entire width of the twenty-five-foot cabin was dedicated to two impossibly lavish suites. The suites were surrounded by partitions that completely enclosed them, secluding their occupants from the rest of the plane. The flight attendant turned to them.

"Welcome to the Meridian Airlines private suites, Miss Morgan and Mr. Matthews. My name is Kaya. I have the pleasure of being your personal flight hostess on this trip. The suite on the right is yours. The other suite will not be occupied during this flight."

She pointed at the leather reclining chairs inside the suite. "Please make yourselves at home. You will find complimentary slippers, pajamas, and toiletries in the nightstand at either side of the bed."

She waited for them to enter the suite. "We ask that the door remain open during boarding, takeoff, and landing. During all other times you are welcome to close the door for complete privacy. The entertainment system is controlled with these devices," she handed them two tablets. "If there is anything at all that I can get you, please only ask, or press this icon on your tablet."

She smiled. "While we wait for takeoff, may I bring you a refreshment? Champagne, perhaps, or a mimosa?"

Alyssa looked up from the tablet. "Uh… yeah, sure! A mimosa would be great."

"Make that two!" echoed Paul.

"With pleasure," she said. "I shall be right back."

Alyssa glanced at Paul as she absorbed their home for the next seven hours. Their plush leather chairs faced the front of the plane where a fifty-inch flat screen hung suspended above a queen-sized bed. A single long-stemmed red rose lay in the center of the gold-embroidered white comforter. The plushy pillows made it almost irresistible to Alyssa. The interior walls were accented with rosewood and paintings hanging on either side of the door. Freshly-cut roses in a vase secured in the corner of the suite completed the décor. If it weren't for the airline-sized windows along the right wall, Alyssa would have never believed that she was inside a plane.

Paul looked at Alyssa and grinned widely. "This is posh."

Alyssa slipped off her shoes and put on the fuzzy slippers from the nightstand. She pressed a button to recline her seat and bring up the footrest. A moment later, Kaya returned with the drinks. Alyssa took the crystal glass and clinked it with Paul's.

"Here's to traveling in style," she said.

She took a sip and allowed the combination of the freshly squeezed orange juice and champagne to burst in her palate. As she savored the taste, she heard Kaya greet another passenger and walk toward the front of the plane. Lazily, Alyssa turned her head and caught a glimpse of a tall man dressed in an impeccably tailored suit. She spotted a brown leather-bound notebook in his hand a moment before he disappeared into the private cabin across the aisle.

She turned to Paul. "I thought Kaya said the cabin across from us was going to be empty."

He shrugged. "Maybe somebody else used their miles at the last moment."

"Unlikely. Did you see that suit? That getup alone will buy this ticket."

"Whatever you say," he replied. "Don't worry. If we're not safe on an airplane, we won't be safe anywhere. Besides, I'm sure we'll have enough personal attention from Kaya even with another passenger here."

"I'm sure you're right," she said, stretching. "I want to get to work when we're airborne and the door is closed. Until then," she put on the noise-canceling headphones, "I'm going to make the best of this."

Alyssa leaned her head back into the soft pillow and closed her eyes. She was asleep after three breaths.

———

IN HER SLEEP, Alyssa was blissfully unaware of the man wearing dark sunglasses who had been following them since their arrival at the airport. He walked into the first class cabin and sat in his seat. He took off the sunglasses revealing raw burns in his eyes. Grimacing with pain, Gavriel dialed a number on his cell phone.

———

DRAKE SAT in his office chair. He answered the phone on the first ring.

"I'm on the plane. They are in a private suite," Gavriel said.

"You know what to do," Drake replied. "Do not fail me again."

He hung up the phone and faced Tasha.

"It's only a matter of time now," he said.

She took a deep breath, "Will, perhaps this... this is too dangerous. George said—"

"Perhaps we should reconsider Lord Renley's commitment to the Society?"

"He feels the risk is too great."

"He is a coward."

"Some things are too dangerous. They can't be controlled."

He studied her impassively, a threatening glow creeping into his eyes. "Is that why Renley sent you to me? To control me? To spy on me?"

She returned his gaze silently, intently aware of the hair lifting on the nape of her neck and on her arms.

Drake leaned forward. "Did you tell Renley about their flight to Cairo?"

Tasha pressed her lips into a fine line.

"Did you?"

"I owe him my life." She moved her hand to his face. He brushed it away.

"Get out."

"Will, please—"

"Leave now," he said, his voice quiet and menacing.

———

ALYSSA WOKE to the hum of the engines. Startled, she looked at Paul. "How long was I out?"

"Not even an hour. We just got up to cruising altitude," he replied. "Hungry?"

Alyssa felt her stomach growl. "Starving. The ham and egg biscuit this morning didn't do the trick." She swallowed hard.

Paul smiled and handed her the leather-covered menu. She opened it. *Marinated lamb loin with coriander jus... Spicy tuna tartare... Veal paupiette stuffed with dried fruits...* She beamed at Paul.

"I know, right? Sure as heck beats 'Chicken or Pasta' in coach," he said. "I was really hoping you'd wake up soon. I don't know how much longer I could have kept myself from drooling all over the menu." He grinned. "So, what shall it be?"

An hour later, Alyssa looked at Paul guiltily as she nibbled on the post-dessert cheese plate and popped a grape into her mouth. She took a small sip of her espresso. "I haven't eaten this well or this much since the dig in Carnac in January," she said. "Good God, can you imagine doing this all the time?"

Paul rubbed his stomach and gave a satisfied sigh in reply. He opened his mouth, but his words were interrupted by a knock on their door.

"Come in," they said in unison.

The door opened slowly. Alyssa felt a sudden chill as she recognized the tall man from the other suite standing in the doorway. He was as slim and elegant as a flamenco dancer; his dark eyes and glossy hair produced a striking contrast to his pale skin. Standing with perfect posture, he seemed as comfort-able in his crisply pressed suit as Alyssa was in her favorite sweatshirt. He held a cognac snifter in his left hand and swirled it slowly.

"My apologies for intruding," he said, his voice ringing with the Queen's English, his cool expression at odds with his gracious words. "May I request a minute of your time?"

Alyssa felt Paul tense in the seat next to her. She gently put her hand on his arm. "It's been a very long day," she said with forced politeness. "My friend and I were just about ready to take a nap."

"Indeed, the hour has grown late," the man replied as he entered the suite. He extended a flawlessly manicured hand to her. Alyssa caught sight of the impossibly thin Patek Philippe watch around his right wrist.

"Miss Morgan." It was a statement more than a question.

Alyssa inhaled sharply. "You have me at a disadvantage," she took his hand, her skin tingling.

"George Renley, at your service," he said with the slightest bow of his head. His handshake was cool and measured.

Renley faced Paul. "Mr. Matthews," he said.

"What do you want?" Paul said.

If Renley took offense at Paul's harsh tone, his measured smile did not betray it.

"Very well, then. Let us dispense with the formalities," he replied. "You have something in your possession that is rightfully mine."

Before Alyssa could react, Paul leaped out of his seat and grabbed Renley's jacket, pushing him against the wall. "Paul, no!" she yelled.

"You would do well to heed Miss Morgan's advice," Renley said, his arms at his side, his cold gaze a silent warning to Paul.

"You tried to have us killed, you bastard!" Paul snarled, his nostrils flaring.

Renley's expression shifted for an instant.

"You misjudge me, Mr. Matthews. I assure you, I had absolutely no involvement with the events at the World Health Organization. I employ more—*sophisticated*—methods to achieve my goals. Now, please, unhand the suit."

"You mean you buy people," Alyssa said, contempt filling her voice. "How can we trust that you weren't the one who hired that killer?"

Renley fixed a steely gaze on Alyssa. "Miss Morgan, I am a collector, I safeguard rare items. I admit that I have gone to great lengths to obtain the objects of my desire. However, killing or paying to have somebody killed is not among my practices."

Alyssa studied him coolly. His eyes were intelligent—calculating, even—but they lacked the flatness of a killer's empty stare.

"Let him speak," she said.

"Alyssa—"

"Paul, please, I want to hear what he has to say."

Paul shot her a dismayed glance but remained silent. He released Renley and took a step back, crossing his arms across his chest. "You have two minutes," he said coldly.

"Thank you," Renley replied. He smoothed his jacket and swirled his snifter before taking a slow sip of the cognac. "It may be of interest to you that your father and I have had numerous mutually beneficial business arrangements."

Alyssa stared at him. "You know my father?"

"I became interested in Dr. Morgan's research several years

ago and have since provided financial auspices for three of his and Dr. Wallace's expeditions."

"What?" Paul shot back. "You've been sponsoring Alyssa's father's expeditions?" He turned to Alyssa. "This is absurd. How do we know that what he's saying is true?"

"Two weeks ago, I provided a substantial donation to the Egyptian Supreme Council of Antiquities," Renley continued, ignoring Paul. "The letter accompanying the donation pronounced my keen interest concerning Dr. Morgan's studies of the Hall of Records."

"You mean—" Alyssa started.

"Yes, Miss Morgan," he replied, steadily. "I enabled your father's pursuit of his studies and passions. So, as you can undoubtedly understand, from my standpoint, I am entitled to a certain claim—"

"I don't care what you think you're entitled to," Paul interrupted. "You have no idea what we've—"

"Did you have anything to do with what happened to my father's expedition?" Alyssa asked.

"My dear Miss Morgan," Renley spread his hands, "please tell me what would possess me to sabotage an expedition I'm financing."

Alyssa considered the reply. "Why are you so interested in the Hall of Records?"

Renley reached inside his jacket and took out a brown leather notebook.

"My great-grandfather, Lord George Renley II, became obsessed with the idea of discovering the hall." He held the notebook out to her. "He recorded all his research within these pages." Alyssa squinted as she tried to make out the embossed sigil on the front cover.

"Ultimately, he collected enough evidence to mount an expedition to the Giza Plateau in 1913," Renley continued. "Regrettably, his entire party vanished without a trace. Over a decade of his research was lost and, for almost a century, nobody has been able to follow his trail of leads or recover any of his work."

"Until my father," Alyssa said. "So that's why you've been financing his research. You wanted him to pick up the pieces."

"Dr. Morgan demonstrated remarkable capability as both an archeologist and a researcher," Renley continued, his tone flat and unhurried. "His methods proved quite successful in retrieving many of my great-grandfather's leads and ultimately provided sufficient evidence to convince the Egyptian Council of Antiquities—with some additional enticement—to grant the permits for the excavation."

"You mean you bribed the council. And now my father is in the hospital and we have people after us who want us dead."

Renley's expression turned dark. "You do not know with whom you are dealing. I can provide protection for you."

"And you're offering this purely out of the kindness of your heart," she sneered.

"I am simply asking for what should have been in my possession in the first place."

Paul faced Alyssa. "This is ridiculous. Why are we still listening to him?"

Renley regarded Paul in silence. Finally, he said, "Mr. Matthews, do you know that the Hall of Records was so named because it is rumored to have contained records created by

Thoth, the scribe to the Gods? It is said that the person who can decipher the knowledge and use it to their advantage will be invincible. And immortal."

"Yet you just want to lock up the key to this power with the rest of your precious artifacts." Alyssa raised her eyebrows. "To safeguard it."

"I believe that certain things are better left alone."

"This is nothing more than a game to you, isn't it?" Alyssa said as she slowly stood up. "You dress in your fine clothes, wear fancy watches and drink expensive cognac. You've used people as pawns all your life. You don't even realize how sick your games are to the rest of us." She crossed her arms. "We both have lost a great deal because of the Hall of Records, Lord Renley, but I cannot permit the only item that may hold the answer to my father's cure to leave our possession. I'm sorry, this particular object of your desire is not for sale or barter."

She turned to Paul then back to Renley. "Thank you for your visit. Mr. Matthews and I are ready to retire for the evening."

Renley scowled, which consisted of the barest downturn of the corner of his lips. He remained silent for several moments before slowly nodding. "As you wish, Miss Morgan," he replied, his voice flat. He turned around unhurriedly and left the suite.

After Renley closed the door behind him, Alyssa let out a sigh and fell back into the chair. She felt her hands tremble and gripped the armrests tight. She took a deep breath and looked up at Paul.

Paul rubbed the back of his neck. "You don't seriously believe a word he said about his great-grandfather. Renley may have financed some of your father's expeditions, but the story about the lost expedition sounds far-fetched. Seems like a perfect sob story to get sympathy from us."

"Did you see the sigil on his notebook?" Alyssa said, straining her memory. "It was a griffin. I could have sworn I've seen it somewhere before."

"An entire party lost on the Giza Plateau," Paul continued. "That just sounds—"

Alyssa pointed at the phone in the seat.

"Kaya did say the calls were complimentary, right?"

————

JACOB'S PHONE lit up and the signature theme from *Halo 3* cut through the silence of the pitch-black hotel room. His hand appeared from under the bed covers and reached toward the nightstand. Groggily, he fumbled for his phone and brought it to his ear.

"Hey, Jake."

He bolted up at the sound of her voice. "Alyssa!"

"I didn't wake you, did I?"

Jacob stifled a yawn. "No, no… why would I be sleeping? That would be a silly thing to do at four a.m." He rubbed his eyes, half asleep. "Where are you?"

"Long story. I need a favor."

"I'm shocked."

"I need you to find anything that you can about a Lord George Renley and an expedition to the Giza Plateau in 1913."

"That all?"

"Yes—no, wait!"

"Uh-huh…"

"See what you can find about a griffin coat-of-arms."

"Griffin?"

"The mythical creature. The head, wings and front legs of an eagle, and the body and tail of a lion."

Jake stifled yet another yawn. "So, kinda like a platypus, except a lot more badass?"

"Bye, Jake."

———

ALYSSA SHOOK her head and hung up the phone. Paul looked at her for several seconds with a curious expression.

"Who was that?" he asked, sheepishly.

"Who, that?" Alyssa replied, sounding more self-conscious than she cared to admit. "That was Jake… Jacob, I mean. He's Kade's student. He stayed behind in Peru to manage the dig."

"Are you two…? Is he your…?" Paul stumbled.

"Jake?" She laughed, feeling a flush creep across her cheeks. "No, of course not." Her gaze lingered on Paul a heartbeat longer than she intended before she continued, only too happy to change the topic, "Anyway, if Renley is right—"

"We're bollocked."

She grinned. "But we do have an advantage."

"Our youthful exuberance?"

"We can see into the future. In the past."

Paul frowned as she stood up and moved to the locker with the carry-on luggage. He let out a long sigh when she pulled out the big duffel bag.

"Alyssa…"

"There's only one way to find out what we're up against," she said. "I do believe it's time for work, Mr. Matthews."

She pulled out the LIDAR and held it out to him. "You did pay attention when Clay was teaching you how to work this, right?"

"WHERE IS HE?" I close my fingers around the man's throat and lift him off the ground. Tears of pain and rage streak down my cheeks. My hand is an iron vise, squeezing each breath from the islander. Fear drowns his bulging eyes as he fights for air, a quivering rag doll in my hand. He may know the answer, but I shall never hear it. Life slips away from him as his windpipe collapses beneath my grip, and his stare turns to glass. I thrust him aside like a spent flask of wine, oblivious to the pounding of my heartbeat against my temples. He hits the ground, and the sound of death reflects from the high-domed ceiling of the audience chamber.

Slowly, I raise my head and take in the crowd that surrounds me. The dread in their faces bears a stark contrast to the splendor of the magnificent murals on the marble walls and gilded columns that fill the hall. I look to my commanders and advisors, to the lords and lordlings who have served me for decades, yet not a single one of them will hold my gaze. Slowly, one person breaks their ranks. Horemheb, the commander of my armies, steps forward and sinks to his knees. His face is etched with pain and shame as he lifts his head toward me.

"We had no warning, my lord. They—"

I do not hear his words. I tear the golden helmet from my head and swing it at him. The helmet strikes hard, and he hits the ground, blood streaking from his cheek and lips.

"They murdered my wife and took *my son*!" The skin of my face stretches into a snarl as I scream, white spittle flying from my mouth. I lift my arm again to crush the heavy helmet on his skull. Horemheb raises his head, fearless, willing to pay the price for having failed me.

"Horus!" A voice rings out behind me. "Horus, my lord! My blood!" The voice quivers with old age, yet it is filled with power and authority. I hold the blow and remain motionless.

"He speaks true!" I hear my grandfather's voice through the red mist of my rage. "He was powerless to avert this evil. He would have given his life a thousand times over to protect your wife and son, but slaying your finest warrior now will not bring them back to you."

I keep my back to him, my chest heaving, and slowly lower my arm. "Do not presume to lecture me, old man," I growl, my voice filled with poison. "For seventy long cycles I have listened to your every word. For too long, I have followed your teachings." I pause, the pounding in my ears clouding my vision. "To what end?"

I turn to him, straining to focus. His ageless eyes mirror the pain in my heart. His lined face speaks of hard life and labor. My breathing slows and my words now come in a whisper, yet each word strikes his ancient heart like a dagger. "The blame lies with you as it does with him. Was it not you who counseled peace between our people? They deserved death for killing our flesh and blood decades ago, yet you spoke of peace. They do not know the meaning of that word!"

He studies me with a distant stare. When he opens his mouth, his voice is trembling and quiet. "I have failed you, Horus, my grandson. I have failed to protect you and your kindred blood. The night we fled our home, I vowed to keep you and all whom you shall love safe from harm. Yet I failed you." His voice cracks as he remembers the night that will forever be engrained in our memories. "But my greatest failure is that I did not succeed in freeing you of your anguish—and hatred." He pauses, taking a deep, pained breath. "For that night I also vowed never to kill again or wage war."

The memories awaken once more in my head in agonizing detail. Once again, I am haunted by the bleeding faces of the men as they died, their screams piercing through the night air. I stare into the distance, wrestling the memories from my mind. *I am Horus, son of Isis and Osiris.* A welcome numbness spreads through my body. *I shall know no fear.*

"Return my son to me unharmed," I command Horemheb, my voice flat, "or do not return." I drop my golden helmet to the floor. "All of you—out!"

Dozens rush out, only too eager to obey my command. I face my grandfather and stalk toward him, each step a trial of my inner strength.

"The night in the harbor. When Mother… when we escaped. I have asked you about that night more times than I can remember, yet each time you have refused an answer. This day, you shall not deny me. You will tell me what you did that night. What cruel fate befell those men?"

His gaze rests on me for a long time. His breathing comes in shudders as he stands before me silently, his shoulders slumped.

Finally, he speaks, "A weapon, Horus. Savage and merciless. Unleashed, it slaughters your enemies and dooms those who shall draw near the dead."

"Yet you and I passed by them, close enough to touch!"

"It was a living weapon, my grandson. Devised by our people, it was meant to protect us. The weapon could never harm you, or those with your blood. The others outnumbered us a hundred to one, but they knew of our power, and so the fragile peace was kept between our two peoples. Two cultures living side by side on our island."

"*Pureans*. The Pure Ones." My lips curve into a grimace as I recall the name by which our enemies called each other.

"Yes," he continues, "and our people, the Hybrids, born to accept the gift of an animal sentinel and destined to live their lives as a cross between two species. A long time ago, there was respect between our cultures, but they grew jealous of our knowledge and fearful of our power. We knew there were those among them who wished us ill, but none could have foretold the extent of their hatred. They attacked us when we were most vulnerable."

"Why did they come here? Why did they not grant us peace after we fled?"

For a long time he does not speak. He closes his eyes. When he opens them again I see shame... remorse.

"That night, I did not merely slay the men in the harbor," he says, his voice shaking. "I condemned those men to eradicate their kin, as the same curse that ravaged their bodies surged across the island. Eventually, the Pureans prevailed and contained the sickness, but not before it ended the lives of thousands of their people."

I stare at him, my mind refuses to grasp the words I am hearing.

"Horus, I have raised you as my own son since we have arrived in this strange land. Your powers, the gift of the falcon, have crowned you a king—a god—among these people. The Pureans knew they could not capture you here, at the seat of your power, so they took your son."

He pauses, his face a mask of pain.

"They seek to use him as a pawn against you, to provoke you into battle, so they can destroy you, for as long as you live you are a threat to them. You must not let them succeed. Enough blood has been shed. You must vow that you will not wage war."

I stare at him, my fingernails leaving bloody imprints in my palms. "This is your sage counsel to me? You, whose daughter was butchered by these savages? This is your guidance? That I vow to abandon my flesh and blood?" I slam my fist against the stone column, cracking its gilded frame. I ignore the searing pain in my hand as I speak through clenched teeth. "In the name of my first ancestor, in the name of Ra, hear this vow, old man. If any harm befalls my son, I shall know no rest until they have learned a hundredfold the anguish they have brought upon me."

His shoulders slump. "I lost a daughter, and I killed for it. And for the past seven decades I have lived with the memories of having extinguished countless lives because of a single moment of weakness. A single moment when I was powerless to control my rage. Not a day passes when I am not haunted by the memories of the terrible evil I unleashed. Every day I crave to undo what I have done. Slaying the islanders will not bring your wife back to life and it will not bring your son back to you."

His gray eyes lock onto mine. "There is another way to honor her memory. To remember your son. To preserve the legacy of our people. But it shall not be through war and annihilation, but through immortalizing her, your son, and every person you have ever loved—and you will ever love."

I stare at him wordlessly, my body rigid.

"Since the night we left our island," he chooses his words deliberately, "I have dedicated my life to immortalizing our culture, our people, inside your mind. I have taught you about our history, tutored you in the arts, the study of the heavens, and the art of healing. I have shared with you nearly everything I know." He looks at me warily. "But I have also kept secrets from you, my grandson. On this day, I shall reveal my greatest secret to you. On this day, you shall learn why I will be remembered as Thoth, the Scribe, for I have succeeded in not only creating records of words and images, but also records of minds."

He moves toward me until he is close enough to touch, his eyes a bright spark of hope against a sea of pain. He reaches inside his robe and pulls out an object. He holds it up to me with trembling hands.

"This is the key, Horus." He looks at it reverently, his voice growing stronger. "This is the key to preserving our culture, our legacy. Your memories of our people and of your life shall continue long after we are gone because of this, the monument to my existence. One hundred and thirty long years, devoted to a single purpose." He takes a deep breath. "To scribe life."

I stare at the object, a crystal in the shape of a pyramid, smaller than a man's fist. I shake my head, unable to comprehend.

"Our memories, our most cherished thoughts, our lives... scribed into this crystal, stored for all ages, to be witnessed by others as if they had lived them. My perseverance shall be my final gift to you, Horus. This is the legacy I shall bestow upon you." He stands taller, his back straight, his ancient eyes sparkling. "Immortality."

Slowly, I raise my hand to the crystal. The tips of my fingers graze the cool surface. A hot needle sears into my head, scalding my eyes. I scream.

———

ALYSSA GASPED FOR AIR. She felt the helmet come off and a pair of hands grasping her face. Gradually the pain in her head began to subside. She slowly opened her eyes, the images of the past blurring with the present. She tried to hold on to her memories, but they were disappearing like sand drawings in the wind.

Slowly, she focused on her surroundings. *I'm in a hotel room. No. The hum of the airplane. Paul.* She winced as Paul lifted her from the leather chair and laid her on the bed.

She put her head back on the pillow and inhaled slowly. Gradually, the sharp pain was turning into a dull headache.

Paul sat next to her. "You screamed," he reached for her hand. "What happened?"

She waved him off. "A pain in my head, but only for an

instant. It's gone now," she replied. "I'm feeling much better." She tried to smile.

"I don't want you using this thing anymore."

"But we're so close to finding out what's going on! We can't stop now."

"It's too dangerous. I won't just watch while it's continuing to hurt you."

"I'm fine. Remember, Clay even said that there might be some short-term effects. A little headache is a small price to pay for—"

"We'll just have to figure out what we need to do without using the equipment again." He held up his hand. "I won't argue with you about this—please don't try to convince me otherwise."

Alyssa nodded slowly, too tired to argue. She stared at the ceiling trying to recall the memories. "I could use some water," she said quietly.

Paul reached to the head of the bed and pressed the flight attendant call button when Alyssa bolted up, pain and exhaustion forgotten.

"It was his grandfather! Thoth, the Scribe. He is the one who developed the technology to capture memories!" Her eyes were glowing. "And Horus was a grown man," she continued breathlessly, her voice trembling. "He must have been seventy, but he seemed half that age. I think he was in Egypt, a king or a pharaoh. My God, Paul, do you know what that means?"

Paul stared at her, trying to absorb her words. "Alyssa, slow down."

Alyssa felt her pulse racing. She recalled the magnificent

hall and people surrounding Horus. Her face darkened when she remembered his pain.

"Something terrible happened. They killed his wife. I think they kidnapped his son. The islanders, the *Pureans*..." She was surprised at the sound of her voice, quivering, suddenly filled with Horus's rage.

"What? What are you talking about? Why would they do that?"

"His rage was terrifying, Paul. He killed one of their spies with his bare hands. I felt his rage, his agony. He wanted to kill them all, but his grandfather..." She gasped, remembering the pieces. "His grandfather also developed the weapon. We were right, it is a bioweapon. It won't harm Horus or his people, but it spread, killed thousands of the islanders. Paul... we have to stop it before it happens here."

He frowned. "And how are we going to do that?"

Alyssa studied him silently, teeth biting at her bottom lip. She shrugged and swallowed hard, trying to clear the lump in her throat.

Paul pressed the call button again. "Where is Kaya when you need her?" he asked, impatient. He stood up. "I'll get you some water."

She grabbed his arm. "No, I'll get it. I need to stretch my legs. Besides, I think splashing some water in my face will help."

"Sure?"

She swung her feet over the bed and stood, smiling reassuringly.

Paul nodded. He walked over to the chair and sank into the

plush leather seat, letting out a long sigh. "Then I'll try to catch some shut-eye," he said, bringing up the footrest.

Alyssa opened the door and stepped into the aisle. The soft hum of the engines was the only reminder that she was in an airplane as she headed down the corridor to the lavatories. *I guess Kaya must be catching a quick nap*, she thought, glancing into the small kitchen area, her vision adjusting to the soft overhead lights that illuminated the narrow corridor between the two suites.

Alyssa stopped in mid-stride. Just ahead of her in the luggage closet, Kaya's face stared back at her, eyes glossy and unseeing, lips blue as if she had just eaten a handful of ripe blueberries.

Her mind screamed a warning an instant before the hand closed around her throat. The other hand covered her mouth and she was shoved hard into the lavatory, her assailant close behind her in the rough embrace.

A bolt of panic went through her, pure and undiluted. *Renley!* she thought but knew instantly that she was wrong.

The vicious man wasn't much taller than Alyssa, but his fingers and sinewy arms were unyielding as they covered her mouth and squeezed her throat. He closed his fingers around her neck, and she felt a needle attached to his ring press against her throat. She could hear his coarse and rasping breath behind her head.

The rough stubble on his cheek scratched her earlobe as he brought his lips to her ear. "One push of this needle and you will die before you can count to five," he whispered menacingly. His tone suggested that he would not hesitate in following up his threat.

"No sound. Do you understand?"

Alyssa nodded, paralyzed with fear and unable to breathe. The man moved his hand from her mouth and roughly twisted her left arm behind her back. Alyssa winced, but remained silent.

"Back to the room."

She felt the needle press against her neck as she stepped out of the lavatory and back through the dark aisle, smelling the breath of Kaya's killer behind her. She stopped in front of the suite, hesitating.

"Inside, now!" the man said and twisted her arm harder.

Alyssa bit her lip to stifle a scream and edged the door open. Paul was dozing in the seat. He stirred lazily, and his eyes drifted open.

The sleepy expression on his face shifted into disbelief when he saw Alyssa and the man behind her with his hand around her throat. He leaped up.

"One more step and she dies where she stands," the man hissed.

Paul froze when he recognized her attacker. Alyssa turned and gasped.

"It's you—"

"Shut your mouth!" Gavriel spat. "Close the door," he ordered Alyssa. She complied, and he faced Paul. "You know what I want. Give it to me. I will not ask again."

Paul glared at him but nodded his head and walked toward the LIDAR.

"No, Paul—" Alyssa started, but the sentence turned into a loud scream when Gavriel twisted her arm high behind her back.

"I told you to shut up, bitch!"

From the corner of her eye, she saw his lips curl up in a sadistic smile as she felt the waves of pain from her shoulder to her little finger.

"One more sound and I will break your arm."

Paul fumbled with the LIDAR, struggling to extract the crystal from the mount.

"Get moving!" Gavriel yelled.

Paul removed the crystal and turned to Gavriel. He stretched out his hand, the crystal in his open palm.

"Here it is. Just don't hurt her… please."

Alyssa heard Gavriel's breathing speed up. Instead of relaxing his grip, she felt his hand tighten around her neck.

"Do you know what it felt like to be blinded for hours? Not knowing if—"

There was a tap on the door. "Is everything all right in there?" Alyssa recognized Renley's voice as he cautiously opened the door. "I heard screaming—"

Gavriel switched his attention from Paul to Renley, and Alyssa felt the pressure relax on her throat for an instant.

She grabbed his thumb with her right hand and yanked it back toward his elbow until she heard the bone snap. Gavriel's howl ended in another sickening crunch as Paul hurtled toward them and rammed his fist into Gavriel's nose in mid-leap. She felt the hold on her left arm loosen. Spinning, she twisted out of his grip and brought her knee up into Gavriel's groin with full force. His bloody face contorted as he doubled over. At the same instant, Renley lifted a bottle of port from the tray and shattered it on Gavriel's head in one smooth motion.

Alyssa watched the killer's limp body slide to the floor, the pounding of her heart the only sound in her ears. Panting, she looked up at Renley, unable to speak. Paul grasped her, and she sagged into his arms.

Renley's lips curled downward as he looked from the man to the neck of the shattered bottle in his hand. "Damn fine vintage," he muttered and dropped the remainder of the bottle on the tray. He used a white cloth napkin to wipe his hands. He turned to Alyssa. "Are you hurt, Miss Morgan?" he asked, his voice ringing with concern.

Alyssa gasped, suddenly remembering the image of the flight attendant in the luggage closet. "Kaya," she said and gently pushed Paul to arm's length. "My God, Paul, I think he killed her." Alyssa realized she was shaking uncontrollably.

"Please sit down, Miss Morgan," Renley said. "I will return in a moment."

———

FIVE MINUTES LATER, the aisle between the two suites was crowded with flight attendants, the air marshal, and the captain. Gavriel, still unconscious, was strapped into the flight crew jump seat, his slumped body held upright by the four-point harness. His wrists were handcuffed to the metal bars behind the backrest. His face, now a bloody mask, drooped onto his chest, a lake of blood mixed with port staining his shirt.

"That's correct. I have never seen this man in my life," Alyssa answered the captain's question, darting a glance at the jump seat.

The dark-skinned pilot studied her, his chin jutting out,

making his hard jawline appear even more stern. He raised his eyebrows, unable to absorb the events just described to him.

"That bastard killed my flight attendant," he spat with barely contained rage, "just so he could rob you?" He sounded like he would rather sit in the cockpit troubleshooting two engine failures and a broken rudder than face this scenario.

"Captain, we are all as stunned about what happened as you are." Renley jumped in. "The death of your flight attendant is devastating. Miss Morgan and Mr. Matthews are fortunate to be alive."

The pilot closed his eyes and inhaled deeply. When he opened them again, his voice was calmer, and he was once again in complete control.

"Since this incident does not constitute an immediate threat or medical emergency, we are not required to divert the flight. We shall continue to Cairo. Per protocol, what happened here does not leave this compartment until everybody is off the plane," he said to the flight attendants then glanced at the air marshal, who nodded in agreement. He sighed, exasperated, "I can't imagine the media circus this will create."

The captain took another deep breath and stared at the killer's limp body. "And somebody see to that piece of trash and put some bandages around his head before he bleeds all over my floor." He spun and stalked back to the cockpit.

As the flight crew dispersed, the air marshal turned to Alyssa, Paul and Renley. "I shall have the Egyptian authorities meet us upon arrival. Please remain in your suites until they have taken your statements." He scrutinized them wordlessly for several seconds. "Do you have any questions?" When nobody responded, he nodded curtly and left, returning to his seat.

Alyssa stood motionlessly, hugging her shoulders. She swallowed hard, struggling to contain the wave of nausea that was building in the pit of her stomach. After a several long moments, she faced Renley. "Thank you," she said, the earlier contempt in her voice replaced by gratitude. "I don't know what would have happened if you hadn't shown up when you did."

Paul extended his hand to Renley. "I am in your debt," he said as Renley grasped it.

Renley reached into the pocket of his jacket. He pulled out a card and handed it to Alyssa. "If you change your mind, you can reach me at this number." He turned and disappeared behind the privacy partition of his suite.

Alyssa closed their door and sagged against it. "How did they find us here?" She stared at Paul. "If Renley is telling the truth, maybe he can help us?"

Paul pulled a face. "He's a toff. I don't trust anything about their kind," he said. "We don't know what he'll do once he gets what he's after. At least as long as we have something he wants, he's predictable."

Alyssa stood silently, chewing at her bottom lip, watching the dark sky outside of the small windows. Finally, she sighed and nodded slowly.

"I'm sure you're right," she said.

HE LOOKS LIKE I FEEL, Alyssa thought, spotting Kamal across the arrivals terminal. Her head was still spinning from the two hour-long grilling she and Paul got from the Egyptian police and the Meridian Airlines security officers. *Can you say Spanish Inquisition?*

She shook off the thought and waved at Kamal. His usual crisp clothes were beat and wrinkled, his chin covered with salt-and-pepper stubble that matched his unkempt hair. Despite the dark circles under his eyes, he flashed a tired grin when he saw her.

"Welcome back," he said, embracing her affectionately.

Alyssa returned the hug. "It's good to see you again." The pressure behind her eyeballs made her attempted smile feel more like a grimace.

"Kamal, this is Paul Matthews," she said. "Paul, meet Dr. Kamal Khanna."

The men shook hands.

"Is everything ok?" Kamal asked. "Your flight landed three hours ago."

Alyssa's tired smile wilted completely. "Kade isn't the only one they're after," she replied. She glanced at Paul and hesitated, bracing herself for Kamal's reaction to her next words. "We were attacked on the plane."

"What?" Kamal's expression shifted in a heartbeat, the tired look wiped from his eyes. "Are you—?"

She held up her hand. "Later... I will explain everything later." She took a deep breath. "Kade first. What happened at the hospital?"

Kamal's face tightened as he seemed to consider pressing her then slowly relaxed. He shook his head. "I wish we had an answer. The police have launched a full investigation, but so far, nothing."

"I want to see him," Alyssa said.

"Alyssa, you know that—" Kamal started.

"Kamal," she cut in. "We barely made it here." She rubbed her temples, slowly losing the struggle with the pounding inside them. "Please... I know you can make it happen."

He looked at her for several moments. "Let's get you into the car." He sighed. "I'll make some calls."

They exited the terminal and strode toward Kamal's white Mercedes Benz parked at the curb. The driver opened the doors and took their bags.

As Alyssa stepped into the car, she spotted Renley strolling up to a silver Rolls Royce limousine. He glanced briefly at her and nodded before disappearing inside.

"Nice ride." Kamal said catching the exchange. "New friend?"

"Everyone starts out as a friend," Alyssa replied, eyeing the car as it drove off. "Until they prove otherwise."

———

ALYSSA'S TEETH tugged at her cracked lower lip as she moved timidly toward the hospital bed, covered by a clear plastic canopy. She cringed when she saw the man lying in it. Her father's face was ashen and his cheeks hollow. Each shallow breath left a trail of condensation on the inside of the oxygen mask covering his mouth. His eyes were closed and he looked like he was sleeping.

She tiptoed closer, not wanting to wake him, but he stirred and slowly opened his eyes. He turned his head to her and she saw his dark brown eyes twinkle with recognition.

"Ally…"

Alyssa flinched at the sound. She was expecting his usual Southern drawl with an air of hardness, a measure of cool superiority. Instead, his voice seemed weak and vulnerable.

Dad…

"Kade…" The word came out as a whisper.

"Hey… don't you worry." His lips attempted a smile. "Heaven won't have me, and Hell is afraid I'll take over." His weak laugh turned into a wheezing cough. When the spasm stopped, he was breathing hard. He wiped his eyes with the back of his hand. Steadying himself, he fixed on Alyssa with a glassy stare.

"Ally, we found it," He struggled with each word, but his gaze remained locked on her. "You should have been there… I mean…" He took a deep breath. "I'm so glad you're safe."

"We got it," she whispered. "We got the crystal."

His eyes widened at her words.

She looked at Paul. "I couldn't have done it without him."

Kade smiled weakly and strained to nod.

Paul gave an awkward wave. He looked to Alyssa and cleared his throat. "I should give you some time alone."

Alyssa faced her dad as Paul left the room. "There's more," she said. "So much more."

She leaned as close to him as the plastic between them allowed. "You were right, Kade. All this time. The Hall of Records, the origin of the Sphinx… The crystal you found, it stores thoughts, memories." She struggled, not knowing where to start. Her eyes prickled with tears as the experiences of the past few days threatened to overwhelm her.

Her father stared at her, newfound strength in his eyes.

"Tell me everything," he said.

————

PAUL TRUDGED along the corridor to the lounge when he heard Kamal's muffled voice around the corner. The other man's hushed tone made him slow down and strain his ears.

"…yes, I understand," he heard Kamal say. "The girl is the highest priority."

Paul's skin tingled as he rounded the corner just in time to see Kamal disconnect the call. Kamal's posture stiffened when he spotted Paul.

"Paul!" he said. "I thought you were with Alyssa and her dad."

"I reckoned they'd welcome some alone time," Paul replied,

keeping his voice flat. "Can you point me to the cafeteria? I'd love a cup of Egyptian coffee."

Kamal laughed. "You've come to the right place. The cafeteria at the El Aini has the finest coffee in the city!"

"Splendid," Paul said, the tight-lipped smile evaporating from his face as he turned.

———

ALYSSA WATCHED her father as he struggled to absorb everything she told him, dozens of questions lingering in his eyes.

"I know what's making you sick," she continued. "It's a biological weapon made by Thoth."

"Thoth, the Scribe?" He swallowed, his face knotting with the pain and effort. He took a slow breath, as if to gather all of his remaining energy.

"In all these years... since I've started dragging you with me all over the world, I know I haven't been the father I should have been... the father you needed." He looked at her through glassy eyes, his breathing slow and shallow. "I'm so sorry."

Alyssa drew back. "Why are you saying this?"

"Ally... I don't think I'll—"

"Stop, Kade. Don't even—" Her stomach twisted.

"Please, Ally... just listen." Another agonizing pause. "To find the Hall... it was always your mom's dream."

"But you were always the one..." she said, puzzled.

"It was her passion, Ally." His lips curved into a weak smile. "She tried hiding it from your grandfather, of course."

"Why would she do that?"

"He didn't think it was safe." Kade face caved. "He was

right." He took another slow breath. "The night we lost your mom, she was following a lead... by the time I got there, it was too late."

"Grandpa must have known! But he still blamed you for her death!"

"Losing his daughter completely destroyed him. His scorn toward me kept him alive... helped him survive the pain."

Alyssa stared at him and shook her head. "All these years... Why did you keep this from me?"

"I didn't want you running off, chasing Anja's ghosts." He lifted his head. "But you deserve the truth."

Alyssa stood silently, her breath caught in her chest.

"That night," his words came out slowly between labored breaths, "she found something... she..."

"Kade!"

He took another slow breath. "The hall, all the digs, everything I've done... it was all to find out what happened to her." His eyelids fluttered, mothlike. For a fleeting instant he was somewhere else.

"Kade?" Alyssa tried to keep her voice from trembling. Her stomach sank deeper with his every wheezing breath.

His eyes slowly lost focus. "The dig... the suits..." He spoke haltingly now, the words individually formed and separated by a perceptible pause. "They weren't working properly."

"What?"

"The filters..." He worked hard for each syllable. "They were deactivated." He took a deep breath, shuddering as he fought off a cough.

"Why would anyone do that?"

"It had to be someone close... very close. Someone with

access." His voice began to fade again, his breathing turning to slow, rattling gasps.

"I don't understand. Who?"

He locked his gaze on her as his eyes began to grow distant. "They will stop at nothing…" he whispered.

"Who?"

He swallowed. His mouth opened again, but his voice failed him.

"Kade?"

He stared into an empty space between them before his face closed in a grimace.

"Dad?"

Alyssa didn't feel the nurse pull her away from the bed or see the team of physicians swarming into the room and surrounding her dad's bed.

Panic rose in her chest, sharp and hot. Alyssa's hands began to tremble. The empty feeling in the pit of her stomach was as abrupt as it was intense. *First Mom… now…*

She turned and ran to the bed.

"*Daddy!*"

The nurse rushed after her and pulled her back again. Alyssa's eyes filled with tears as she let the nurse guide her out of the room to Paul and Kamal.

Paul approached her and reached out, then stopped, suddenly uncertain what to do next. He looked at her, his soft eyes in contrast to his tight posture. "He will pull through," he said gently.

She stared at him for several seconds, ignoring the heat behind her eyelids. She nodded softly then slumped into him and buried her head into his shoulder. He hesitated for a moment then wrapped his arms around her tightly. They stood, embraced in silence, as Kamal watched the medical team inside Kade's room.

"Alyssa," Kamal said softly after a minute. Alyssa looked up and broke the embrace, surprised at the effort it took to step away from Paul. He kept his hands on her an instant longer and gave her a wavering smile.

Kamal pointed at an older physician who stepped out of the room. The physician's face was a mask as he approached them.

"Alyssa, this is Dr. Ahmed Farag," Kamal said. "Dr. Farag is the attending physician in charge of your father's care. You met during our video call."

Alyssa looked at the physician, suddenly embarrassed. "I'm sorry about... during the video call... I know you're doing everything you can."

Dr. Farag extended his hand to Alyssa. "Please, Miss Morgan. Do not give it another thought." His English was flawless. "I am glad to meet you in person."

"Thank you—for everything," Alyssa managed to reply.

"Unfortunately, it seems the disease has continued to progress." He scrubbed his hand over his face, as if trying to wash away the frustration. "Despite all our efforts, his condition remains a mystery. Instead of finding answers, we uncover more questions." He moved to a computer terminal and beckoned them to follow.

He brought up two images on the display. "We compared Dr. Morgan's blood samples taken on the day he arrived to samples taken earlier today. Whatever pathogen is causing his illness appears to be modifying its structure. It is also causing an autoimmune reaction in his body."

"What does this all mean?" Alyssa asked.

Farag sighed. "I'm truly sorry, but I'm afraid it's just a matter of time before we run out of options."

Alyssa remained silent for several seconds. She glanced from Farag to Kamal. Finally, she said, "I'm sorry, this is a lot to take in. Can you please drive us home?"

Kamal peered at her, lips pressed flat. He responded with only the slightest hint of hesitation. "Of course, Alyssa. The car is waiting downstairs."

PAUL SURVEYED THE SPACIOUS, elegantly-decorated living room of the condominium. He strolled to the floor-to-ceiling windows and took in the panorama of the city skyline before turning to Alyssa, nodding approvingly.

"Ritzy digs," he said and fell back into the white camelback sofa with a sigh.

Alyssa dropped into the plushy chair across from him. She swung both legs over one armrest and arched her back against the other one until she heard the familiar pop-pop-pop of her vertebrae. Sighing, she took out her cell phone and tossed it on the coffee table then reached into the other pocket and held up the card Renley handed her. Renley's name and a single telephone number were embossed in an elegant black font on a snow-white background. She studied it for several moments before slipping it back into her pocket.

"You don't trust him," Paul said. It was more a statement than a question.

"Who?"

"Renley."

Alyssa looked at him, her silence an answer.

"What about Kamal?" Paul asked.

"He's one of my dad's best friends," she said. Her shoulders sagged. "I don't know who to trust anymore."

Paul took a deep breath as if to say something then hesitated. He shook off the thought.

"What is it?" Alyssa asked.

"At the hospital. I thought I heard…" He stopped. "I'm sure it's nothing."

Alyssa stared out of the window as she replayed the conversation with her father in her head. "All these years, I've blamed him for what happened to my mom." She shook her head. "Why didn't he tell me what really happened?"

Suddenly she sat up, her jaw set. "We have to get inside."

"Uh… Please tell me you're not thinking of the same *inside* that I think you're thinking of," Paul said.

Alyssa looked at him wordlessly, teeth tugging at her bottom lip.

"Okay, then." Paul stared at her. "You are thinking of *that* inside." He turned away and curled his arms over his head. "Are you completely insane?" He whirled. "Your dad came from *that* inside! And now he is infected with—"

"Kade said the filters in the suits were rigged," Alyssa interrupted.

"He what?"

"The filters," she repeated. "He said somebody deactivated them."

"What? How? And how can he be sure?"

She stared at him silently, brows pulled in.

"And even if that was the case, Alyssa, that would require access to biosuits... which we currently lack, and a really good plan for getting past the security at the site... which we also currently lack." He gave her a pained stare.

"We can try to get close," she said. "Once we're there, we'll think of something."

Paul's voice shook. "This isn't like breaking into a storage room! We'll either get caught before we get inside and get thrown into an Egyptian prison, or—worse—actually make it inside and get infected by some ancient killer bug." He paused. "Neither of those sounds particularly appealing... or conducive to a thriving, heterosexual adolescence!"

Alyssa looked at him for several moments then shrugged dejectedly.

"What Kade said—about the filters," she said. "We can at least start there. If somebody actually tampered with them, it must have been somebody close. Somebody with access to the suits."

"We don't even know if he's right about the filters."

Alyssa swung her legs down and leaned forward in the chair, a scheming smirk on her face.

"Why do I have the feeling you already have something in mind?" Paul asked.

"So, Clay is the smartest guy you know, right?" she asked.

Paul pressed his lips together in a tight knot. "And why do I have a distinct feeling I won't like where this is going, either?"

"He could test the filters, and we'd know for sure."

He scowled. "Yep, I was right."

"We don't have anything else, Paul. You have to ask him."

Paul stood and paced toward the door then spun and

returned to the sofa. "How is he even supposed to get his hands on them? After everything that happened!"

"Paul, it's our only lead."

"After what we put him through, I expect him to just tell me to go to Hell. And with good reason." He started toward the door again but stopped and turned in mid-stride. He stood quietly, looking out the window.

He remained motionless for a long time, the conflict plain in his face. Finally, he gave a long, low sigh and pulled out his phone. He dialed a number and hit the speaker button. The phone rang several times before it was picked up.

"Paul! How are you? How's Alyssa?" Clay's voice rang through the speaker.

"Hey, Clay. Things are… a bit tense." He grimaced. "Listen, mate, I need you to do something."

"What is it?"

"I need you to check Kade Morgan's biosafety suit."

"You… uh… Come again?"

"The filters may have been tampered with. I need you to examine the filter in the suit."

"Are you…? How do you suppose…? And just how am I—"

"Mate, please—"

A ripple of groans echoed from the speaker. "Everybody is arse over tit about what happened last night! I've already been shot at… and now you're trying to get me arrested for tampering with evidence?"

Paul pinched the bridge of his nose and squeezed his eyes shut. "Alyssa's dad's life is at stake. Maybe countless others."

He forced a deep breath. "Clay… we're gutted… It's all we've got."

Clay was silent for a few seconds. "I am so going to regret this, aren't I?"

"If anybody can pull it off, it's you."

Clay groaned again and hung up the phone.

Paul pushed the speaker button. "Well, that was blinding…" He collapsed on the sofa and rubbed his neck.

"Strong work," Alyssa said and moved over to him. She stepped behind the sofa and put her hands on his neck.

He spun, startled.

"Relax." She smiled. "Let me." She began kneading the muscles at the base of his neck.

Paul closed his eyes and a soft moan escaped his lips.

She moved her mouth close to his ear. "'Thriving heterosexual adolescence,' huh?" she whispered seductively.

Paul jolted. He opened his mouth an instant before her grin hit him like a ton of bricks. Alyssa looked at him like the cat that ate the canary.

"Not funny," he said, his skin flushed. "For a second I really thought you were coming on to me."

"Disappointed?" she asked, smoothing her long hair away from her neck before moving her hands back to his shoulders, pressing down hard.

"Maybe." He paused for a heartbeat. "Besides, I've ticked off enough people already. Don't need to add Jacob to my list."

"Jake?" Alyssa stopped kneading.

"Yeah, you can't seriously tell me that there's nothing—"

"He's like… my big brother, Paul."

Paul digested her words. "So… there isn't somebody?"

"With all the traveling—*somebody*—would be…" she searched for the right word, "complicated." She started drumming her fists on his upper back. "Enough with the interview."

Paul was quiet while she continued working on his back. The silence felt comfortable as he sat quietly, the tension ebbing from his back under her hands. He yawned. "How long has it been since we got some real sleep?"

Alyssa glanced at the clock. "I dunno. Thirty hours?"

"It's going to be a long day tomorrow, isn't it?" He looked up at her.

Alyssa met his gaze halfway, her dark, serious eyes silent.

"You sure your dad would approve?" he asked. "Me staying here?"

"Don't be ridiculous. If I can't trust you by now to behave yourself—"

"I was more worried about you." Paul stretched out on the sofa. He grinned to himself as his head hit the pillow. He was asleep a moment later. He didn't see Alyssa's mouth falling open, glaring at him with mock indignation before her expression shifted into a tired smile.

She turned her head to the window and surveyed the city. The sun was beginning to set, its brilliant bands of red and purple a gleaming contrast to the bleak reality of the last three days. She lazily pushed her head against the armrest of the plushy chair and yawned, struggling against her heavy eyelids before finally drifting off.

———

JACOB'S BUTT ACHED. He shifted in the wooden chair, trying to ease the throbbing, and adjusted the screen of his laptop that sat on the old metal desk. The single working light bulb in the four-bulb overhead lamp barely managed to illuminate the cramped hotel room and keep him awake. He reread the headline of the last article in the stack of images of old newspapers that filled his screen: Blueblood Explorer Perishes in Ill-fated Expedition!

He zoomed in on the picture, cropped it, and pasted it into the email message when he spotted another headline. *Arab Revolt?* He opened up a Wiki page.

Jacob ruffled his hair and shifted again. He took another swig of the coffee and reached for his phone. Alyssa answered on the second ring.

"Jake!" he heard her voice as she stifled a yawn. "What have you got?"

"Turns out the griffin was the sigil of Lord George Renley. I just sent you an email."

A few seconds later he heard Alyssa draw in a sharp breath. "The picture looks just like the man we met on the plane. So it was his grandfather! That's where I saw the sigil—on the ring in the video!"

"What?"

"The video, from the dig! Did you find anything else?"

Jacob opened up another window on his desktop. "I also looked into the time frame of the expedition. It took place a year before World War I and the Arab Revolt. The entire region was in upheaval."

"No wonder nobody went looking for them and all traces of the expedition vanished!" She pondered for a moment. "Wait, World War I? Wasn't there a big epidemic right after it?"

"Hang on," Jacob typed into the web browser. "1918 Flu

Pandemic, also known as the Spanish Flu," he read. "Believed to have been brought to Spain by soldiers returning from Egypt."

"The Spanish Flu?" Alyssa's voice sounded aghast. "Jake, that pandemic killed over fifty million people. What if the expedition was the cause? Somehow released the virus?" Jacob heard her collapse into a chair. "My God, what if these events are somehow related?"

Jacob shook his head, dumbfounded, trying to find words.

"Thank you, Jake," Alyssa said and ended the connection.

"Alyssa?" Jacob called out. "Alyssa!" He shook his head and threw the phone on the desk, trying to ignore the painful lump growing in his throat.

———

ALYSSA SAT IN THE CHAIR, staring at the wall.

The Spanish Flu? If Renley's dig and that pandemic are somehow related...

She pinched her bottom lip. It wasn't until she felt something wet on her fingers that she realized she'd been biting it so hard it bled.

She turned to Paul sleeping on the sofa and watched his chest rising and falling in slow, deep breaths. She pressed her lips together, the taste of blood pushing her to dismiss the fluttering feeling in her stomach. Slowly, she stood and moved quietly to the bag with the VR gear. She picked up the bag and tiptoed toward her bedroom, locking the door behind her.

Alyssa was too aware of the sound of her heart throbbing against the cage of her chest when she took out the LIDAR and the VR set. She booted up the laptops and opened the control software, scanning the parameters. She didn't realize her hand was trembling until she moved to adjust one of the sliders.

Laser Beam Intensity: 90%

She put the VR helmet on her head. *I'm sorry, Paul,* she thought and toggled the switch.

THE STARS FLICKER on the surface of the water as the twin bows of the catamaran slice relentlessly through the waves under my watchful vigil. At three hundred feet long, each one of the two hulls of the *Ra* is larger than most ships, easily accommodating the four hundred warriors who spent the last six weeks with me on the flagship of my fleet. The pyramid-shaped structure built into the sixty-foot wide center deck is home to my palace and my personal guard.

I raise my head and scan the darkness ahead, toward our destination, toward the island kingdom I called home in another life. Empty water stretches for miles. I focus the gaze of the falcon into the distance, and a tall tower rises from the horizon, bringing evidence that our long voyage is nearing its end.

My breathing slows as memories take over, filling my senses with images that will forever be engraved in my mind. My body tenses as my thoughts turn to the last time I gazed upon that island. The night my mother was murdered, the night my grandfather and I were forced to abandon our home. The last time I looked at the place of my birth, my eyes were filled with tears. Tonight, they are filled with rage.

A deep voice breaks the silence. "It is time, my Lord."

Slowly, I turn to the man who spoke the words. His black eyes are at one with the night, set deeply into his finely chiseled features. His head, face and eyebrows are shaved, a single long braid the only hair growing from his head, his mark as the general of my armies. His only other mark is a red scar he bears on his left cheek, a reminder of his failure to me.

One long year he has spent in exile, searching for my son. It was not until after my grandfather's burial that he returned, alone and nearly starved, clutching a map to the island kingdom in his hand. Within days of his return we set out for the long journey west, to the place of my birth. Now, after weeks at sea, we are almost upon it.

Horemheb gazes at me, as if to read my thoughts. "We shall bring him back." His voice is strong, his jaw set.

I remain silent but grasp his shoulder and look to the stern of the *Ra*. Hidden behind the pyramid is the secret that will lead us to victory in a fight against an island thought to be impenetrable. I breathe slowly, trying to steady my racing heart.

I nod, and his command rings out into the night. Twenty soldiers move as one, forming a line before me. Dressed in the color of the night, they are more shadows than men, their faces painted dark, only the whites of their eyes shine brightly in the darkness.

I step closer and study each face. Their gazes meet mine, their eyes unwavering.

"Each one of you was chosen by Horemheb." My voice is quiet. "Each one of you a warrior worth dozens of ordinary soldiers." I point my hand east. "One year ago, your prince, my flesh and blood, was torn from his home. Your queen, my wife, was slain where she slept." I hesitate as memories return. *I am Horus. Son of Isis and Osiris.* I close my eyes. *I shall know no fear.* When I open them, my voice rings out into the vast darkness. "The hour of recompense is upon us. On this night, we shall descend upon our enemies and answer their savage attack. We shall finish their treachery the only way it can end. We shall destroy them and bring back my flesh and blood and return to our homes with honor. On this night, we shall not know failure. On this night, we shall not know fear!"

My gaze falls upon Horemheb in a silent command.

"Prepare the airship," he says, his voice steady. Twenty men work as one as they lift the platform, revealing an airship in the shape of a falcon, a marvel constructed by my grandfather. Black and silent as the bird of prey it embodies and lighter than the air through which it glides, it shall carry us as we slip undetected past the island's formidable defenses and descend upon our enemies like a wraith from the sky. Two dozen men, strong as an army, with their king leading them to victory.

The men are quiet as they move into the airship. If there is hesitation in their hearts, their eyes do not betray it. Horemheb follows his men. I glance at the *Ra* one last time then step inside. Before I can count to a hundred, the lines tying it to the *Ra* are cast off, and the catamaran grows smaller beneath us while we rise silently into the darkness.

I look to the east, at the single column of ships trailing the *Ra*, stretching behind us as far as I can see. The formation masks our true numbers as we approach the island. Four hundred ships. Forty thousand men. All sworn to me, all willing to die without hesitation.

We ascend for a long time and glide toward the island. Silently, we cross the outer ring, the first perimeter of the island's defenses. We pass high above the sentries watching the sea. I know that they cannot imagine an airship, gliding silently through the night air, hundreds of feet above their heads, and the twenty-two men who slip undetected across their border.

I turn to the men, recalling the lessons from my grandfather.

"Two separate landmasses enclose the center island, forming almost perfect concentric circles around it." I keep my voice low. The cool air carries sound far into the quiet night. "The combination of the outer and inner rings creates a formidable defense against any ships that dare to mount an attack from the sea. A single channel has been dug into each ring on opposite sides of the island, both of them heavily fortified. Any ships that could penetrate the outer ring will be trapped in the waters between the two rings, exposed on all sides."

I point to the single spire rising high above the island, still hidden in the darkness. "Yet the most devastating weapon on the island rests upon the crown of that tower. A vast mirror and lenses constructed to harness the heat of the sun and turn it upon any fleet of ships that threaten the island, trapped between the two rings. Any enemy ships doomed to be within its path will be burned instantly.

"The island has but a single weakness. They cannot conceive an attack from above. We shall destroy the weapon, enabling our fleet to mount an attack on the island. And while all will pay heed to the battle rising from the sea, we shall strike from within and reclaim your prince—my son."

Once again, I center the gaze of the falcon on the tower in the distance. Four men stand on the large platform that makes up the apex of the spire, each pair of eyes focused on the dark ocean stretching below them.

"Four sentries," I whisper. Horemheb waves four men toward us, each of them with a crossbow strapped to his back. He speaks quietly and they reach for their weapons. Each crossbow is equipped with a farseeker, giving ordinary men a sight almost worthy of the falcon. They are my best marksmen, but I know even with the farseekers they cannot yet spy the sentries, so we wait as we silently descend upon the tower.

Minutes seem like hours as the men stand motionless, unblinking, fixed on the tower. One by one, they raise their crossbows and focus their sights on the targets in the distance. I hold my breath. A single missed shot, and our raid is at an end before it has begun.

"Make your shots true," Horemheb says when the last man raises his weapon.

"*Loose.*"

Four bolts whisper as they fly. A second later four dead bodies collapse on the platform. The raid has begun.

"Anchors," Horemheb orders. The men aim two large cross-bows mounted on the bow of the airship at the tower and fire. A pair of metal bolts, each the length of a man's forearm, fly for the tower, each dragging a thick line behind it. The sound of the metal striking the stone rings out into the night. The men pull the lines tight and move out, each attaching a small pulley to the thick line before sliding down to the tower. My breathing quickens as I follow them, grasping the wooden grips of the pulley.

I step onto the side of the airship and push off. I squint as the wind whips my face, and my body races for the tower, hundreds of feet above the ground. When the flat surface of the tower appears beneath me, I release my grip and drop onto the stone, my feet striking hard. I turn my fall into a roll and come up, one knee on the ground, a curved dagger in my hand. My breathing slows as my eyes find Horemheb.

"The sentries?"

"Dead before their bodies hit the ground."

I nod and rise. We stand on the apex of the tower, a large circle, sixty feet across, a raised platform in the center. I approach the structure in the middle. The mirror is in the shape of a bowl, made of polished steel. Its diameter as large as three grown men standing head to toe. The enormous glass lenses in front of it complete the terrifying weapon.

Silently, the men position the black powder charges around the mirror. I recall grandfather's stories about the ill-fated fleets that dared to attack our island, their ships burned by the heat of the sun, the men on board screaming as the sun scorched their flesh.

I look to the east across the empty water. I focus the gaze of the falcon, and the *Ra* appears before me, the long column of ships trailing into the distance. I bring out a light and shine it toward them, toward their farseekers aimed at the tower, awaiting my signal.

From the distance, a speck of light no brighter than a firefly flickers back in answer. The ships fan out slowly, forming a crescent surrounding the island as they prepare for the assault.

The men finish arranging the charges, a trail of black powder leading away from the central platform to the side of the tower. We anchor our ropes to the wall. I move to the edge of the tower and point at the domed structure below.

"We start at the palace. Spare those that do not resist. Kill those that oppose you," I say. "Find your prince."

Horemheb strikes the fire starter and touches it to the black power. A sizzling trail of sparks rushes for the center platform.

"Now," I command. As one, twenty men leap over the wall. The ground rushes at us as we glide down our ropes along the side of the tower.

The silence of the night is shattered by the deafening explosion above us only seconds before we slow our descent and reach the ground. My feet touch the soil of my home for the first time in seven decades.

Atlantis!

Familiar smells fill my nostrils, and memories from a past life awaken. The grand square leading to the royal palace and the magnificent statues lining its sides, the marketplace, filled with daring performers in their motley costumes—

I shake off the memories, and we turn to the palace.

We race for the outer gates, and the first wave of our enemies rushes out to meet us; a dozen soldiers, their blades drawn. Horemheb shouts a command, and each man sinks to one knee and fires his crossbow, leaving twelve enemies dead. Our company is back to full sprint before the dead men's bodies hit the ground.

My men form a ring around me as we burst into the courtyard and speed for the inner gates. Surprise is on our side. Our enemies are confused. Most are cut down by the deadly bolts from our crossbows before they can get near us.

Without warning, arrows begin falling on us.

"Phalanx!" Horemheb's command cuts through the night.

Instantly, the ring tightens, and the men lift their round shields from their backs to protect us against the arrows. Our shields tight, we continue on for the entrance of the palace, almost out of reach of the falling arrows.

A deafening sound splits my ears. I am thrown to the ground. My ears ring as I lay face down, stunned and blinded. I shake my head, trying to see through the haze.

Slowly my vision returns. I turn to my side. The men who guarded my left flank are gone, their mangled bodies strewn across the marble grounds of the courtyard. Their shields and bodies protected me from the force of the explosion.

Black powder? But Thoth—

Strong hands lift me to my feet. I look into Horemheb's face, marred with dirt and blood, but his eyes burn fiercer than ever. Four of my men cover us with their shields as we back up toward the gate.

The door flies open, and ten islanders pour out like angry ants, steel in hand. Horemheb leaps forward and pulls his swords in a single motion. The long, curved blades slice through two breastplates as though they had been made of silk instead of steel, and two men collapse, lifeless. Eight guards remain against my finest warrior. The islanders lie dead on the ground before I take another breath as the men at my back continue to shield me against the onslaught of the arrows.

"My Lord!" One of the men's voices rings out. He points to

the far end of the square and the dozens of soldiers rushing at us.

Horemheb scans them then turns to me. "You must get inside." His voice is steady. "Find your son!"

Before I can reply, he and the other four men speed off toward the approaching horde. I hesitate for an instant then turn and rush through the gate.

As I stand inside, I struggle to recall my grandfather's words and remember his drawings. Ahead of me, a stairway leads to the throne room. I turn to my right—the stairs leading deep below the castle.

I slow when I reach the stairs. My breathing is labored, and my vision narrows to a pinprick. I grasp at the wall for support, the marble cold beneath my hand. I take a deep breath before turning into the dark stairway. The shadows flicker on the walls as I descend along the curving stone staircase.

My breathing steadies when I reach the bottom. A long hallway stretches before me. To my left, a dozen spears wait in a wooden rack, lined up like soldiers eager for battle. To my right, a thick door, wide open. Inside the room a long table and chairs, toppled over on their backs, witnesses to the frantic scurry of the guards rushing out to the battle.

I continue along the hallway. I hear the noise an instant before the thick reinforced door opens at the far end. The three guards talk in loud, agitated voices then fall silent when they see me.

For a long second, nobody moves. Then one man rushes forward, his eyes wild, a scream escaping his lips. An instant later, another follows, his sword in his hand.

I stand my ground as the first guard charges me, his mouth

twisted in a snarl. The dagger flashes in my hand only an instant before it flies through the air. It strikes true and buries itself to the hilt in the first man's chest.

The second guard stumbles, trying to avoid his slain companion. His attack turns careless, his sword thrust uncontrolled. I glide aside and let his momentum carry him forward. My hands lock around his head, and I twist it as he rushes past me. He collapses at my feet. I turn to the third man.

His glance darts between his dead companions and me. He approaches warily, the point of his sword aimed at my eyes. With his other hand, he draws a dagger.

My sword remains sheathed on my back as he lunges at me, his strikes fast but controlled, determined not to make the same mistake as the other men. He cannot know that his fastest movements are but a slow lumbering to me. I control my aggression, letting my fury fuel it rather than consume it as I avoid his strikes. He continues to attack relentlessly, like an avalanche made of flesh.

Soon, his chest begins to heave, his exhaustion forcing him to hesitate for an instant. I move into him before he can swing again, my advance lightning fast. I grip his sword hand, twisting the weapon out of his hand and whirl, holding the sword at the level of his neck.

His helmet hits the stone and rolls noisily into the corridor. His body slumps to the ground. I step over it and continue to the door. I drop his sword as I pass his helmet, his lifeless eyes staring at me from inside it.

I pass through the thick door and onto a large platform. The smell of blood, excrement, and rotten flesh hits my nose at the instant the horrific scene strikes my eyes.

My mind is sent reeling, unable to comprehend the evil before me. Beneath me, countless cages stretch out row after row. My body grows rigid when I grasp the full extent of the depravity.

Hybrids... My kin...

My legs begin to tremble as I pore over their forms, naked and ravaged. Their bodies are chained onto metal cots, and thick rubber lines pierce their skin, draining their lifeblood into metal containers.

I sink to my knees, unable to breathe—

My head jerks forward and stars burst in my eyes. The pain explodes in my skull an instant before everything goes dark.

———

"WHO ARE YOU?" A voice in the darkness.

Pain. Sharp. Tearing. I scream. I cannot move. I writhe against the chains. My chest heaves in shuddering breaths. My body fights to control the agony.

Slowly, I focus. A face, dark-skinned and angular, glistening with sweat. The pupils in his ice-blue eyes flare as they burn into me.

"Who are you?" he asks again and raises my own dagger, its black obsidian blade stained red with my blood.

Then I remember. The pain in my body pales at the rage spawned by the memory. My face twists into a snarl as I strain once more against the iron shackles. The sound that escapes my lips is that of a wounded animal.

A gloved fist shoots out and strikes my jaw like a steel

mace. My vision blurs, and I taste blood. I struggle to focus once again.

"What have you done to my kin?" My voice is a growl.

"Your kin?" His expression shifts as recognition fills his face.

"You," he says. "You came back." The sound of his laughter is more menacing than the dagger a hand's width from my eyes. "I should have known. The eyes. Little Horus, who fled the island with his traitorous grandfather, returns at last."

"Who... who are you?" I ask.

"You truly do not know, do you?"

I remain silent, my jaw tight.

His posture stiffens, and he glares at me for several heartbeats, chin held high.

"I am Set, the First of My Name. Rightful Heir and Sovereign Ruler of the Island Kingdom of Atlantis."

A bitter chill sweeps through me at the sudden recognition. I stare at him, stunned at the hatred spilling from his unblinking eyes.

"Where is my son?" My voice trembles. "Why are you doing this?"

"Your grandfather kept so much from you, young Horus. Thoth, *the Scribe*." His words mock me as his scorn builds. "Did Thoth tell you what truly happened that night, the night you and he abandoned the island?"

"You slaughtered our families!" I growl and lunge at him against the chains, my teeth bared.

"Your grandfather condemned every Purean man, woman and child you left behind on this forsaken island." The hatred in his face is complete. "The men he infected at the harbor. The disease never stopped. It continues to ravage us every day. Only the blood of the Hybrids can keep us alive. Those of your kind we did not kill, we bred to harvest their blood."

He stops, his gaze distant and voice strangely calm, before he speaks again. "What a sad irony that the Pure Ones' sole recourse to escape certain death is to pollute their own bodies with Hybrid blood."

Dizziness threatens to overwhelm me, my mind unable to grasp the words I hear. My shoulders slump and numbness blankets my body.

"Release my people, Set. Release them, and I shall reveal to you how to stop this illness, end this suffering, once and for all time. A cure, devised from my blood—"

"We shall have your blood," he says, his voice low. "We shall have all of it, Horus. We shall drain you—as we have drained your son."

Dread creeps down my spine like the legs of a sun spider, her delicate feet descending on my skin until I'm frozen to the ground. "What have you done with him?"

"He was harvested, yet he was young and the power of his blood limited. He tried to be brave, but his tears flowed when his young body failed."

Burning rage hisses through my body, yet I cannot speak. I cannot move. Each of his words fuels my silent fury, pounding into me like wave after ferocious wave.

"His mother's blood made him weak," he continues. "But you, Horus, *the Falcon.* What powerful Hybrid spirit courses through those angry veins!"

He appraises me, his slow smile filling my throat with bile.

"We shall breed you. We shall tear every half-blood cell

from your body and harvest it." His gaze is pure evil as he lifts the dagger to my eyes.

My howl of rage is terrifying. I do not feel the blade as it pierces my left eye, and half of my vision perishes, never to return. Somewhere, I hear the high-pitched scream of a falcon. He pulls out the dagger and holds it to my right eye.

"Remember my face, Horus, son of Isis and Osiris. For it shall be the last image engrained in your half-breed mind."

I am Horus.

Son of Isis and Osiris.

I shall know—

Explosions shake the building.

Bells ring loudly in alarm.

Our fleet has arrived. The sea assault has begun.

Set's face betrays his shock. My shackles fall as two metal crossbows bolts strike the chains. The men behind Set fall to the ground, their hearts pierced with bolts.

I tear my dagger from his grip. His face contorts in surprise, then pain, as the tip of my blade enters his nape and emerges from his throat, just below his chin.

I pull him to me and twist the blade then wrench it out. I feel the warmth of his blood as it pours down my naked chest, mixing with my own. His eyes bulge, and he reaches up with his hands, trying to stem the tide of blood as his life spills from him.

Finally, I break the deadly embrace, and he collapses at my feet.

Slowly, I lift my head. Horemheb stands before me, his face a mask of terror.

"My Lord, your eye!" He moves toward me then stops as I raise my hand commanding him to stay.

My blood is on fire, yet there is no pain. There is no rage. There is... *nothing*. I stand, a statue, a blood-soaked dagger in my hand.

"My Lord! I must tend to your wound!"

My voice is calm as I sense the blood from my empty eye socket flowing down my cheek.

"Kill them all." I hear my own voice. "Every man, woman, and child."

"My Lord..." Horemheb's face pales.

"After you have killed every one, burn them and scatter their ashes into the ocean. Burn every building on this island, then bring down what is left. Destroy every brick, every stone, every cup. Destroy every trace of them. If it takes you a decade to tear down this cursed island, it shall be done. When the ships turn back east, barren land shall be at our back."

Horemheb's eyes are pure terror. "My Lord—"

"You will obey!" My scream carries through the night as the suffering overwhelms me, and I slip into the tender arms of oblivion.

TASHA'S SKIN tingled under William Drake's finger as he lazily followed a bead of sweat along her back before it dripped into the silk sheet. Her skin glistened as she laid next to him, her breathing finally beginning to slow down. He lifted a matted strand of auburn hair from her damp neck and leaned into her ear.

"What happened on that plane?" he asked.

Tasha tensed for an instant before she drew in a deep breath and turned around languidly, eyeing Drake through heavy lids.

His gaze rested on her face—cool, unblinking, unreadable. She waited, knowing the value of both silence and patience, until finally he sighed. "Those two have proven to be more resourceful than anticipated—and more aggravating."

She exhaled slowly.

"I'm done playing games," he continued. "Do whatever it takes. Get me the artifact."

"And the kids?" she asked.

"Whatever it takes," he repeated.

She nodded. "I will prepare a team."

"I want you there. As backup."

"As you wish," she replied.

He slowly wound her long hair around his hand and gently pulled her toward him.

"Do not let me down," he said quietly.

———

CLAY STOOD WORDLESSLY in the biosafety laboratory of the World Health Organization, a dazed look on his face. His mouth was a thin line as he set down the last HEPA filter at the table in front of him, having checked them all for the third time. He looked at the five air filters, his mind still refusing to accept the results. It wasn't only Kade Morgan's filter that had been tampered with. All but one had been compromised. He picked up the working filter and clenched it in his fist. He glanced to the suit from which he extracted it and focused on the name stitched on the white fabric: *Edward Wallace.*

———

PAUL STIRRED at the sound of a buzz. Working to blink the sleep from his eyes, he noticed the flashing red light of his cell phone beckoning him an arm's length away. He reached to the coffee table and brought the phone to his face. Struggling to focus on the display, he read the message from Clay.

FOUR FILTERS BUGGERED, INCLUDING KADE MORGAN'S. ONLY ONE FILTER STILL WORKING:

EDWARD WALLACE. WASN'T HE THE BLOKE THAT DIED??

"I'll be damned," Paul muttered drowsily and sat up, trying to make sense of the message. "Alyssa…"

His voice trailed into silence when he realized he was alone. He glanced at his watch: *4:09 a.m.*

A dismal suspicion stirred in his chest. Paul held his breath and looked toward the corner of the room. The bag with the LIDAR and VR gear was gone. His stomach sank.

You didn't…

He got up and rushed out of the room. A faint line of light under another door broke through the darkness.

"Alyssa?" he repeated, quietly knocking on the door. No answer. He knocked again, louder.

"Alyssa! You in there?" He pounded on the door, alarm creeping into his voice. He pushed down the knob only to find the door locked from the inside. "Open up!" Weighing his options for a heartbeat, he backed up half a step and put all his weight behind him as he slammed his shoulder into the door.

He grunted as the door crashed open, and he staggered into Alyssa's bedroom—and froze at the sight of her body lying life-lessly on the floor.

———

THE GRAY TESLA rolled noiselessly to a stop across from the El Maadi building. Tasha studied the elaborate, horseshoe-shaped driveway of the luxury apartment complex through the driver's side window then brought the com to her lips. "I'm in position," she said. "You're clear to move in."

"Copy." The simple reply came through the earbud when she spotted a white Mercedes Benz pulling up to the entrance.

"Hold," she said.

She watched a man step out of the rear passenger door and walk inside the building. Moments later, the car slowly cruised to the far end of the portico before the driver got out and lit a cigarette.

"Status?" the man's voice came through her com.

"Single male, a driver, waiting outside at a car," she replied. "He just dropped off somebody at the entrance."

"Do we abort?"

She considered. "Negative. Proceed."

A minute later a dark gray SUV turned into the driveway. It rolled to a smooth stop in front of the entrance, and two men stepped out. The driver of the white Benz glanced up lazily before turning again to his cigarette.

Tasha said into the com, "I want all three of you inside. No room for mistakes."

The voice on the other end hesitated only a brief instant. "What about the exit?"

"I will cover the exit," she said.

"Understood," came the reply. Seconds later the third man got out of the car. Tasha watched the three men as they disappeared into the building.

Her lips were a tight red knot as she placed her hand on the high-powered sniper rifle on the passenger seat.

———

PAUL DROPPED DOWN next to Alyssa and tore the VR helmet from her head.

"Alyssa!" he gasped. He gently lifted her head, cradling it in his arms.

"Wake up!" he pleaded. He pressed his fingers against the side of her neck. A relieved sigh escaped his lips when he felt a pulse. He gently lifted her eyelids. Her pupils were large and dilated, but they constricted when the light hit them.

"Alyssa," he repeated again, gently patting her cheek.

Alyssa moaned softly. Her eyelids fluttered, and she winced. "The lights," she murmured, "they hurt…"

Paul stretched his arm and flipped the light switch, engulfing them in darkness. As his eyes gradually adjusted, her features became clear once again in the faint glow of the light flowing in through the large window.

"Paul, I'm so sorry." Her voice was a whisper. "I had to."

"Shhh…" He cradled her head in his arms. "I know."

"No, Paul. You don't… Cayce—and my grandfather—they were right." She hesitated, taking in the weight of her words. "Atlantis was real. Horus destroyed it, all of it." Her voice shook as the memories rushed back.

"The Pureans killed his son. When Horus found out, he slayed them all. Destroyed every trace of them." She grabbed his arms, shuddering. "Paul, he wiped them from history."

Paul stared wordlessly at her as she took in a slow breath.

"The people who are after us, they're trying to harness Horus's powers. I think they want to reconstruct his DNA and combine it with their own." She looked at him, sudden clarity in her eyes. "Paul, we can do the same to help my dad. Horus's grandfather said that once the disease was unleashed, it would continue changing, spreading. That Hybrid blood was the only thing that could stop it. What if it's using him as a host? Mutating into something much more dangerous? The Hall of Records was opened before. Renley's grandfather... the dead people we saw in the video... I think the disease got out, it spread."

"What?"

"Jake found out about Renley and his grandfather's expedition right before World War I. The first cases of the 1918 influenza pandemic were found in Egypt, before the disease was carried to Spain by soldiers during World War I. If Renley's expedition had anything to do with it..."

Paul's face caved at the sudden realization.

"Paul, we have to stop this. This is much bigger than my father." She sat up, her jaw set. "We have to get into the Hall of Records. It's our only chance to prevent this. We must find a way to get inside... safely."

Paul studied her in silence. Her features were soft and indistinct in the darkness, but her eyes glowed with determination, the small crease between her eyebrows somehow making her appear even more beautiful than she already was.

"Your dad was right," he said finally. "His filter was deactivated. Clay confirmed it." He felt her tense at the news.

"But who would do that? And why?"

"That's not all. Clay also said that—"

Alyssa put a finger on his lips and looked toward the other room.

"What is it?" he asked.

"I heard something at the front door," she whispered.

Paul peeked into the foyer. His skin tingled as he watched a shadow move inside the condo. He slowly pushed the bedroom door closed with his foot until only a crack remained.

He helped Alyssa sit up with her back against the bed then quietly got to his feet. He stared through the crack at the man stalking across the corridor. Paul stood frozen in place, his mind racing, considering his options.

Paul's heartbeat hammered against his temples as he waited breathlessly for the man to pass the bedroom. He ripped open the door and hurled himself at the stranger. Surprise gave him the edge, and he felt the man slump to the ground. Without warning, the man shifted his weight, and Paul found himself flying through the air past the intruder, crashing painfully onto the floor.

He ignored the wave of pain in his back as he staggered to his feet, disoriented, but ready to fight.

"Paul, wait!" He heard the man's familiar voice.

Paul gasped when he realized the man in front of him was Kamal!

Kamal opened his mouth again an instant before his eyes glazed over and he slumped heavily to the ground. Alyssa stood behind Kamal's limp body, the heavy VR helmet in her hand. Her chest rose in rapid breaths, her expression blank. She looked down at Kamal, her mouth falling open in sudden recognition. Paul bent over the body.

"Is he—" the word stuck in her throat.

Paul pressed his fingers against Kamal's neck. He glanced up at her. "He'll wake up with a mammoth headache, but he should be okay," he replied. "Remind me never to tick you off."

Alyssa's concerned expression shifted to disdain. "Now we know what happened to Kade's filter!" Alyssa's face tensed.

"What if he wasn't alone?" She hurried to the front door and peeked through the small crack into the hallway. She whirled.

"Paul!" she whispered, alarm filling her voice. "Three bad-news guys just got out of the elevator!"

"Close the door!" His scanned the large foyer. *The dresser!* He leaped to it and began shoving it toward the front door. Catching on, Alyssa hurried to help him barricade the door.

"The crystal!" she yelled, turning to her bedroom.

He grabbed her arm. "There's no time!"

She struggled, pulling toward the bedroom door.

"Alyssa, now!" He held tight as she resisted.

She whipped her head around and hissed at him, dark, fiery eyes burning into him. Then they heard the noise outside the front door.

"The balcony!" he yelled, pushing her ahead of him. She groaned, her eyes darting back to the bedroom door as she crossed the living room toward the French doors. She pushed them open and rushed out onto the balcony.

Paul came up behind her and looked over the wide marble railing to the street below.

"That's a good thirty feet! Way too high to jump!" he yelled. He checked the balconies on either side and frowned. *Too far.*

Alyssa leaned out over the railing and looked down to the balcony on the floor beneath them.

"The balcony below," she said, her voice flat.

"You're out of your mind," Paul stared at her. "One slip and we're dead."

"We're out of options!" She climbed over the railing without hesitation. "I'll take my chances over those guys."

The front door burst open and slammed into the heavy dresser.

"Go—now!" she called out to Paul, over the sound of the dresser scraping across the floor, as the front door was being forced open.

Paul squeezed the railing until his knuckles turned white and followed her gingerly, swinging one leg over the wide balcony railing.

Alyssa kept her feet firmly planted and inched her hands down one of the big stone columns of the railing, lowering her body into a crouching position. When her hands were just above her shoes, she kicked off with her feet, using her hands as a pivot. As her feet swung back into the empty space between their balcony and the one below, she released her hands and arched her back, landing gracefully on the lower balcony. She looked up at Paul.

"Your turn!"

Paul's heart pounded against his chest as if it was trying to crack a rib. "Have I mentioned to you that I hate heights?"

He desperately tried not to think about the drop beneath him as he attempted to copy Alyssa's graceful maneuver. Just as he swung back into the lower balcony, he heard the men bursting into the room above. He cringed and his right foot caught the railing, plummeting him headfirst toward the stone floor. Alyssa leaped to catch him an instant before they both crashed onto the balcony.

"Well, that was exciting," he said breathlessly, lying on top of Alyssa. "Thank you," he mumbled.

Alyssa grimaced, struggling to catch her breath. "No time for anything more." She rolled him off her and jumped to her feet before staring down at him, rubbing her back. "Next time I'll be the maiden in distress."

Before he could reply she turned to the balcony door. It was cracked open. She glanced inside when they heard the voices above them.

"Go!" Paul whispered.

She gently swung the door into the room and quietly hurried across, Paul at her heels. They tiptoed to the front door then dashed through it and sprinted down the hallway.

Alyssa tore open the stairway door and charged through it. They raced down the stairwell, taking three stairs at a time until they burst through the door on the ground floor and bolted across the empty lobby for the exit, drawing bewildered stares from the night clerk behind the counter. Before he had time to react, Paul and Alyssa slipped through the tall glass door into the portico.

———

TASHA WATCHED with a hard smile as Paul and Alyssa emerged from the front entrance and tore down the street, away from the building. She lifted the sniper rifle from the passenger seat and cycled the bolt back to eject the high-powered round from the chamber. Her mouth was tight as she reached into her pocket and her fingers locked around the low-energy cartridge before she loaded it into the firing chamber.

She took a deep breath and cleared her mind as she lowered the driver's side window a hand's width. She focused the sights on Alyssa's head then moved the crosshairs down, visualizing the contour of the girl's body. She waited for the pause between her heartbeats—and squeezed the trigger.

———

ALYSSA CRIED OUT, a searing pain tearing through her insides. She grabbed her left flank and gasped when she felt something wet between her fingers.

"Alyssa! *No!*" Paul's horrified voice sounded distant. The night started closing in around her, shrouding the street in a crimson haze.

What a beautiful sunset, Alyssa thought as she felt Paul hands guiding her to the ground. Then darkness enveloped her.

GEORGE RENLEY STOOD at the tall window, dressed only in his bathrobe, and surveyed the city below him. He took a sip from his teacup and savored the flavor of the Darjeeling as he scanned the desert in the distance. The panorama from his thirty-fifth floor penthouse suite provided a stunning view of the rising sun, a golden disk that cast shimmering mirages across the dunes and lit up the Nile like a million fireflies dancing on the surface of the water. He scowled when a buzz behind him interrupted his thoughts. Reluctantly, he turned from the window and picked up his phone.

"Yes?"

"George Renley?" The voice on the other line was breathless and trembling.

"Yes."

"It's Paul Matthews. I need your help."

Renley's face remained a mask as he continued to listen. When Paul finished, Renley took a deep breath.

"Stay where you are. I will be there in ten minutes," he said, his lips curving upward in the barest of smiles.

————

PAUL SAT on the cold pavement of the side alley as the white Rolls Royce Phantom approached and pulled smoothly to a stop next to him. He glimpsed down at Alyssa, her head cradled in his lap, and his stomach dropped for the tenth time in as many minutes. The dark circles around her eyes stood out against her pale skin, glistening with beads of sweat. Her chest rose and fell in shuddering breaths.

"They're here," he said, fighting off the dizziness and forcing a smile.

She smiled weakly in reply and licked her dry lips.

Paul lifted his head and watched Renley and his driver get out of their car and approach them. He squeezed Alyssa's hand.

Renley's expression was a mask as he stared at Alyssa.

"How is she?"

"I managed to stop the bleeding," Paul replied, straining to sound calm. "I put a pressure wrap on her, but the bullet is still inside her body."

"She needs a hospital immediately," Renley said. "We'll go in my car."

"No hospitals." Paul's voice was firm.

"She needs a doctor!"

"Then get her a doctor. I know you have connections. No hospitals."

Renley pursed his lips in thought for several moments.

"Very well." He turned to his driver. "Let's get her into the car."

The man moved toward Alyssa but stopped at Paul's stare.

"I'll get her," Paul said.

The driver looked at Renley who gave him a small nod. The man lifted his arms, palms-out, and took a step back.

Paul faced Alyssa. "Everything's going to be okay," he said softly, lifting a strand of hair off her cheek. He stroked her head. "Are you ready?" he asked.

She nodded. He gently slid one arm under her legs and the other under her back. She winced as he lifted her and carried her to the Rolls Royce.

Renley grimaced at the blood on her clothes. His expression warmed up when his eyes met hers.

"Thank you," she said quietly. "That's two I owe you."

Renley gave her a tense smile and opened the rear door of the Rolls Royce. He reclined the rear seat and raised the footrest. He moved aside to let Paul ease her down into the seat.

"I'll sit with the driver," Renley said.

Paul looked at him gratefully. "How far?"

"Less than thirty minutes. I will have a doctor waiting for us."

————

HALF AN HOUR LATER, Paul watched Alyssa and the gray-haired man standing at the side of the bed. Alyssa's black bra and tan skin stood out against the white sheets as the man's gloved hands gently touched her left flank. He studied the wound from behind his round metal-rimmed glasses, his sharp black beard thrust forward like a dagger.

He opened a sterile package and bent over her arm. She winced as he inserted an IV line into her arm and connected it to a saline bag that he hung on the post of the bed.

Paul flinched at the hand on his shoulder. He turned.

"She is in good hands." Renley's voice was reassuring, but there was a strange light behind his eyes. "Dr. Nazari is the British ambassador's personal physician."

Paul glanced at Renley. He had delivered on his promise and brought them to this sprawling manor house on the outskirts of Cairo, yet Paul could not shake the feeling they were in the lion's den.

Paul's thoughts were interrupted by the physician's voice. "Are you allergic to any medications?"

When Alyssa shook her head, he squirted the contents of a syringe into the IV line.

"What is that?" Paul asked.

"Ceftriaxone. A broad-spectrum antibiotic," Nazari replied. "Bullet wounds are relatively sterile, but she has been moved around quite a bit. The Ceftriaxone will serve as a preventive measure against any infections."

He put his hands into the bag and pulled out a laptop-sized device connected to a small, razor-shaped probe.

He looked back to Alyssa. "This is a portable ultrasound machine. It will allow me to determine the extent of the damage the bullet caused to the inside of your body."

Paul's fingers plucked at the stubble on his chin as Nazari glided the probe across Alyssa's stomach while he watched the display. He positioned Alyssa on her right side and examined her left side and back. After several minutes he exhaled deeply.

"What is it?" Paul asked, unable to remain silent.

"The bullet missed all vital organs and major blood vessels. The spleen, kidney, and their blood supplies have all been spared. The damage is limited to connective tissue. Just as fortunate is the fact that the bullet wound is relatively superficial."

Paul let out a sigh as the physician turned to Alyssa and used his forearm to adjust his glasses. "You had a guardian angel looking out for you, madam. A couple inches higher and you would have exsanguinated from a ruptured spleen, a couple inches to the right and your spinal cord would have been shattered."

Alyssa turned her head to Dr. Nazari. "So you'll be able to get it out?"

"I will be able to extract the bullet without much risk to the surrounding structures, but it will have to be removed in a sterile fashion." He faced Paul. "I will have to prepare an operating field. It may be best if you wait outside."

"No." Alyssa reached out and squeezed Nazari's arm. "I want him to stay." She turned to Paul. "Please don't go."

Paul met her gaze, unblinking. "Don't you fret. I'm not going anywhere."

The physician glanced at Alyssa, then Paul, his lips pursed. He cleared his throat. "You may stay, of course, but please stand clear of the sterile field."

"Understood," Paul replied. He looked at Renley whose face was as expressionless as a slab of granite.

"I will wait outside until Dr. Nazari has finished," he said.

Paul nodded absentmindedly and watched the physician gently touch Alyssa's shoulder. "I will need you on your stomach for this procedure. Can you turn over for me?"

Alyssa nodded and bit down on her lip. She winced softly as Nazari helped her turn onto her stomach.

"I will administer a local anesthetic for the procedure," Nazari said. "You'll feel some discomfort initially, but it will help with the pain."

Paul saw Alyssa grimace when the man injected the anesthetic around the wound site. After he finished he looked down at Alyssa and smiled.

"The worst is over."

Paul edged around the bed and took her hand. Beads of sweat followed the curve of Alyssa's spine, her upper back trembling with shallow breaths. She looked up at him, her face pale.

"Everything is going to be okay," he told her, giving her a small smile.

Paul's nose wrinkled at the faint smell of the antiseptic as the physician cleaned the area around the wound. He pulled out a tray and surveyed the instruments before slipping on the sterile gloves and picking up a scalpel. "Please try to be as still as possible, Miss Morgan." He leaned over her, bringing the scalpel to the wound.

Paul's chest tightened as he watched Nazari make an incision into Alyssa's skin, opening up the small hole made by the bullet. His movements were smooth and efficient. He put down the scalpel and picked up a pair of long-nose pliers from the tray. Alyssa gasped and squeezed Paul's hand hard when Nazari inserted the instrument into her wound.

A heartbeat later Nazari removed the instrument from Alyssa's body, a small metal slug between the pincers. "Here is the culprit," he said and dropped the bullet into the tray.

Alyssa continued holding her breath, her fingers still locked around Paul's hand. He touched her head gently. "It's over," he said.

He felt her grip relax slowly as she exhaled.

"I'm going to examine the inside of the wound to ensure there aren't any remaining fragments," the physician said. "Then all we have left is to suture the wound."

Alyssa's eyes slowly lost focus. "That's swell," she said softly. She looked from Nazari to Paul. "I'm going to pass out now." Then she closed her eyes.

Paul stared at Nazari, alarmed.

Nazari gave him a reassuring look. "She will be fine. Everything went well. Sleeping is the best thing she can do now. She will feel much better when she wakes up."

PART 3

REVELATION

DR. AHMED FARAG shivered as the cold blast of air from the inside of the minus-eighty degree freezer met his skin. He quickly scanned the shelves and removed two small vials before closing the heavy door. He crossed the laboratory to the long blacktop bench and reached for the DNA extraction kit. Absentmindedly, he threw a glance at the updated test results on the laptop. *Still nothing.*

He grabbed his water bottle and brought it to his lips. *Empty.* He didn't remember finishing it. He swallowed, trying to wet his irritated throat.

The sound of his phone made him jump. He answered it.

"*Ahlan*, Ahmed." He recognized Kamal Khanna's voice. "Any progress?"

Farag tried to hide his frustration. "The cursed thing keeps mutating in front of our eyes, but we can't make any sense out of it! Any news from the CDC and World Health Organization?"

"They are still having problems isolating sufficient amounts of stable RNA. The molecular structure of this bugger is more fragile than a teenage girl's heart. Anytime we think we're getting close, it just shatters on us."

Farag scoffed and rubbed the back of his neck. "We're running out of time, Kamal. We can't afford to botch this up."

"We will get to the bottom of it." Kamal said and hung up.

Farag put the phone down and slid the tubes into the DNA processor. He cleared his throat, but it turned into a cough. He shielded it with his arm. When he brought his arm down, he gasped. His sleeve was covered in bright red blood.

―――――

PAUL'S HEAD BOBBED DOWN, and he jerked up, again, struggling to stay awake. He watched Alyssa, the steady movement of her chest rising and falling beneath the silk cover when the door slowly opened. He turned and eyed Renley as the tall man quietly entered the room.

"How is she?" Renley asked.

"She's been sleeping, mostly."

"You have been sitting in that chair all day. The room across the hall is set up for you. You should take a rest."

"I'm fine," Paul answered.

"As you wish," Renley turned, heading for the door.

"Wait."

Renley stopped and faced him.

"I never thanked you for what you did for Alyssa—for both of us," he said. "Why did you help us?"

"My motives are my own, Mr. Matthews, as are yours."

Paul's gaze moved to Alyssa. He studied her, watching her

sleep peacefully in the luxurious bed. He took a deep breath. "We planned to enter the Hall of Records."

"And what would you do once you got there?" Renley asked.

"I'm not sure," he hesitated. "Alyssa says the answers lie inside."

"But you remain doubtful?"

"The crystal. It contains information. We managed to decode some of it," Paul said, "but they were only snapshots. It became too dangerous for Alyssa to continue. She was too stubborn to let anybody else take the risk. She insists that the cure to her father's illness is in the Hall of Records. Something about Horus's blood."

Renley gazed at him silently.

Paul shrugged. "I know it sounds crazy." He rubbed his temples. "I think you're right. I'm going to go rest for a bit."

Renley continued staring at Paul with a strange expression.

"What is it?" Paul asked.

Renley shook his head wordlessly and stepped out of the room.

Moving as quietly as his stiff joints allowed, Paul slowly got out of the chair and inched to the bed. He studied Alyssa's face, trying to ignore the waves of emotions welling up inside him. He ran a hand through her hair, moving the strands away from her eyes. Quietly, he turned and left the room.

———

PROFESSOR BAXTER MOVED the VR helmet with his foot and

knelt beside the body sprawled on the floor. He studied the man's lifeless eyes for several seconds then stared up at Drake.

"What the hell happened to him?"

"You tell me, you're the doctor," Drake scoffed.

"I'm a molecular geneticist, not a physician." Baxter replied, frowning. "What did you do to him?"

Drake pointed at the helmet and cables connecting it to the computers on the desk. "The whiz kid from the WHO put this together. We found it in the apartment." He pushed a button on the LIDAR and a small panel slid open, revealing the crystal. "Apparently, they figured out how to access information stored in the artifact."

"They what?" Baxter gave a bark of laughter. "You can't be serious."

"It seems there may be truth to the old prophecies after all, Professor."

Baxter opened his mouth then shook his head. He closed his jaw with a snap and ran his hands through his gray hair. "So, what happened?"

Drake pointed at the man on the floor. "One of our men volunteered to access the information."

"Ah…" Baxter nodded. "You'll have a harder time finding a second volunteer."

"He started seizing within seconds of putting on the helmet," Drake continued. "We shut it down but couldn't bring him out of it. He was dead in two minutes."

Baxter bent down and scrutinized the fully dilated pupils in the man's frozen eyes.

"My professional opinion?" He frowned. "Sensory overload. Guy's nervous system is fried. Whatever the hell that thing is, clearly it didn't agree with him."

"I need the information stored in the crystal," Drake said. "The girl accessed it, repeatedly, and still lives." He regarded Baxter with an expectant look.

"I want to know why," Drake continued. "Can you figure it out?"

Baxter pondered the question. "Possibly," he replied. "If I can get my hands on her and perform a thorough—"

Drake snorted. "No." He shook his head. "As long as she's the only one who can get us the information, we need her intact —and cooperating."

"At least get me a blood sample, so I can run some tests, then," Baxter shot back.

"That can be arranged," Drake replied, a cold smile building on his face.

———

THE ORNATE HANDLE creaked softly under Tasha's hand as she gently pushed the heavy oak door into the room. She glided inside, carefully closed the door behind her, and studied the young woman sleeping in the bed. *You should never have come to Egypt*, she thought, pressing her lips together wistfully.

She moved across the carpet and sat on the bed. Alyssa stirred, but her eyes remained closed. Tasha's gaze traveled across Alyssa's body, following the graceful curves under the thin white blanket. Her hand hesitantly moved to Alyssa's face, almost touching it as her fingertips skimmed the contour of her cheek. Her fingers tingled as they drifted over Alyssa's body, slowly descending toward the wound on her left side.

Alyssa stirred again. Tasha's hand jerked back. She took a deep breath and took out a pen-shaped item and removed the plastic tip covering the tiny blade. Gently, she grasped Alyssa's hand and moved the item to her finger.

Alyssa lifted her eyelids sluggishly. She recoiled, wild-eyed. "What are you doing?"

Tasha flinched and pulled her hands back. Her eyes narrowed imperceptibly for an instant before her lips curved into a disarming smile.

"I'm sorry. I didn't mean to startle you. Dr. Nazari assured me that the sedative would keep you asleep for another couple of hours. He asked me to check on you."

Alyssa looked dazed as she processed the other woman's words. She stared at the object in Tasha's hand. "What is that?"

Tasha slowly brought it closer to Alyssa, allowing her to examine it. "This? It's just a lancet pen. It pricks your skin and takes a drop of your blood. Dr. Nazari wants to check it to make sure you don't have an infection."

Alyssa tried sitting up then winced and clutched her back. Tasha reached out to help, but Alyssa waved her off.

"Where is Paul?"

"The young man who brought you here?"

"Where is he? I want to see him."

"He's been at your side since you arrived. He was finally convinced to rest for a while. Would you like me to wake him?"

Alyssa looked down and sighed. "No, that's all right." She shook her head softly. "Let him rest."

Tasha smiled. "He's a good man. And he cares about you."

"Who are you?"

"I'm Tasha. Renley said you're friends?"

"No," Alyssa replied too quickly. "I guess, maybe…"

"You're lucky to be alive. He saved your life by bringing you here, you know."

Alyssa's body stiffened again. "I want to see Paul." She tried pushing herself up but staggered. Tasha caught her and gently lowered her onto the bed.

"Your body is full of sedatives. You're in no shape to get out of bed right now." She put her hand on Alyssa's arm. "You need to recover. It will give your boyfriend a chance to rest, too."

Alyssa moved her arm away from Tasha. "He's not…" she shook her head. "It's complicated."

Tasha grinned. "Always is with men."

Alyssa blinked, puzzled.

Tasha considered her for several moments. "I should let you rest," she said, finally. She held up the lancet pen. "Would you like me to come back later to do this?"

"No," Alyssa held out her hand. "Go ahead." She grasped Tasha's arm. "I hate needles," she said.

"Don't worry," Tasha replied, gently squeezing Alyssa's hand. "I'm good with sharp objects."

PAUL WOKE UP WITH A START.

How long have I been out? He checked his watch. *Only a couple of hours. I must have passed out as soon as I got into the room.*

He sat up on the bed and rubbed his face to clear his head then stood and lumbered into the bathroom. He glanced at his reflection in the mirror. He looked haggard, eyes sunken. His beard looked as if he hadn't shaved in two weeks. He fixed on the dark stains on his shirt. *Alyssa's blood.* He lifted his hands to undo the buttons and flinched as he spotted the dried blood on his palms. Paul's fingers trembled as he fumbled with the buttons, rushing to get away from the blood and the memories. He finally gave up and lifted the shirt over his head and threw it on the floor.

He turned on the faucet and scrubbed his hands, desperately trying to erase the image of Alyssa lying bleeding on the pavement from his mind. He scrubbed harder until his knuckles were red raw. Only when the water drained perfectly clear did he stop.

Paul opened the glass door to the shower and started the water. He stood for several seconds, eyes closed, keenly aware of the air conditioning against his bare skin and the soft splatter of the water hitting the marble floor.

Did all of that really happen today?

He opened his eyes and took a deep breath. He reached into his pocket and took out his phone. He had switched it off when he was with Alyssa, so it wouldn't wake her. Absentmindedly, he powered it on and placed it on the sink. As he started unbuttoning his jeans, he heard the phone buzz with a new voicemail.

He glanced at the display. *Unknown number.* He tapped the screen to listen to the message.

"Paul, this is Kamal." He tensed at the voice. "You and Alyssa are in great danger. I came to warn you in the apartment. You must call me back. Your lives may depend on it."

Paul rested his hands on the sink and gaped into the mirror, studying his own reflection. *What the hell is going on?*

There had to be a connection somewhere. The thought hovered over him, as if waiting for permission to descend.

Frustrated, he reached for the phone and pushed the callback icon. The phone on the other end was picked up on the first ring.

"Paul?" Kamal's voice sounded tense.

"Yeah, it's me."

"Is Alyssa with you?"

"Yes. Well, not right here. She's in the other room."

"What happened?"

"She was shot, Kamal. Alyssa was shot."

He heard Kamal inhale sharply.

"How is she?"

"I think she'll be okay. The doctor said she was very lucky."

"Where are you?"

"I… I didn't know what to do. I called Renley. He picked us up and drove us to—"

"Renley?" Kamal interrupted, alarm in his voice. "Paul, listen to me carefully. You are both in grave danger."

"What?"

"We haven't told you everything because we didn't know whether we could trust you."

"What are you talking about?"

"I'm trying to protect Alyssa. Damn it, Paul! We tried to keep her in Peru. Keep her from entering the Hall of Records with her father!"

"You're behind the attack on her camp?"

"Nobody was supposed to get hurt! We just had to keep her out of Egypt long enough to miss the dig."

Paul's head was spinning as he processed the news. "That's insane! And who is 'we'?"

"There is no time! You have to trust me. We have reasons to believe that Renley was linked to what happened at the dig site."

Paul slammed his hand on the sink, his nostrils flaring. "I knew it! That aristocratic prick. He's been behind this all along!"

"He may be involved with a group of fanatics that are extremely dangerous."

Paul's mind raced, reliving the events from the last three days.

"The filters..." Paul started, "something doesn't add up... They were all deactivated, except one. Ed Wallace. But he's the one who died! That doesn't make any sense!"

Paul heard Kamal breathe in sharply as realization hit him.

"Good gods," he said, his voice trembling, "you're in more danger than you can imagine."

"What? What are you talking about?"

"Listen to me. You both have to get out of there, now." He paused. "Wait! No, don't do anything. Don't give them a reason to suspect that you know anything. We can track your location using the GPS on your phone. Don't do anything, do you understand?"

Kamal waited for several seconds. "Paul? Did you hear me?"

Paul remained silent and frozen, watching the door to his room open slowly. He turned off the phone and put it on the sink and quietly slipped behind the bathroom door. Watching through the doorjamb, he tensed as a man entered his room and softly closed the door behind him. He remained motionless for several seconds listening to the running water. *He thinks I'm in the shower.* The man slid his hand into his jacket, pulling out a large, black, sinister-looking auto pistol, and stalked across the room toward the bathroom door.

———

DRAKE STOOD next to Tasha and stared at the computer display over Baxter's shoulder, trying to make sense of the multitude of color-coded shapes and sequences of letters. It was complete gibberish to him. "What is all of this?"

Baxter ran his hand through his hair. "These gene sequences are completely degraded. Even the promoter regions are incomplete." He scrolled through the results. "And the coding segments don't exhibit any homology with known exons."

Drake stared at him. "In English."

Tasha looked up. "It appears the girl's blood sample does contain several unknown genes, but they are quite splintered," she explained. "What's even stranger... even the individual pieces don't match any of the known genes in the databases."

"Maybe the sample was damaged during processing in the lab," Drake said.

Baxter sat up, his chin out. "I can assure you, my sample processing protocols are flawless. There was no degradation or contamination."

"So what else can it be? And what does it mean?" Drake asked.

Baxter cleared his throat. "It means reconstructing the genes and getting any useful information is going to be painful."

Drake's eyes narrowed to slits as he turned to the door.

"You will learn the meaning of that word, Professor, if you fail," he said and left the room.

———

ALYSSA WOKE with a vague and eerie sense of panic. *Where am I?* She opened her eyes, darting her gaze around the room as she lay perfectly still, too afraid to move. Gradually, her memories returned. *Paul?* She looked for him. *Tasha?*

The room was empty.

Alyssa clenched her teeth and gently slid her hand along her left side and probed the wound dressing on her back.

I guess I can cross off getting shot from my bucket list, too.

She pulled back the silk covers, shivering when the cool air hit her skin. She cringed when she realized she was dressed only in her bra and panties. Moving tentatively, she swung her feet over the side of the bed and sat on the edge, earning a grumpy complaint from her wound.

She took a deep breath and glanced out of the window at the setting sun, its fading rays casting a crimson glaze onto the white interior of the spacious bedroom. *I must have been out for a while.*

Alyssa slid her feet to the floor and used her right arm to push herself up. She scrunched her toes into the plush carpet and held her breath, dreading a wave of sharp pain. Surprised at the absence of it, she slowly exhaled. The carpet tickled the soles of her feet as she crossed the room to the dresser. She looked into the large mirror above it and cringed. She moved closer, scrutinizing her reflection. Her long hair was tangled and her face looked pale, with dark rings circling her brown eyes. She ran her tongue over her chapped lips and frowned. *I look like shit.*

She spotted a pair of white pants and a blouse wrapped in a clear plastic bag, hanging from the back of a chair. She approached the chair and took the clothes out of the bag, holding them up. *My size*, she thought, surprised. She bit her lip as she gingerly slipped into the pants and put on the blouse. Working on the last buttons, she moved to the door and opened it, taking a cautious step into a wide hallway. The slate floor under her foot was cold, and she quickly took another step onto the thick rug in the middle of the corridor.

Alyssa absorbed her surroundings. She stood at the end of a long wood-paneled hallway. To her left, a large window revealed a magnificent view of the desert and its ruby-colored sky, lit up by the sun's waning rays. To her right, the long hallway continued for at least a hundred feet, lined with statues and suits of armor. Paintings decorated the walls between four pairs of large wooden doors. *A British manor home in the middle of Egypt,* she mused. As she moved along the corridor, the faint sound of voices rang from the hallway ahead of her.

The voices grew louder when she reached a large granite stairway that spiraled gently under a dome-covered foyer. She followed the sound of the voices to a room on the left side of the foyer where she spotted Renley, sitting in a brown leather armchair facing the stairway. He was talking to a man who sat in a second armchair facing him. Alyssa couldn't see the man's face, but her skin tingled as she stared at the back of his head. Something oddly familiar about his posture and his dark, slicked-back curls struck her.

Renley looked up at her. "Ah, Miss Morgan," he said. "How delightful to see you on your feet. We just sent up for Mr. Matthews. Please, join us."

"It seems like I owe you my gratitude and an apology, Lord Renley," Alyssa said, moving gingerly down the stairs, holding on to the railing. "I was wrong not to trust you."

"My dear Miss Morgan, not trusting me was the wisest thing you have done since we met." Renley's cold expression matched his voice when he spoke. "Please allow me to reacquaint you with my associate. I believe you two have met before?" Renley said as the other man turned around.

Alyssa's knees weakened. Her hand clenched the railing, her brain struggling to process the image sent to her by her eyes. She felt the hall spinning as she stared into the familiar face of the man sitting across from Renley.

"Ed?" she muttered. "I don't... I thought..." Her voice trailed off as the words stuck in her throat.

"I believe you're mistaken," Edward Wallace said with a menacing smile, his voice sending an icy chill rippling up her spine. "Dr. Wallace met an untimely demise. I prefer William Drake."

KAMAL FROWNED as he redialed the number for the third time. Once again, the call went straight to Paul's voicemail. Frustrated, he tossed the phone onto his desk. He propped up his elbows and held his head in his hands. Absentmindedly, his right hand moved to the back of his head, feeling the massive lump. His head felt like it was going to split in two. He grimaced. *It's like the worst hangover in my life, without actually having done anything worthwhile to earn it,* he thought, irritated.

He rubbed his temples, trying to clear his mind. The answer had been staring him in the face for three days. How could he have been so stupid? If what Paul said was true, he and Alyssa didn't realize the danger they were in. He had to get to them at all cost.

He reached across his desk and picked up the bottle of painkillers. He shook out four tablets into his palm and threw them in his mouth, washing them down with cold coffee. He grimaced at the bitter taste, then took another sip. He stood and started for the door when it swung open, revealing his assistant. Her expression made him stop in his tracks.

"What's going on?" he asked, a tight knot building in his chest.

"It's Dr. Farag from the hospital. He needs to speak with you right away," her voice cracked. "Morgan's virus broke containment."

Kamal froze. "Contact the Ministry of Health and quarantine the hospital," he said, his throat thick. "Nobody goes in or out. Tell Farag I'm on my way and will call him from the car." He grabbed his phone from the desk and rushed past her. "And tell the biocontainment team to meet me outside the hospital with Level 4 suits." Kamal's face was white as he raced down the glass-enclosed corridor.

PAUL WAS ACUTELY aware of the sound of his heartbeat thrashing in his ears as he watched the armed man through the crack in the doorjamb. He advanced on the bathroom with a silent, predatory walk. Paul stood completely frozen, his mind racing. The man reached the half-open door, and his gun arm slowly came into view as he stalked into the bathroom.

Paul slammed his body against the heavy wood, crushing the intruder's arm between the massive wooden door and the edge of the doorframe. The gunshot mixed with a loud scream as his arm shattered, and the pistol fell to the tile floor.

His brain on autopilot, Paul rushed out from behind the door and grabbed the man by his broken arm, pulling him into the bathroom with all his strength. The man screamed again, his face twisting with pain. Paul used his body as a pivot and swung the intruder at the shower by his arm—then he let go.

The man slammed violently against the glass enclosure and burst through it. He threw his arms over his head, desperately trying to protect himself from the rain of shards plummeting toward him as he fell onto the hard floor.

Paul lunged for the Glock and snatched it from the ground.

"Don't move!" he yelled, his heart pounding, and pointed the weapon at the other man.

The intruder froze, his cold blue eyes beneath the short-cropped blond hair locked on the gun in Paul's hand. His flat nose looked to have been broken more than once. His thin lips were contorted as he clutched his arm, the fresh cuts on his face growing into faint red lines.

"Get up. Slowly," Paul said, stepping back, trying to keep his voice steady.

The man awkwardly regained his feet, holding his broken arm close to his body. He glowered at Paul, but remained silent.

"Go," Paul pointed with the Glock, motioning him to move out of the bathroom.

"You cannot win," the man said through clenched teeth, his voice ringing with a German accent.

"Then why are you the one bleeding?" Paul replied flatly.

————

KAMAL KHANNA STOOD in the middle of the deserted lobby of the Kasir El Aini hospital, his stomach twisted into a tight knot. Without the usual clamor of the bustling crowd, the gentle sound of the three-story waterfall seemed eerily loud and out of place as it reverberated through the empty space.

He felt a bead of sweat from his forehead move down toward his eye. He brought his arm up to wipe it off and cringed when his gloved hand hit his visor. Snorting, he shook his head. The Level 4 biosafety suit sealed him off completely from the outside environment. He looked at the small heads-up display in the visor, informing him of the suit's status. The suit's independent air supply, a twelve-liter tank on his back, provided him with breathable air and positive pressure inside the suit, ensuring that any air exchange with the outside environment was going only one way, away from his lungs. Regardless of whether the filters on the Level 2 suits that Kade and his team wore at the dig were working, he wasn't taking any chances.

He heard a chime as the elevator doors opened and Ahmed Farag stepped out. He approached Kamal, his ashen face a glum mask.

"Are you all right?" Kamal asked when Farag reached him. *What a stupid question,* he thought as soon as the words left his mouth.

Farag nodded silently. "Is the hospital contained?" he asked.

"It's locked down, and we have guards stationed at every exit," Kamal replied.

"I just talked with the ministry. The Minister of Health formally declared the hospital a quarantine area."

"How the hell did it break containment?"

Farag shook his head. "We took all the precautions…"

"How many symptomatic people do we have?"

"So far, me and one ICU nurse. We've quarantined each of the floors and each of the departments. All visitors have been moved away from large areas. We're trying to keep people in small groups. From what we've been able to learn so far, it appears that the incubation period for the mutated version is about twenty-four hours."

"We won't be able to handle this alone," Kamal said. "We need the CDC and WHO for backup."

"The Minister of Health doesn't want this to get out until we know what we're dealing with."

"Damn it, Ahmed, look around you! We've been trying to figure out what we're dealing with for four days now. By the time we know what we're up against, it's going to be too late!"

Farag grimaced. "I told him the same thing. He insists on more information before calling on anybody from the outside for help."

Kamal gave him a pained stare through the visor. "This goes deeper than any of us envisioned. The whole thing was a setup. I think Edward Wallace created this entire situation and faked his death. The two kids are in danger." He swallowed. "I need to go after them, but that'll take resources. I can't do this on my own."

Farag stared back at him in disbelief. "What are you talking about? This isn't some game. You can't just run off!" He looked at him, pleading. "I need you here to help us deal with this before it's too late and this whole thing spirals out of—"

He started coughing violently. His breathing turned into a wheeze. He stared at Kamal between fits of cough.

"Ahmed!" Kamal rushed to him as the other man collapsed to the floor.

———

ALYSSA HEARD A GUNSHOT AND A SCREAM.

"Paul!" she yelled, leaping from the chair. She yelped in pain when Drake pulled her back down roughly.

"Why, Ed?" she asked, blinking. "Why are you doing this?"

Drake smiled as if Alyssa were an elder daughter who'd asked a clever question. "You will understand soon enough," he replied, his calm words at odds with the fire in his eyes.

"My dad, and everybody else," Alyssa tried to keep her voice steady, "they trusted you."

"Kade," his lips curled into a snarl as he spat the name. "He was nothing but a pawn."

"He was your mentor!"

"He never respected me. He kept so much from me… about your grandfather, about the hall." He scrutinized Alyssa for several long moments. "Do you know that your grandfather founded this Society?"

Alyssa stared at him. "You lie!" She turned to Renley. "Please tell me this isn't true."

"But it is, Miss Morgan," Renley said. "It was only after your grandmother passed away and Francis Chaplain disavowed the Society that William's father stepped in and salvaged it from the brink of extinction."

Alyssa shook her head in disbelief.

"William's father knew of my keen interest in the Hall of Records," Renley continued, "so he reached out to me and suggested an alliance. Under his guidance and my considerable auspices, the Society was finally able to pursue Edgar Cayce's original vision." He sighed pensively. "We tried to convince your grandfather to join us again, of course."

Drake scoffed, cutting in. "But the old fool had closed

himself off completely," he said. "Fortunately, your father came along at just the right time."

"My father would never help you!"

"And yet he did," Drake said. "He worked for the Society without suspecting a thing. It was my father's idea to place me under Kade's care as Ed Wallace, his student. After your mother... vanished... we knew that he was too unpredictable on his own, so the Society brought him here, where he could be controlled."

Drake glanced at Renley then continued, "We arranged for the university to offer him a faculty position. When I proposed a collaboration to locate the hall—which Lord Renley generously funded—he rose to the bait like a speckled trout to a fly. Ultimately, our patience and your father's persistence paid off... Yet even he could never conceive the true potential hidden inside it. Only the Society—"

"How could you betray him like that? He taught you everything!"

"There was so much more." Drake reached into his pocket and took out the crystal, staring into it. He shook his head as if trying to ward off an old memory. "Once I learned the truth, I could not allow this to be locked up, probed by imbeciles, unaware of its true power."

"You betrayed him. You betrayed all of them! And now they're all dying."

"Their sacrifice is nothing compared to the enlightenment we shall receive soon," he said, a dangerous gleam in his eyes.

"You are a lunatic!" A sob escaped Alyssa's lips. "All you've done is unleash a devastating weapon and put everyone on the planet at risk! You'll never be able to harness Horus's power!"

He looked at Renley. "You see? She has seen it. With her help we will—" Drake's next words stuck in his throat. His expression shifted as he stared past Renley into the foyer. Alyssa followed his gaze to the top of the stairs. Tears of relief welled up behind her eyelids at the sight of Paul looking down at them from the landing of the winding staircase. He was shirt-less, pointing a handgun at another man who stood next to him, clutching his arm, bleeding from numerous cuts.

Paul glared at Drake, sudden revelation in his face. His glance darted to Renley for an instant then back to Drake.

"So it's true. You really deactivated the filters."

"Ah, Mr. Matthews—so nice of you to join us," William Drake said calmly. "Put down the weapon. You have no chance of escaping."

"What else is new?" Paul said. He pointed the Glock at the man's head.

"Alyssa," he motioned to her, "get up and come up here."

Drake stood and stalked behind Alyssa.

"No, I don't think she will do that, Paul." He grabbed Alyssa's hair and pulled a compact Kel-Tec auto pistol out of his jacket.

Paul yanked the soaked man in front of him and pressed the gun against his head. "Let her go," he said. "Nobody has to get hurt."

Drake looked at the man with a detached glint. "Yet some-body always does." He raised the Kel-Tec and shot the man in the head in one smooth motion.

Alyssa screamed as the man collapsed in front of Paul, his

lifeless body tumbling down the curved staircase. Paul's eyes betrayed his shock as he stared at Drake in disbelief.

Drake jerked Alyssa's head back and pressed the gun to her temple.

"Drop the weapon, now!"

Paul's eyes were locked on Alyssa's as he slowly bent and placed the pistol on the floor.

KAMAL RUSHED along the floor of the intensive care unit as quickly as the suit and the forty-pound tank on his back allowed him. Struggling to catch his breath, he burst through the door and into the ICU suite.

Kamal slowed and approached the bed. He winced as he stared in disbelief at Ahmed Farag's lifeless body.

He turned to the physician. "How... how could he deteriorate so fast?"

"The mutated version is even more lethal than we anticipated," the physician replied softly.

Kamal stared at him silently, his face blank, then he turned and sped out of the room. He stormed into an office and dialed a number on the video phone. A few seconds later the Minister of Antiquities appeared on the screen.

"Ah, Dr. Khanna," the other man said. "I have just spoken with the Minister of Health again. He assures me the ministry's full support. How is Dr. Farag?"

Kamal stared at him blankly.

"Dr. Khanna?"

"Dr. Farag is dead."

The minister gasped in surprise. "Dead?"

"We must bring back the CDC and the WHO," Kamal exclaimed, "before it is too late and we lose the hospital!"

"We shouldn't be hasty in our decisions, Dr. Khanna. We don't want to alarm—"

"With all due respect, Minister, the quarantine simply delays the inevitable. If we don't act now—"

"This is a very delicate situation, Dr. Khanna. We must give it more time."

"This goes much deeper than we thought! The accident at the dig was a setup. Wallace faked his death!"

The minister's face drew into a tight pinch. "That is highly doubtable. We must collect additional information. The Minister of Health and I think that—"

Kamal snorted and disconnected the call, then stormed out of the room.

————

ALYSSA'S HEAD jerked up at the sound of the turning lock. She rose from the chair that constituted the solitary piece of furniture in the small, windowless room and stared at the door as it slowly opened. She focused on the face of the young woman entering. Her features made the notion of make-up seem garish, like using highlighter to trace over a butterfly's wings. Her violet eyes were locked on Alyssa's, the dark auburn hair in perfect contrast to her pale skin and the short white dress that covered her slender body.

"Tasha? What—?" she started, then scowled, sudden realization dawning. "You're one of them!"

Alyssa lunged at her.

Tasha nimbly danced aside and grabbed Alyssa's arm and hair, letting her momentum carry her into the wall. She pinned Alyssa's arm behind her back and pulled her head back by her hair. Alyssa screamed as the jolt sent a flash of searing pain through her injury.

"Stop!" Tasha said. "I'm not going to hurt you!"

Alyssa struggled against her grip, surprised at Tasha's strength. "Let me go!" she hissed.

Tasha relaxed her hold, and Alyssa squirmed out. She backed into the corner of the room and glowered at the other woman.

"Why are you doing this?" Alyssa asked, her voice shaking.

Tasha appraised her silently, a stony expression on her absurdly beautiful face. Then her eyes softened. "George Renley," she said.

"Renley?"

"He saved my life... gave me everything I could have dreamed of. The best education, finest training."

"Trained you how to lie and do his dirty work."

"You have no right to judge me," Tasha shot back. "I came from nothing."

"You're still nothing," Alyssa spat back. "Just Lord Renley's little whore."

Tasha slapped her. Alyssa gave a bark of laughter. "Seems like *Drake* isn't the only one who can't control his anger."

"The only reason you're still alive is because you're useful to him."

Alyssa looked at her silently.

"He tried the gear on one of his men. It... didn't end well. He needs you to help him get inside and find Horus's body."

Alyssa's gasp betrayed her surprise.

"Did you really think you were the only one who knew the truth?" Tasha asked, her voice taunting. "The Society has proclaimed it for decades. The crystal is the key to—"

"Fuck you and your society."

Tasha regarded Alyssa with a steady gaze, her expression distant and unreadable. Finally, she spoke. "It wasn't always like this, Alyssa. When William's father was in charge of the Society, he and George Renley shared a vision. He respected George, valued his council. Now, with William at the head— things are changing. We are at a knife's edge—"

"I don't care about your petty quibbles—" Alyssa cut in, scowling.

Tasha moved closer. "Alyssa," she said quietly, leaning into her, "listen to me—" She stopped when the door opened and William Drake entered the room. He studied them with a condescending look.

"Enough girl talk. Let's go."

Alyssa sneered at him. No words, just protest. Her eyes burned into him.

Drake grasped her by the front of her blouse and brought his mouth close to her ear. The smell of the expensive Scotch on his breath turned her stomach.

"You will do exactly as you're told," he whispered and spun

her around then shoved her out of the room ahead of him. He turned to Tasha. "Bring her friend."

Drake moved alongside Alyssa and motioned her to walk.

"It seems that you are still of use to me, Miss Morgan. For reasons I can't fathom, you seem to be the only one who can access the information on the crystal and live to tell about it."

Alyssa looked straight ahead, her lips a thin line.

"Edgar Cayce—and your grandfather—predicted this discovery many decades ago. We are merely fulfilling their destiny." They stopped in front of a tall wooden door. Drake turned to her. "You should feel quite honored, Miss Morgan. You are contributing to the evolution of the human race." His voice was clipped and filled with a dark fervor. "We stand at the threshold of the birth of a new species. Humanity is about to be awakened from its ashes of complacency."

Alyssa trembled as the fire in his eyes froze the skin beneath her clothes. "You are insane," she whispered.

Drake's eyes narrowed in a harsh squint before his lips curved up in the barest imitation of a smile. He opened the door. "Get inside."

Alyssa peered into the wood-paneled room. She gasped at the dozen men and women sitting at a long table. They turned to her as she entered.

The head of the table was empty. Renley sat at the right of the head, the leather-bound notebook on the table in front of him. "Ah, Miss Morgan," he said. "We have been anticipating your arrival."

Alyssa flinched at his voice. "How could you?" She glared at him. "We trusted you. I—" she stopped as Tasha walked into the room through another door, her gun pointed at Paul walking in in front of her, his face bruised.

"Paul!" Alyssa yelled and rushed to him. Drake jerked her back.

"Enough!" He pointed at the empty chair at the foot of the table with the VR setup in front of it. "Now you will tell us how to enter the Hall of Records."

Alyssa tensed and shook her head. "You are all lunatics," she said, lips trembling.

Drake pulled the Kel-Tec auto pistol out of his jacket and pointed it at her head. "You will do as you're told or you will die right now."

Alyssa hugged her shoulders and gave a half-hearted shrug. "You'll just kill me, anyway."

Drake flashed a mocking smile. "Very perceptive." He nodded at Tasha. She hesitated, seeming to fight an internal battle. Drake stared at her, his eyes burning into her. Finally, she pulled out her pistol and pointed it at Paul—and fired.

Paul screamed and clutched his left arm. He glowered at Tasha, as his chest rose and fell in ragged, shallow gasps.

Tasha pointed the Ruger at Paul's head, a rueful expression crossing her face.

Drake stared at Paul. "The next one won't be as painful," he said quietly.

"Stop!" Alyssa yelled, sobbing. "Please stop!"

"I'm sorry, Paul," Alyssa said between sobs. She slumped into the chair. Her hands trembled as she pulled the VR helmet to her. She turned on the LIDAR and booted up the laptops. As she calibrated the settings, she hesitated an instant then keyed in the setting for maximum power.

She met Paul's gaze as he stared at her, pale-faced, cradling his arm to his body.

"Ally, no…" he whispered.

Alyssa closed her eyes and lowered the helmet over her head.

I HAVE BECOME DEATH, destroyer of worlds, king of a thousand enemies.

I open my eye. The sun beats down with brilliant intensity as I behold the hybrid statue in the distance. Carved out of the native limestone bedrock and covered with black onyx, it is almost two hundred fifty feet long and seventy feet high at its head. Half cat, half human, this monument shall be a fitting tribute to my people... to my mother. It shall be the only homage to my race that I will leave behind for all to gaze upon. Another rests in my hand, and shall remain unseen.

I descend the stairs to the tunnel. Twelve years in the making, the Sphinx is now complete, as is the Hall under it, my resting place beneath the sheltering arms of my mother. I smile for the first time in a decade. For the first time in ten years, I feel at peace.

I glance to my side. Horemheb strides beside me, pain carved into his strong features. We enter the long tunnel that will lead us under the statue. Horemheb turns to me, his dark eyes glistening.

"My Lord, I do not understand. Why?"

I stop and face him, my single eye meeting his pair. I place my right hand on his shoulder, his posture rigid like a carving under my touch.

"For the past thirty years, you have been my finest warrior and most trusted advisor." I pause, the sound of my voice ringing through the tunnel. "My loyal friend."

His expression shifts at hearing the word. He lowers his head.

"My Lord, I do not deserve—"

"I would have been dead a long time ago if it had not been for you. And on this day, yet again, I must ask you to bear the burden of my trust."

I bring the pyramid-shaped crystal in my hand to him. "My memories, my feelings, my life—all inscribed into this gem. One day, it shall be unearthed by my descendants, and I will live again. But today, my final memory shall be written. And I have entrusted you, my loyal friend, to carry out this final bidding."

I turn once more to the door ahead of us, and we stride side by side in silence, the soft sounds of our steps echoing in the tunnel.

We reach the stone door to the massive chamber beneath the statue. I study the falcon carving. *My companion, my sentinel... my birthright.* I have lived with the blood of the falcon for more than eight decades, bestowed with the gifts of his magnificent sight, his strength and speed, his intuition. I move my hand to the ornate patch that covers my left eye. How close I came to losing these gifts completely. The memories of my other losses threaten to rise. I breathe deeply and control them. *Not on this day. Not now.*

I lift the crystal to the door. It sinks smoothly into the triangular opening beneath the falcon's talons, and the familiar blue light fills the tunnel. I extend my hands in the blessing of our people, my two hands forming a single triangle between the thumbs and forefingers, and place them against the crystal. I feel its warmth pulsing under my skin as I steadily press on it until it glides effortlessly into the door. Moments later, the sound of stone grinding over stone fills the tunnel as the heavy door slides open, revealing the entrance.

I remove the crystal from the talons and enter. The illuminated walls guide our steps deep into the tomb to the vast inner chamber. We stop at the threshold of the hall, and I behold the cavern that stretches beneath me, and the stone pyramid that fills it. It is the same pyramid that I ascended the day I was reborn as a Hybrid, the day I felt the blood of the falcon coursing through my veins for the first time. Thousands of my men labored for years to disassemble the sacred symbol of my people. They carried it on a hundred ships on our voyage home to be reassembled brick by brick in this subterranean hall. It is the only memory of my cursed home that is worthy of my race. It is the only structure that shall remain from the island kingdom of Atlantis, and it shall be buried deep beneath the earth, hidden from view.

We follow a stone ramp to the bottom of the chamber and draw near the stairs of the pyramid. Our feet stir the thin layer of fog that covers the base of the structure, created as the warm air near the ceiling collects moisture when it cools and falls to the ground. We reach the stairs and begin the long climb. Three hundred and forty-three steps separate us from the summit.

My memories turn to the first time I ascended this hallowed structure. My mind fills with images of a time long dead.

When we reach the peak, Horemheb stares at the ornate sarcophagus and the inscription device resting at its side.

"After my memories of this day have been inscribed into the crystal," I say to him, my voice steady, "after I am frozen in time, you will destroy the device."

He nods silently.

"You will release the weapon in the tunnel and bury the door."

His jaw clenches, but he nods again. He sinks to one knee and lifts the golden helmet up to me.

I take the helmet and place it on my head. I give the crystal to Horemheb, and he places it into the inscription device. He bows his head as I enter the sarcophagus.

I am Horus.

He looks up. One last time he meets my gaze, his eyes unwavering and hard, his tears slow and silent.

Son of Isis and Osiris.

"Now," I say and close my eye.

I shall know no fear.

PROFESSOR BAXTER'S assistant jumped at the sound of his boss's hand slamming into the lab bench.

"The genes from her blood sample are too fractionated to reconstruct," Baxter said, the veins in his forehead straining against his skin. "How the hell am I supposed to…?" He stopped and scrutinized at the display. "Yuri?" he said. "Come look at this."

His assistant scurried over and stood next to him.

"What does that look like?" Baxter pointed to a region of the DNA sequences on the monitor.

Yuri took off his glasses and leaned forward. He contemplated the display intently for several moments. "That appears to be an attachment sequence for a virus." He stared at Baxter. "It almost looks as if…" He shot a glance at the biosafety hood that contained the samples of the virus extracted from Kade Morgan's blood.

Baxter stood up and took out his phone and dialed it. He tapped his fingers on the back of the chair, listening to the ringing. After the fifth ring he threw the phone on the bench and groaned, irritated.

"We need to amplify the DNA from the girl's blood sample. Start the cycle on the amplifier. When it's completed, introduce the virus into her DNA and then run them through the sequencer again."

"But exposing the DNA to the virus will only destroy—"

"Don't argue. Just do it." Baxter spat back. "I'm going to the dig site. Call me with updates."

———

ALYSSA'S BODY was on fire, stars bursting behind her eyelids. She screamed, sealed up in a universe of constant pain. Slowly, much too slowly, the pain began to recede and her screams turned to shuddering sobs. She felt a hand touching her cheek. She tried opening her eyes. Her eyelids would not obey.

A distant voice cut through the agony. "Alyssa! Alyssa, can you hear me?"

Gradually, the blaze in her body transformed into a dull ache. The absence of pain was a blessing. She slowly opened her eyes and focused on Paul. His expression was pure terror.

"Alyssa..." he whispered and gently lifted a strand of hair from her face. "Are you okay?"

"No." She eyed the crude dressing on his arm. "You?"

He looked down wordlessly, his tight lips an answer.

She put her hand on the ground and lifted her head. She started as her fingers dug into soft sand. She looked past Paul and took in her surroundings. *I'm in a tent.* Tasha stood over them holding a pistol, staring down.

"Where are we?" Alyssa asked.

"You were unconscious for over an hour," Paul said. Alyssa winced as she slowly got to her feet, Paul straining to support her with his uninjured arm. "They brought us to the dig site."

Alyssa frowned, confused. "I thought the entire excavation site was quarantined."

"Haven't you learned by now that I achieve my objectives, Miss Morgan?" George Renley's voice rang out as he and William Drake entered the tent.

She whirled and faced them, sneering.

"Tell us what you saw," Drake said.

She remained silent, glaring at her captor in a futile act of defiance.

"I will not ask again."

Alyssa's shoulders slumped as she willed the anger out of her voice. "I know how to get in," she said. "I will take you to Horus."

Drake pointed to the biocontainment suits on the floor next to them. "Suit up. Both of you."

He turned to Tasha. "Make sure our guests suit up properly. It would be a shame if something happened to them while we still have need of their services."

————

TEN MINUTES LATER, Alyssa trudged along the smooth stone floor of the tunnel, encased in the white biosafety suit. She tried to ignore the throbbing from her wound as she focused on the lights from her headlamp cutting bright slices into the darkness ahead, bouncing off the stone walls with each shuffling step.

She glanced to her right. Drake marched next to her, holding the gun awkwardly in his gloved hand, staring into the tunnel ahead. Behind him, Paul trailed with staggering steps, nursing his arm in a makeshift sling, flanked by Renley and Tasha.

As they approached the end of the long tunnel, Alyssa spotted the figure on the ground. Renley cautiously moved to the body and knelt beside it. Alyssa watched him leaning over the remains of his grandfather, his expression unreadable. After several seconds he rose.

She felt a push from Drake toward the door. "Open it."

She moved up to the magnificent carving in the center of the door. "I need the crystal."

Drake handed it to her wordlessly, and she slowly inserted it into the opening beneath the talons of the falcon. She gasped as the talons locked around it, and brilliant blue light illuminated the corridor.

Alyssa touched the thumb and forefinger of one hand to the thumb and forefinger of the other, forming a triangle. She brought her hands to the crystal. She held her breath and pushed evenly along its perimeter, her fingers grazing the blue light.

The light turned white and the crystal slid, without any resistance, entirely into the door.

For several seconds nothing happened.

Then the sound of the airtight seals releasing filled the tunnel, and the door slid back with a grating sound.

THE HELMET of the biocontainment suit bounced in the passenger seat as Kamal steered the white Land Rover onto the moonlit desert, leaving the comfort of the paved four-lane highway behind. He sped through uneven terrain toward the large tent that stood halfway between the Great Pyramids and the Sphinx. He tightened his grip on the steering wheel and shot a nervous glance at the large oxygen tank that was squeezed tightly between the passenger seat and the dashboard. He wiped the sweat from his forehead and turned the air conditioning to maximum, trying to ignore his soaked clothes underneath the Level 4 biosuit.

As the vehicle approached the dig site, he turned off the engine and dimmed the lights. Silently, the Land Rover drifted to a stop a hundred meters from the site. Kamal scrutinized the two parked sedans outside the tent.

Where are the security guards?

He remained seated for another minute, staring at the cars, looking for signs of any movement.

He opened the door and took a deep breath, letting the cold desert night air fill his lungs. Kamal regarded the towering statue in the distance. With the body of a lion and the face of a man, the eyes of the Great Sphinx cast an enigmatic gaze over the moonlit plateau before him.

He lifted the tank from the floorboard and strapped it to his back then grabbed the helmet and set off across the soft desert sand to the large tent. He drew near the entrance, ears on alert for any sound, and cautiously lifted the flap. The interior was completely empty. Most of the floor of the fifty foot wide tent was excavated, revealing a thirty foot deep pit with a ramp zigzagging down its side. He focused on the tall stone door on the far side of the pit. The door was completely enclosed by a small chamber, separated from the outside by transparent plastic, accessible only through a set of sealed double doors. He glanced around and swallowed before walking down the ramp.

He reached the plastic enclosure and studied the biocontainment bubble and the access mechanism of the double doors. He took his last breath of fresh air, opened the oxygen valve on the tank and secured the helmet on his head. As the suit began to inflate, he focused on the small heads-up display in the helmet. The cursor of the optical interface followed his eye movements to the *Status Check* box on the small display.

"And what the hell do you think you're doing here?" Kamal jumped at the voice behind him. He spun. The man standing at the top of the pit stared down at him from behind a lazily raised revolver. "This site is quarantined. Get up here. Now."

Kamal's mind raced as he slowly moved toward the ramp, watching the man above him.

"That's good." The other man's patronizing voice rang with

an American accent. He watched Kamal walk up the ramp and ran a hand nervously through his gray hair. "Nice and slow."

"Who are you?" the man asked brusquely when Kamal reached the top.

"I am Dr. Kamal Khanna of the Genetics Institute," he replied, his voice flat.

"What are you doing here?"

Kamal remained silent as he moved his eyes toward the small heads-up display in his helmet and blinked, activating the cursor.

The man stalked closer. "I asked you a question."

Kamal slowly moved his eyes, the cursor on the display trailing his pupils toward the box marked *Headlamp*.

"Don't make me ask again." He pointed the revolver at Kamal's head.

Kamal blinked and the Xenon headlamp came to life, its brilliant twin beams focused directly into the man's eyes. He screamed and brought up his hand to shield himself from the sudden glare.

Kamal rushed him, reaching for the revolver. The suit slowed his movements, and he barely managed to lock his grip around the barrel. His breathing quickened as he felt his gloved hand slip and slowly lose grip. The man stared at him with a triumphant expression.

In a final effort, Kamal twisted his body rapidly, his hand still clutching the revolver. The man refused to let go of the gun for a split second too long, causing him to stumble into Kamal.

The heavy tank on Kamal's back drove hard into the other man's side as Kamal continued turning, flinging the man to the edge of the pit. The man's face froze as he stared at Kamal, teetering at the edge of the pit, his hands grasping at an invisible hold, an instant before he plunged backward with a scream.

Kamal rushed to the side of the pit and looked down. The man lay at the bottom, his body twisted at a grotesque angle.

He rushed down and crouched next to the body. Kamal removed one of his gloves and, already knowing the answer, pressed his fingers against the man's neck.

He checked the man's pockets and pulled out a wallet. He flipped it open. *Grayson Baxter.* Kamal sighed before he brought his fingers to the dead man's eyelids and closed them slowly.

He reattached his glove to the suit and started the checklist procedure. As the suit inflated, he stood up and lumbered to the isolation bubble then released the seal on the first door and stepped through it. A few moments later, a green light appeared above the second door and he opened it, entering the bubble.

His heart beat furiously against his chest as he crouched and crawled through the opening in the stone door. He stood up on the other side, peering into the tunnel ahead of him.

Trying to steady his breathing, he took a step into the darkness.

ALYSSA'S SKIN TINGLED, the anticipation flowing through her like electrical sparks on the way to the ground, prickling her toes with each shuffling step. They slowly advanced through the corridor, brilliant white light illuminating the smooth surfaces. She studied the walls and ceiling, seeking out the source of the glow. It was as though the stone panels themselves were lit up.

"The corridor leads to a large chamber just ahead," she said, unaware that she was whispering.

Alyssa peered around the corner and gasped. A vast subterranean hall opened before her. Inside it was an enormous stone pyramid, more than two hundred feet wide on each side, its base covered by an eerie fog. Alyssa recalled Horus's memories. Three hundred and forty-three stairs led to the top of the structure, brought to Egypt stone by stone from his home island.

She turned to Drake, struggling to ignore his triumphant stare. "Horus's sarcophagus lies on the summit. That's where

Horemheb sealed him into his final resting place." Her voice trailed off as she recalled Horus's last memories.

They ascended the pyramid wordlessly. When they reached the top, they gathered reverently around the rectangular stone tomb.

Drake pointed at the sarcophagus, his eyes glinting in the dim light of the cavern.

"Open it," he said, unable to contain the tremor in his voice.

Alyssa, Paul and Tasha stepped forward. Alyssa clenched her teeth, ignoring the protest from her wound as she pushed on the heavy stone plate covering the sarcophagus. She heard Paul groan beside her, straining to move the lid using his one good arm.

The lid inched aside with a harsh grating sound, slowly revealing the interior of the sarcophagus, before it fell to the floor with a loud thud that reverberated through the vast cavern.

Alyssa looked into the sarcophagus. Surprise and confusion registered first, and then a tired smile appeared on her face.

She chuckled quietly, shaking her head. Drake stared at her, bewildered. She was laughing out loud when he pushed her out of the way and leaned over the sarcophagus.

William Drake began to cackle. Slowly the cackle crescendoed—not into a laugh of joy or elation, but the shrill howl of a quivering madman. Seconds later, his scream echoed through the vast cavern.

Renley looked inside the sarcophagus. "Oh, for goodness sake," he said and turned away.

"Where is he?" Drake roared at Alyssa.

His gaze was like a lit fuse, scorching the air between them. With a snarl, he pulled out his Kel-Tec. "What have you done with him?" he thundered, his face contorting into a grimace. He pointed the gun at her. "Tell me, or you will die where you stand."

Alyssa shook her head. "It's over," she said, her voice steady.

Drake grunted when Paul slammed into him from the side, the impact knocking the weapon out of his hand. They both crashed to the ground heavily. Fury flashed through Drake's eyes. He drove his fist into Paul's injured arm.

Paul howled in agony. Drake gained his feet and pulled a knife from his boot. He stalked toward Paul.

Alyssa lunged at him, trying to grab the arm holding the knife.

Drake lifted his arm, and the blade cut through her glove and palm, slicing deep into her flesh. She screamed, and light trembled behind her eyelids at the searing pain. She barely noticed Tasha diving for the Kel-Tec on the floor as Drake lunged at her, the blade raised, ready to plunge into her body.

"No!" Her ears registered the desperate cry an instant before Paul leaped at her, putting himself in the path of the knife. Paul's face contorted as the blade buried deep into his side. Drake howled in frustration, a menacing look fixed on Alyssa.

"Shoot her!" he screamed at Tasha. "Finish her now!"

Tasha raised the Kel-Tec. She hesitated and turned to Renley then back to Drake.

"No," she said softly, lowering the weapon.

Alyssa jumped at the sound of a shot. Tasha grimaced and looked down. Confusion rippled through her face as she took in the growing stain forming on her chest, the crimson color at odds with the bright white of the biosuit. She lifted her head, glassy eyes straining to focus—then she saw Kamal, standing at the edge of the platform, holding Baxter's revolver in his outstretched hand.

"Tasha!" Renley's face caved. He reached for her as she crumpled to the floor. "Dear God, no…" He pressed his trembling palm against the dark red spot on her suit, desperately trying to slow the bleeding.

Alyssa gasped as Drake grabbed her and brought the knife to her neck, backing toward the empty sarcophagus.

"Drop the gun!" he screamed at Kamal.

Kamal froze. He slowly bent down and placed the revolver on the floor. He lifted his arms. "Let her go…" he said.

"Kick it over to me," Drake spat.

Kamal hesitated.

"Do it!"

Kamal kicked the gun toward him. Drake shoved Alyssa hard toward the sarcophagus and lunged for the weapon.

Alyssa saw the edge of the stone sarcophagus an instant before her visor struck it, shattering the fragile glass. She heard the rush of the clean air escaping her suit. Dread flooded her mind and whiteness washed across her vision as the scent of the ancient air filled her nostrils.

She groaned and put her hands on the ledge of the sarcophagus. She slowly dragged herself to her feet, breathing heavily. Her right hand left a bloody imprint on the stone, the blood forming a thin trail as it streamed inside the sarcophagus.

William Drake raised the revolver, backing up to keep Kamal and Renley in his view.

"Killing you won't make up for the disappointment," Drake

spat. He pointed the weapon at Alyssa and cocked the hammer. "But it's a start."

————

YURI SILENCED the beeping of the alarm on the DNA amplifier and carefully removed the sample. He shuffled to the biosafety hood and inserted the sample through the sliding door. He put his arms inside the long gloves secured to the glass enclosure and used a pipette to collect a tiny amount of the virus. He held his breath as he meticulously introduced the virus into the DNA sample then inserted the container into the sequencer and focused on the monitor.

He zoomed in on the fragmented gene sequences and the virus particles. For several long seconds nothing happened. He shrugged.

Waste of time, just as I thought.

He leaned in closer as a virus capsule attached to a region of the DNA strand.

What in the world?

Yuri stared at the capsule traveling down the strand, repairing the sequence as it traveled along the gene. Then a second virus capsule moved into another spot on the DNA strand and repeated the process. He zoomed out and staggered back, staring open-mouthed as the virus particles swarmed the DNA strands and began reconstructing the fragmented pieces of Alyssa's genes.

————

ALYSSA GLARED at Drake through the shattered visor of her helmet. She tasted the stale air, its bitter scent filling her mouth and lungs. Her body began to throb as Thoth's weapon surged into every cell of her body.

Behind her, the thin trail of her blood reached the bottom of the sarcophagus, forming a small pool on the polished interior of the tomb, before vanishing completely into the stone—soaked up without a trace by the smooth surface of the sarcophagus.

The first thing Alyssa noticed was the pounding of her heart in her temples. Next came the wave of heat that surged through her marrow, rippling from the top of her head to the tips of every finger and toe, plunging into the pyramid beneath her feet. Time seemed to slow as her panic subsided and in its place something else stirred.

Rage.

All the air inside the cavern seemed to rush into her body. For an unimaginably long second, there was nothing but silence, as if time itself had stopped. Then everything erupted.

A blaze of light exploded behind her, like a star coming alive. Blinding rays washed over her, and a brilliant beam burst out of the tomb up to the ceiling, bathing the vast cavern in a dazzling glow.

William Drake stared at Alyssa, gasping, unable to move.

Alyssa's body filled with electricity, her blood on fire, each breath fueling the blaze inside her. She ripped the helmet from her head. Her hair stirred in the electric current streaming through the air.

Her chest heaving, she stalked toward Drake, the brilliant glow behind her creating a halo around her.

She gripped her helmet tight and raised it. Her voice rang out, echoing through the vast hall.

"I am Alyssa Sarah Morgan!"

She swung the helmet at Drake's head, shattering his visor. He heaved as his suit deflated, and the outside air entered his lungs. His eyes bulged as the deadly virus raged through his body. He staggered, finally able to move, and stumbled backward, gasping for breath.

"Daughter of Kaden and Anja!"

She brought the helmet across his face again. He screamed, crumbling to his knees, trails of blood flowing down his cheeks from his bulging eyes. He gaped at the specter before him through a crimson haze.

"I shall know no fear!"

Alyssa swung the helmet up, snapping Drake's head back and driving him backward over the edge of the pyramid. William Drake's body bounced on the steep slope, tumbling down the pyramid and crashing lifelessly onto the mist-covered ground.

For a brief moment time stood still. Gradually, the glow dissipated. Alyssa sank to the ground, her heart racing and body trembling. Her body began shaking uncontrollably, cold sweat trickling down her back as the rush of her body's defenses against the storm ran its course. Finally, the trembling subsided. She groaned and sluggishly pushed herself up to her knees. Her shoulders slumped, and she stared at her hands, oblivious to the blood streaking from her wound.

She lifted her head and found Kamal's eyes. She fixed a glassy stare on him. "Horus—he's gone. The cure for my dad and the others…" she shook her head, her rich dark hair waving in the air.

"I'm so sorry…" she said, unable to finish.

Kamal stared at her wordlessly, his gaze locked onto hers. Slowly, he sank to his knees, eyes glistening with tears. His voice trembled as he whispered breathlessly,

"The cure… It is in your blood… *Daughter of Ra.*"

THE MINISTER of Antiquities stood on a makeshift platform erected in front of the lavish water fountain. He appraised the large crowd gathered before him in the atrium of the hospital then faced the cameras once again with a well-practiced smile before continuing his speech.

"And so, today marks a historic day in the annals of Egyptian archaeology, as well as in the fields of genetics and medicine. With the help of myself, along with Egypt's world class scientists and doctors, we have devised a successful cure for the mysterious illness that befell Dr. Morgan and his team last week—"

———

ALYSSA STOOD at the tall window, her gaze sweeping over the buildings toward the wind-brushed desert. She tuned out the minister's voice streaming from the TV as she allowed the warmth of the sun to spread across her body like a soft blanket, savoring the rays flooding into the hospital room.

She heard her dad groan before he switched off the TV and threw the remote onto the nightstand.

"Ah! I knew that smug sonufabitch would take all the credit."

Alyssa turned and smirked. She pushed up the sleeves of her freshly washed and patched up Willis and Geiger. "Glad to see you're feeling better... Dad."

Kade Morgan stretched lazily and laced his fingers behind his head. "Never better," he said, blinking, his Southern drawl giving his hard voice a softer edge. "Thanks to you, kiddo. And how are you feeling?"

"A bit tired," she replied.

"Says the living descendent of Ra?" Paul's voice greeted her from the door as he gingerly limped into the room, arm in a sling, Kamal trailing behind him.

Alyssa's cheeks dimpled and her lips skewed into a smile before it turned into a full-faced beam. She rushed to Paul and threw her arms around him.

"Ow! Easy there!" he said, only half-exaggerating his distress. He pointed at his arm, "Gunshot..." then his side, "knife wound... still recovering." He gave a sheepish smile. "Not all of us have divine blood coursing through our feeble, mortal veins, you know."

Alyssa cringed. "Sorry!" She gave a shallow sigh. "Bill Nye never prepared me for this. And I thought he really cared." She turned to Kamal before Paul could muster a reply.

"I'm sorry for ever doubting you." She hugged him. "Thank you for everything you have done."

Kamal looked at her, a flicker of embarrassment crossing his eyes. "It was nothing."

"Nothing?" Kade's voice rang from the bed. "If it hadn't been for the brainiacs at your institute working day and night to isolate the genes from Alyssa's blood, we would have never devised the gene therapy and vaccines in time to stop the Horus epidemic."

Alyssa's smile wilted. "I don't like that name," she said.

"Call it by any name you choose, Ally," her father replied. "We haven't been that close to a major epidemic in decades. What you and Paul did may have saved millions of lives."

Kamal nodded. "It is clear that the immunity comes from your mother's side. Have you reconsidered the ministry's request for consent to sequence your genome?"

Alyssa absentmindedly stroked her right palm, feeling the faint scar from the knife wound beneath her fingers. "Donating my blood to prevent a pandemic was one thing, Kamal. But I'm not sure I want to be a genetic guinea pig."

"I suppose there is no convincing you otherwise, is there?" Kamal asked.

"I don't think it's what he would have wanted."

Paul cleared his throat to break the sudden silence. "So, what's going to happen to all those crackpots?"

"All known members linked to the Society are being investigated for any illegal activities," Kamal replied. "The problem is, there may be dozens of others we don't know about. The manor house was purchased in the early nineteen hundreds by a foundation based in Zurich. It has been seized pending further investigation."

Alyssa shook her head. "I still can't believe Ed Wallace—William Drake—whatever he wants to call himself…"

"I should have seen it," Kade said.

"Why didn't he just take the damn thing in the tunnel, when he had a chance?" Paul cut in.

"He knew the minister and his council were watching our every move," Kade replied. "I suppose he needed a diversion to keep them out… until he got what he wanted."

"But faking his own death?" Paul shook his head.

Kade considered that for several moments. "Once the council got around to checking the footage and discovered that an artifact disappeared from the site, who do you think would be their prime suspect? Killing off the prime suspect was—an elegant solution. I'll give him that."

Alyssa scoffed. "Speaking of elegant, what about Renley?"

"On his way back to England," Kamal replied. "No charges are being brought up against him in exchange for a large donation to the Ministry of Antiquities's new research institute."

He faced Kade with a mischievous grin. "I figured this is as good a time as any to break the news to you. The minister himself has highly recommended you to be the founding director of the new institute. I figured that should give you an incentive to get out of the hospital and on your feet as soon as you can."

Kade swallowed. "Hmmm… that's certainly unexpected." He raised an eyebrow. "So, does that mean I'll get to be chauffeured around in a fancy white Benz?"

"Sure does."

"And get to spend the rest of my time pushing papers?" He

shook his head. "I don't think so, Kamal. I'll leave that job to the minister and you."

"Well, it's funny you should say that," Kamal replied, with a smirk. "I pretty much told him that would be your answer. I'm afraid he insisted. He said that you would, of course, be expected to spend at least half your time doing field work. The principal mission of the new institute, to research the origin of the Hall of Records, would fall under your direct supervision. And to make the offer more attractive to you, you will also have unrestricted access to the hall and all the fiscal and administrative support—"

Kade raised his hand in mock defeat. "All right, all right," he said. "You had me at 'research the origin of the hall'. As long as I don't turn into the bureaucrat you've become…"

Kamal laughed and stepped to the door. He turned to Alyssa and Paul. "I'll wait for you two in the car."

Kade faced Alyssa. "Are you sure I can't convince you to stay in Cairo longer?"

Alyssa shook her head. "I have to get away for a while. Clear my head." She smirked. "Besides, somebody has to pick up the pieces in Peru and finish the Chumbivilcas job you left behind."

Kade's expression darkened, but he nodded. Paul approached the bed and the men shook hands.

"Have a safe trip back to London," Kade said, "and thank you—for everything you've done." He pulled Paul toward him. "Anytime you're sick of the WHO, we'll have a job waiting for you."

Paul smiled and nodded. Alyssa stepped up to the bed and gave her dad a long hug. She took his hand in hers.

"Try to get some rest. You may look better, but you've been through Hell." She leaned down again and kissed him softly on his cheek. "We all have."

———

ALYSSA DIDN'T NOTICE the throngs of passengers squeezing past her and Paul. She tried to ignore her racing pulse and the tightness welling in her throat as they stood wordlessly next to her departure gate in the Cairo airport.

"Got a call from Clay this morning," Paul said, breaking the silence. "Guess who just became the youngest person to be awarded the WHO fellowship in bioinformatics? Apparently, they were so impressed with what he did that they chose to turn a blind eye to him bending some rules... and his father's car."

"That's so wonderful!" Alyssa smiled, but the smile was sad and distracted.

Paul gazed at her with troubled eyes. "You sure about this?" he asked, concern rising in his face.

"I have to know."

"How many of you are left, do you suppose?"

"I don't know, but right now the Society is our best lead. Jake thinks he dug up a good place for me to start." Alyssa looked down at his arm in the sling and gently brought her fingers to it.

"Paul, I will never be able to—"

"I know," he said.

She studied his face. It seemed so much older than when they met. *Was it only a week ago?* She reached out and touched his other hand and their fingers intertwined without thinking.

Her stomach fluttered at the warmth of his skin against hers, and their gazes locked as they faced each other, unsure, neither of them confident enough to initiate the kiss. Slowly, Alyssa leaned in and moved her lips toward his.

"This will serve as the final boarding call for Swissair flight 2012 with non-stop service to Zurich, Switzerland."

She flinched at the overhead announcement and pulled back with a sigh. Paul's face was a mirror of the disappointment she felt in the pit of her stomach. She inhaled deeply and smiled then embraced him.

He stood for a moment, arms at his sides, before he wrapped his uninjured arm around her waist and pulled her close, holding her tight. The feel of his body pressed against hers soothed Alyssa more than she had expected. She squeezed him back, not wanting to let go.

"Miss?" the voice of the gate attendant brought her back. "We are about to close the gate."

Alyssa reluctantly broke the embrace. "I'd better go. I'm done pounding at closed gates." She turned and handed her boarding pass to the agent then stepped toward the jetway door.

"Alyssa!" Paul called after her.

She turned in the doorway.

"So, what's the plan? How are you going to pick up the trail?"

She stared at him for several moments, contemplating the question. A slow, wicked smile spread across her lips.

"Don't you fret. I have seen into the mind of an Egyptian god," she replied, her eyes sparkling for the first time in days. "I'll think of something."

THE WOMAN STOOD up and approached the man kneeling on the floor in front of her. She squeezed the thin scepter hard in her hand, ignoring the dread in the man's eyes as she slowly removed the hood of her robe.

"Your orders for Peru were clear," she said in an icy voice. "The girl was not to be harmed."

"It… it was an accident," the man stammered. "I didn't mean to hurt her… The *Rathadi*—"

The scepter came down on his head, snapping it back. The man sank to the ground.

The woman ignored the pool of blood forming around the man as she watched him, yellow irises burning into his lifeless body.

END OF BOOK ONE

ACKNOWLEDGMENTS

This book would not have been possible without the remarkable support of countless individuals. I owe my respect, gratitude, and admiration to all of you:

First and foremost, Heather, for having lived through every iteration of the manuscript and without whose brilliant intellect this work would have been vastly inferior.

My amazing daughter, Sarah, whose intuition, boldness, and fresh perspective helped shaped every aspect of this work.

Michael Mailer, whose feedback on the screen adaptation provided crucial insights into the story.

My stellar editors, Carol Woods and Philip Athans, for their sharp eyes and astute criticism.

Irene Kraas for her wisdom and guidance during the preparation of the manuscript.

Kornelio Rath and Torsten Weine for endless hours of D&D that helped shape my imagination decades ago.

Rainer Holdhoff for being a real-life version of Robin Williams's character in "Dead Poets Society" and for inspiring his students to never fear to look at the world from a different perspective.

Dr. Zahi Hawass for sparking the love for archaeology and Egyptology in generations of people.

The students at Hampton Roads Academy, Abby B., Avery C., Breanna W., Cerese L., Kaila M., Lexie A., Meghan C., Misha Z., Sarah T., as well as Dominique Adair, Ali Baedke, Scott George, Patti Grayson, Kim Hatton, Alex Marshall, Thomas Marshall, Gene Tracy, and Russ Warnick for taking time to read the early editions and providing honest critiques.

To the person that I am undoubtedly forgetting, my deepest apologies and profound gratitude.

And, finally, Vera, whose optimism, tireless drive, love, and unwavering support made this book possible.

Continue Alyssa's story in

DAUGHTER OF RA

Book Two of Blood of Ra

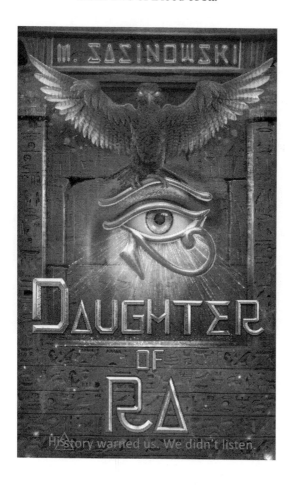

Ra, grant me strength…

My feet pound the marble as I charge the gilded stairs to the door of the sleeping chamber. My heart rings against my chest, echoing the clamor of the palace bells. The bitter scent of ash that hangs in the air sweetens the taste of bile in the back of my throat.

With a snarl, the man leaps forward, and his sword scythes with vicious intent. Weaponless and unable to parry, I dive under his blade. The man reels, surprised at missing his mark, but there is no hesitation in his next move.

He cuts down with his right. The blade scours only marble as I roll aside. His balance upset, he staggers for a heartbeat. It is all the time I need. My fist rams into his face, the brunt of my blow doubled by my fury and fear for my kin.

Blood erupts from his nose and he wavers, eyes glazed. He never recovers as I move in and thrust my fingers to his throat. He crumples, eyes bulging.

I snatch the sword from his limp grasp an instant before

another blade lashes out. With a sharp clash, steel meets steel, and I deflect the savage slice. He turns full circle, leaps and strikes. I parry and counter to his head. When he lifts his blade to defend, I change the angle of my attack, dropping low. My weapon cuts through his thigh, cleaving bone. I reach the door at the end of the hall before he drops to the ground, screaming, clutching his useless limb.

I storm into the sleeping chamber. My breath catches in my throat at the sight. My wife, dagger in hand, besieged by three invaders. My rage swells at the crimson lines on her skin, her wounds numerous and deep. I roar and charge. All eyes lock onto mine, one pair swells with hope, the others flare with hatred. Two men turn to intercept.

We meet in full stride. The first to reach me is the first to die. He moves to defend, and our blades meet in a sharp clash. I spin my weapon and lock my grip, slicing the blade deep across his torso as we pass. He gasps, and the blood bursts out. The second man is on me in an instant, knuckles white on the hilt of his sword. With a growl he charges, cutting low with his left, then spinning about, his sword screaming to my neck. Our blades weave a dance of liquid fire in the glow of the torches, the clash of steel on steel ringing into the night. Then it is over. His hands grasp his throat, blood seeping between his fingers.

I spin to face the third man.

Time stops.

The attacker's blade sinks into the soft flesh beneath my beloved's breasts. He tears the sword free, and she slumps to her knees, clutching the ghastly wound.

My mind rejects my sight.

My soul shatters.

The howl of a wounded beast thunders through the chamber as I close the distance between us in a single leap. The murderer draws back, his sword raised, but his fate is sealed. I know not when I strike the killing blow. The blood flows freely, and the man writhes on the ground, clutching his gut, his sword in my hand.

I sink to my knees at my beloved's side.

Hathor... I mouth her name, the sight before me robbing me of my speech.

"Horus..." Her voice is thin. She coughs, and red spittle mars her lips.

"Be still... do not speak." My eyes are glued to her face. The radiance of her golden skin dims with every slowing beat of her heart. The delicate lines of her face are twisted with pain and fear.

My hand presses to her chest as her life weeps from her, warm and silky between my fingers. "The healers will be here soon." My voice sounds distant to my own ears.

"Horus," she says again. I know the words before she utters them. My eyes beg her to remain silent.

"They took him," she whispers, "they took Imset."

Her pleading eyes turn glassy, but before she leaves, a mother's final appeal.

"Find him... Bring back our son."

Our gazes meet in a last embrace, then she is gone.

My vision fades. The pounding in my ears surges like a wave.

I am Horus.

Son of Isis and Osiris.

I shall know no—

The sound of my son's name rips out of my throat, drowning the wailing of the alarms.

———

"Imset!"

The scream passed through Alyssa's lips, its echoes erupting like cracks of thunder in her head.

Imset...

Her body shuddered as the rush of adrenaline receded. She swallowed, trying to flush down the taste of the ash and bile that lingered in her throat. The memories began to fade from her mind.

No.

Not memories.

She pressed her fists against her temples, willing her mind and body to reject the onslaught of the—

Dreams.

Just... dreams.

When I decided to pursue my dream of writing a book, I set out to create a novel that compelled book lovers to pick it up and start reading it. As Heir of Ra grew into existence, I realized that it was far more difficult to write a book that readers choose to *finish*, given the myriad of alternatives to reading. We're both here, so—unless you're one of those readers who likes to start at the end—congratulations to both of us!

I hope reading Heir of Ra was as enjoyable for you as building the world was for me. This book was inspired by countless works of fiction. Among all of them, one holds a special place: Michael Ende's Neverending Story. When I read it as a ten-year old boy who had just arrived in a strange, new country, I realized there was something magical about reading a book that told a story within a story. If the dream realm of Fantastica could become real for the book-loving Bastian, perhaps there was an enchanted world waiting for each of us. Decades later, sharing Alyssa's journey into Horus's mind with you represents my very own dream-come-true. Thank you for helping me find my Fantastica.

Pursue your dreams and know no fear.
- M. Sasinowski

P.S. If you enjoyed Heir of Ra, please consider taking a few minutes to leave a review or recommend it to a friend. These reviews and recommendations are incredibly valuable for new authors and allow us to continue sharing our worlds with you. Thank you for your support.

I'd love to hear from you! Please visit our social media pages and send me a note. Visit our web site and sign up for the email list for a chance to win an autographed copy of the sequel!

WWW.HEIROFRA.COM

facebook.com/heirofra

instagram.com/heirofra_book

twitter.com/heirofra

ABOUT THE AUTHOR

FROM THE POINT OF VIEW OF HIS
15-YEAR-OLD DAUGHTER
(THAT'S ME! :)

Some say that M. Sasinowski writes until 4 am… fueled by a single cup of decaf coffee. Others say this Polish-born American hyper-nerd absorbs energy from late-night TV space shows. No matter the truth… he's my dad. He will never be cool.

He loves archaeology, Star Wars/Trek, martial arts (especially women who kick butt), and impromptu father/daughter (that's me! :) science debates or music jam-sessions.

He's kind of smart, I suppose (he has a physics PhD, and an MD, or whatever) and likes to build computers for fun.

His teenage daughter (that's me! :) is occasionally a handful to deal with and also served as the inspiration for the main character in his debut young adult novel *Heir of Ra.*

You may recognize him from his glorious hair or his tendency to do the "vacuum cleaner" dance to embarrass his daughter (that's me… :(.

If you ever see this man, approach with care and greet him in a language he understands, like in Klingon or, better yet, in Wookie.

Guurrghghgh!